'You have nothing to fear from me.'

Even if Dania had not already decided, his new tenderness might well have swayed her, though she knew the venture to be fraught with dangers and almost certain heartache. This man was obviously experienced in casual relationships, a cool predator without a heart to speak of, whereas she was vulnerable and emotional with a sad lack of seduction techniques and a growing revulsion for deceit.

He insisted, touching her hand with his fingertips. 'I have seen what lies beneath the façade, remember. You ought to be mistress of a great household. You ought to be in my bed and at my side. You have not found a man with enough dogged persistence to take you, until now. And I don't intend to accept no for an answer.'

Juliet Landon's keen interest in art and history, both of which she used to teach, combined with a fertile imagination, make writing historical novels a favourite occupation. She is particularly interested in researching the Roman and early medieval period, and the problems encountered by women in a man's world. Her heart's home is in her native North Yorkshire, but now she lives happily in a Hampshire village close to her family. Her first books, which were on embroidery and design, were published under her own name of Jan Messent.

Recent novels by the same author:

THE WIDOW'S BARGAIN
THE BOUGHT BRIDE
HIS DUTY, HER DESTINY

THE WARLORD'S MISTRESS

Juliet Landon

MILLS & BOON®

First published in Great Britain 2006
Harlequin Mills & Boon Limited,
Eton House, 18-24 Paradise Road, Richmond, Surrey TW9 1SR

© Juliet Landon 2006

ISBN-13: 978 0 263 84670 6
ISBN-10:   0 263 84670 9

Set in Times Roman 10½ on 13½ pt.
04-0906-81915

Printed and bound in Spain
by Litografia Rosés S.A., Barcelona

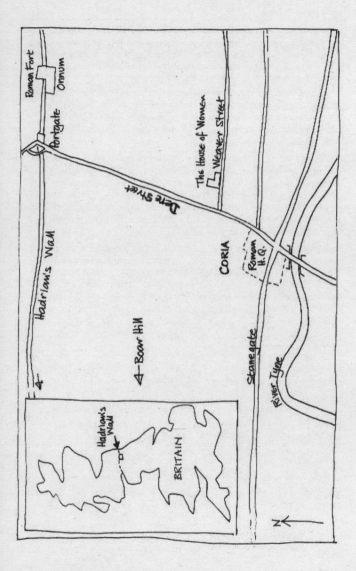

Prologue

❧

The Boar Hill Settlement, Brigantia AD 202

The fires lit to celebrate the festival of Beltane had been kept ablaze for a day and a night to light the revellers' dances and to give them a new kind of hope that the year ahead would be nothing like the last. The cattle had been driven between two fires to purify them, and the Druids had made their sacrifices, but now the flames had died and all the sparks of hope with them, and clouds of white ash drifted up into the morning breeze that swept across the hill-top settlement, blowing the embers into pockets of menacing red. Gaps between the conical thatches and mud walls framed the dark sheen of a recent lake where, by this time of the year, new green shoots should have appeared in the thin soil. Already the greenwoods were holding back their pale leaves, and the surviving ewes had dropped fewer lambs than at any time in living memory. The Druids' living memory, that is, for no one would have challenged what *they* could recall after twelve years' initiation into the mysteries. Since last year's murrain and the disastrous harvest, the settlement had gone quiet except for the bleat of hungry animals and the wail of unsatisfied children, and the sacrifices to Brighid and to the gods of the oak had not been enough to stop the constant rain or the floods from filling the valleys. The Druids, those all-powerful priests, were getting desperate. Their credibility was at stake. Something momentous would have to be done at the close of the Beltane revels.

There was a young woman, however, who was relieved not to have been pulled, willingly or otherwise, into the surrounding greenwood by the lusty young men whose natural urge to procreate fitted so conveniently into the customs of May. For that was how Beltane was always celebrated: in procreation. Having discharged herself from those events, she had watched her hulking husband-of-one-year, Con the Silvertongue, grab the hand of his newest concubine and half-carry her, giggling and squealing, into the darkness and she, Dana, had turned away into her hut for a night of blessed freedom from his groping hands, his noisy rutting and his irritating attempts to make her jealous. To be jealous, she would have had to care for him, and she didn't. But to remain childless after a whole year reflected badly upon her, for few would believe that Con had not done his part. He had, after all, fathered so many of the red-haired brats in the settlement.

Nothing had gone well since Dana's marriage to Con, though she had given them warning how it would be. Her father, chieftain of the Boar Hill tribe, had not taken kindly to the emotional predictions of a mere lass of fifteen summers, nor had the chief Druid to whose eldest son they had married her. It was politics, of course, and nothing to do with preferences.

Dana now stood at the door of her warm timber hut to watch the snaking line of revellers emerge from the forest waving boughs of may-blossom and dragging behind them a pole stripped of its branches. Bellowing like bullocks, they erected it in last year's hole with streamers of twine and bindweed trailing from its summit, leaping and cavorting round it in a last frantic endeavour to recoup the season's flagging fertility. And while the wind tangled their hair into cords and buffed their cheeks like rosy apples, a straggling line of sober-faced elders trudged towards the largest rectangular hall in the centre of the compound to answer the urgent summons of Brigg, their chieftain. Dana's father.

Then she knew that it was serious, that her time of reckoning had come, that she would need all her courage, resourcefulness and more than a touch of inspiration to evade what she knew was to be her fate. This might otherwise be the last time she would see the Beltane fires, or watch the little lads making bows and arrows outside her neighbour's hut, or hear the rooks quarrelling in the pines, or feel the lift of her thick black hair as the wind caught it before she'd had time to tie it up. They would cut it all off, and someone would be wearing it as false hair within the week, without a qualm. Shivering, she reached up to take her woollen cloak from a peg as a youth ran across to her, his face grave and full of the terrible import of his message.

'Lady,' he said, standing rigidly before her, 'my lord your father sends for you and says to be quick about it.' He held his spear upright like a warrior, though he was her junior and one of her many half-brothers. Her father's procreating had not been confined to Beltane nor even to his own wife, to her shame. A chieftain's privilege, he had said. The lad's features crumpled as he forced out a whisper, 'I'm sorry, Dana.'

'Don't be, Bran,' she whispered back. 'Where's your pony?'

Alarm flitted across his eyes. 'No...no,' he said. 'I *dare* not.'

As if they had known he would need help, they had sent men, grown men, to back him up, and now four of them appeared from nowhere to stand some paces behind him, and Dana lifted her chin so as not to shame the lad. 'I will come with you,' she said, loudly, looking at the coiled rope in the nearest man's hand. 'And you'll not need that. Lead me there, Bran, son of Brigg.' Barefoot, she stepped out over the threshold, fastening the cloak on her shoulder with a costly gold pin bright with blood-red garnets.

The revelling slowed to a standstill at the base of the maypole as the group picked its way through the mud towards the chieftain's hall, though one hefty man broke away to challenge them. 'Where are you taking her?' Con the Silvertongue roared. 'Where's she going? She's mine...my wife...' His outrage was brought to a sudden halt, felled by the fist of one of the escort, stepped over by the rest of them, ignored by young Bran and Dana, and by the time Con had regained his feet, they were inside Brigg's large hall, frowning into the dimness.

This was no mean hovel: the floor was thick-layered with straw and a large central hearth was festooned with an array of bronze pots and chains that coiled through the blue smoke as far as the heavy oak cross-beams. Bunches of herbs, bronze-bound buckets and shining horse-bridles dripped from those same beams alongside oblong shields of great worth, iron swords in studded scabbards and spears longer than a man. Curtains of leather and wool screened off cubicles along the aisles, though these were now hidden behind dozens of men and women, many of them related, who had answered the summons that morning, and Dana felt their eyes searching her for signs of fear, puzzlement, acceptance or defiance.

Brigg, chieftain of Boar Hill, was the only person to be seated. Behind his carved wooden chair stood his son Somer and, with one hand resting upon his shoulder, Rhiannon, Dana's mother, whose tearful eyes caressed the lovely young woman, the pride of her life, her youngest and most beloved. She put out a hand to comfort her daughter, but Brigg's strong fingers clamped over her arm, freezing the gesture that he could only have anticipated. His unseeing and clouded eyes swivelled and searched until they came to rest on his daughter's silhouette. 'Dana?' he said.

'Yes, Father.'

'Hear what the lord Mog has to say.'

She knew what the chief Druid would have to say. Her marriage to his son had not been the success he had hoped for, nor had his son won the loyalty or affection of the Boar Hill tribe. Instead, Somer was all set to take the leadership after his father and she, Dana, must be sacrificed ostensibly to appease the gods, but more truthfully to remove the one who had failed to fulfil her intended purpose, namely to link the two most powerful elements of the society. She had announced only last full moon that she proposed to end her marriage to Con, and there was nothing he could do about it. He would have to pay back the huge silver bride-price to her father, and she would be freed to marry again. As the father of a sacrificial victim, however, Brigg could not expect the repayment of her bride-price; it would remain with Con and his Druid father. Some of these truths, of course, would not be spoken, but then, Mog was a dealer in portents, not truths.

'The gods demand a sacrifice, my lady,' he intoned portentously. 'Something of great worth to us all.' His long white beard flapped upon his chest as with a trembling hand he straightened the heavy gold crown upon his snowy brow. Thick twisted torques of pure gold hung about his neck, the discs at each end encrusted with spiralling patterns and specks of coloured enamel. 'Since your marriage,' he went on, 'nothing but disaster has befallen us, no crops have grown through the floods, no honey has been made, no milk has been yielded and no eggs have been laid. Darkness has covered each season and our women have had to abandon their bairns for lack of nourishment. Yet *you* did not conceive.' He recited the catastrophes as if they were poetry, as if the rhetoric would lend truth to a string of exaggerations. Those women who had borne children that winter had been forced to expose them so as not to add to the problem of food shortage in the future, and Dana knew full well that, had she allowed herself to become pregnant, she would have had to do the same. Fortunately, she knew how to prevent conception, but that was a forbidden and dangerous kind of knowledge which she would not share with anyone. The food shortage had been bad, but they could have survived it if they had used some of their vast hoards of silver to buy food from the markets at Coria, some eight miles away, as other tribes did. There was no need for anyone to starve. There was, though, a need for a scapegoat, and who better than the ailing chieftain's unco-operative daughter?

A shadow fell across her father's gaunt face, and Dana felt the heat of her husband's great frame behind her. Not daring to interrupt his father, whose power was as great as Brigg's, Con moved to one side.

With eyes bright blue and fierce with secret knowledge, Mog went on with his ranting. 'And we have a duty,' he said, 'to rid our northern lands, our Brigantia, of the pestilence of Rome, and in this we have failed time and time again. They have divided our homesteads with the abominable Wall and we are forced to dwell apart from our neighbours and relatives, to be stopped, searched, questioned, taxed, imposed upon, beaten and enslaved, killed and maimed for doing what we have been doing since the world began. Not once in this last four seasons—' he glared at Dana as if she were personally responsible '—have our brave warriors been able to prevent the incursions of the Roman armies from the Wall forts and garrisons, or stem their rapacity and domination. Indeed, we have suffered more losses than ever and our brothers are preferring to become their slaves than to die the proud death of opposition. It is shameful,' he cried. 'Shameful! The gods demand a price for their aid. They must be appeased.'

There was a murmur of agreement from the crowd, though there were some amongst them who would have offered themselves, for it might be a better way to go than a lingering death, and all honours to their family. Even so, there were many who would rather Mog had not shown such transparency in singling out Brigg's beautiful youngest daughter, who they loved. They would rather he had chosen Con the Silvertongue as the sacrifice, the Druid's own son.

There was only one man who dare say so, and now his voice found its old strength, taking them all by surprise. Shakily, he rose to his feet like the warrior he had once been, shaking off his son's supporting arm. 'Not so fast,' he said, turning to the sound of Mog's voice and the memory of his white-robed, gold-adorned figure. 'Not so fast, priest. You are eager to lay my daughter upon your altar, but I don't see how she can be blamed for what has befallen us this last twelve-month when she was set firmly against her marriage to your son from the start. Isn't that precisely why she agreed to a marriage-of-one-year, as a trial? And isn't that why she has now announced her intention to end it? And what part does Con the Silvertongue play in this drama? Is he not half of the marriage that failed and therefore is he not as much needed as a sacrifice to the god Belenos? Where *is* my son-in-law when his wife needs him?'

A scuffle alerted him to Con's exact whereabouts, but the young man's attempt to sidle away through the door was prevented, and now his protests collided with his father's blustering denials. For a few moments there was bedlam, the village elders noisily supporting Brigg, and the four other Druids and Con supporting Mog.

Taking the opportunity to go to her daughter's side, Rhiannon placed an arm about her shoulders, but spoke no word except through her eyes. Like Dana's, they were of an astonishing changeable green that seeped unbidden into men's dreams, and the thick black lashes needed no cosmetics such as other women used, soot, red earth, roots, white of egg. The men used lime on their hair to make it stand stiff like spears. The Lady Rhiannon's hair was now streaked naturally with white, and braided, but Dana's black mane poured like a torrent over her shoulders, its waves refusing to lie sleek and obedient like silk. It had never been cut, nor was it yet tamed by the narrow gold circlet she wore over her brow, the entitlement of a chieftain's daughter.

The men's eyes turned to her as the chief Druid raised a hand to stop the argument, and now they saw a new defiance in her proud bearing and a dignity that refused to quake beneath Mog's blatant malevolence. Though not of the same order, the women's admiration was just as great, for most of them had benefited in the past from Dana's healing skills, her generosity and unselfishness, and not one of them would have preferred to lose her rather than her dissolute young husband, Con the Silvertongue.

'Stop!' cried Mog, his face contorted with anger. 'Silence, all of you! This has been decided.'

'No, it has not!' thundered Brigg, clutching at his chair. 'It has been proposed, but it has *not* been decided. This may be my last season as chieftain of Boar Hill, my lord Mog, but it shall not be said that I allowed *you* to rule the roost before I reached my death-bed. If my fair daughter is to atone for my failings as leader, then your son shall do likewise for, as the son of the chief Druid, nothing less will do for the god Belenos.'

'No!' yelled Con above the wave of sound that greeted Brigg's challenge, elbowing aside those who hemmed him in.

He came to stand before Brigg, his father-in-law, red-faced and stinking with the sweat of fear. 'What use would it be to reduce the manpower when it's needed to fight our enemies? I am needed here. The gods know that I am needed.'

'So you would have us all think,' said Brigg. 'Especially the women. I would rather hear what my daughter has to say about your so-called dedication to the tribe.'

'She's a woman. She may not speak on such matters in public.'

'Then it's time we made an exception if the men are as useless as your revered father appears to believe.' He turned to Dana. 'Speak, daughter. Say what you have to say before this husband-of-one-year says it for you.'

Dana took a step forward, pulling the edges of her chequered woollen cloak together across her breast. 'About Con the Silvertongue I have nothing to say except that I desire an end to our marriage. About my own fate, however, I am more able to speak. I am not unwilling to dwell with the gods if my lord Mog truly believes that that will suffice to end the sufferings of our tribe. But I have an alternative, if you care to hear it. It is true that I cannot stay here at Boar Hill, so why not send me to Coria, further down the Wall, where our people mix with the invaders to buy and sell, where I might set up a stall of my own, set up my loom and weave my cloaks? You know how sought they are. Two looms, if you would let me take my woman to help me. Once at Coria, we could gather information about what the Roman army is planning and bring it back here so that you can devise your raids more accurately. Think of the advantages, Father. Men are only too willing to chatter to a woman as long as they believe she can make no use of it. And how much more useful to the tribe would such information be than having my body lie face-down in the bog and my spirit with the gods? Do you not think the god Belenos would approve of my desire to help, after all?'

Con the Silvertongue was impressed, standing with his mouth agape and not unaware that a reprieve for Dana would probably mean his salvation also. 'That makes good sense, Father, does it not?' he said to Mog, gulping.

But now Mog's authority had been challenged and, although he could see the sense in what Dana said well enough, it was against all the rules for a woman to speak without his permission and he could not, would not, give way. 'It makes sense to the lady Dana,' he said, grudgingly, with a sidelong look at his animated daughter-in-law who had never, to his chagrin, showed sufficient respect for his high position, 'but I can see where that clever little scheme will lead, even if you cannot. Roman soldiers without their women, and *her* without a husband's protection. Daily chatter over the counter. Oh, yes, I can see where all that will end. She'll soon forget she's a woman of the Briganti, and in a year she'll come crawling back with some foreigner's brat in her belly.'

'Exactly what are you implying, my lord Mog?' snapped Brigg. '*Do* say it out loud, won't you? Leave us in no doubt of what's in your mind. You are suggesting, I take it, that my daughter will betray her own people by consorting with the enemy? The daughter of a chieftain, no less? Shame on you, man. The lady Dana's suggestion is the most sensible I've heard for some time, a far more positive one than you've uttered these last twelve moons. If she doesn't want your son for a husband, she's hardly likely to want a citizen of *Rome*, is she?' He spat the offensive word out like a plum stone.

Dana's older brother Somer stepped into the hostile pause. 'Put it to the assembly,' he said. 'See what they say.' Somer had none of Con's noisy swagger and, of all the members of their family, he was the one Dana would miss most if her plan was accepted. 'My father is right,' said Somer. 'The lady my sister is virtuous and noble-minded. Everyone here must know of her skills, not only in weaving, skills that the enemy needs as much as our brothers. What better way could there be to gain an advantage than by learning in advance of the enemy's movements, their numbers, leaders, positions, weapons? And if you truly believe she may be tempted to forget her identity, then take a look at this, will you? Look… Here!' He took a fistful of Dana's ankle-length woollen skirt and lifted it just enough to expose her lower leg. 'There. The anklet of a Briganti. If that doesn't proclaim her tribe, then nothing will.'

Necks craned to see the slender ankle with its hoop of intricate gold cords twisted like ropes: only a handful of her friends understood and admired the outer calmness that masked her seething inner turmoil and ice-cold fear.

The chief Druid's glance was still disdainful. 'Anklets can be sawn off,' he proclaimed, unwilling to concede the point. 'The gods require a—'

'Brand her, then!' yelled Con the Silvertongue, panicking as the argument veered once again, sensing his own destiny go with it. 'Burn the mark of the tribe on her as we do on our cattle. That's permanent. Eh? Isn't it?' He looked wildly round at the assembled faces, willing them to agree with him, for once.

And for once, they did. Even Brigg, Dana's chieftain father, whose blindness meant he would never see the terrible mark upon her satin skin, nor would he see her suffering, even though he could not escape the smell of seared flesh or her stifled screams through the gag between her teeth. It was her mother, her brother and, oddly enough, her guilt-ridden and rejected husband who held her fast in their arms throughout the ordeal, who carried her back to the round hut, and who nursed her through the days of her healing before she was allowed to travel eastwards along the Roman Wall to Coria.

Chapter One

The House of Women, Coria (Corbridge) AD 208

The girl knuckled away a tear from one large blue eye that would have melted the hearts of most women, but apparently not this one. She looked up with a growing respect at the lady Dania in whose spacious entrance hall she stood, noting again the woman's elegance and intimidating dignity that were not quite what she had expected when she arrived. She had been treated courteously, but the answer was still no.

'It's not only that you're too young, Lepida,' said Dania, 'and it's not that you don't have the looks. You are on the way to becoming a beauty, I'm sure of it. But this is not the way to punish your parents, nor do I need to be dragged before the magistrate to answer charges of procuring under-age girls, let alone kidnap. Had you thought of that?'

'No, my lady.'

'Then what had you thought?'

'Well, that I'd prefer to live here…the excitement…the

parties, pretty clothes and hair, and no parents telling me what not to do.'

'And men?'

'Yes.' Long fair lashes, damply spiked, swept her cheeks.

Dania smiled and glanced sideways at Etaine, the woman who had come with her from Boar Hill six years ago. 'It's not quite what you think,' she said, kindly. 'We have to work, too.'

'Oh, I know what happens,' said Lepida, using one last flutter of her eyelashes to convince her audience. 'I know why men come here. I'm sure I could…'

'Lepida,' said Dania firmly, 'this is not an orphanage, nor is it a place for young daughters of officers. It's a house of women. And you're going home. Now, Etaine and Albiso will escort you, and your parents need know nothing about your visit here. If you still think the same way in five years' time, when you're nineteen, then you can come to me again and we'll talk. No promises, mind.' With a look, she summoned the man who stood apart over by the pink-washed wall, placing a warm hand on Lepida's bony shoulder and easing her towards him. 'Go home, my dear. Your parents need you there.'

'Yes. Thank you.' The liquid eyes lingered appreciatively over the panels of pink, ochre and white, the shrines alcoved in the walls, the shining mosaic floor whose imagery she only half-understood. The glimpse of a sun-washed garden on the far side of an adjoining room was all light and glamour and a far cry from the noisy squabbling of her siblings at home. 'It's beautiful here,' she whispered, turning away.

Wistfully, Dania watched the slender young Lepida glide along the verandah, cross the cobbled courtyard and disappear into the passageway between two shops that led into the street. Weaver Street, just off Dere Street, was set on the quiet outer edges of Coria, the town that some were already calling Corbridge after the stout wooden bridge built by Roman legionaries across the Cor. There had been ancient settlements here since anyone could remember, but once the great fortified Wall had been built across Britain from coast to coast, Coria had become an important supply base for the army, growing steadily and attracting traders of every kind, integrating local civilians with the foreign military. What had once been a remote settlement of thatched huts, animal compounds and plots, was now an organised network of stone-built garrison blocks and storehouses, workshops, temples and granaries, large merchants' houses and living quarters for all those who serviced the troops along the Wall, all seventy-three miles of it. Including the House of Women.

Dania's establishment had grown from very modest beginnings that were quite unlike young Lepida's innocent imaginings, different in fact from those of all but a select few of the now extensive household. Except for her closest henchmen, no one in Coria knew that the lady Dania was a Brigantian woman from nearby Boar Hill, or that her brother Somer was the chieftain of that local tribe.

It was early morning, a time of rest for the women who worked late and slept late, a time when Dania attended to the business of the house and to the shops on each side of the passageway fronting on to the street. A weaver and a tailor. This morning, however, there was another matter that needed her attention after the business of the volunteer Lepida. Passing through the outer door, she turned on to the covered verandah where Ram and Astinax stood side by side watching the departure of the trio. They stood to attention as she approached, bowing deferentially as she stopped before them. 'How did that child get in here?' she said.

The two men, ex-gladiators from Verulamium, were built like house-sides, but to Dania they represented security, reliability, never letting anyone unsuitable slip past their guard. 'We believe she got into the kitchen, my lady,' said Ram, 'when the cook's lad carried the supplies in earlier. We've spoken to him. Shall you dismiss him?'

'No, Ram. But it mustn't happen again. This is no place for children.' She looked away into the sunny courtyard where tubs of lavender, violets and pansies were already alive with fumbling bees. Climbing roses twisted around the wooden columns that held up the upper storey, and the tree in the centre of the space dripped with white may-blossom that spiralled like snowdrifts beneath the stone benches.

Dania held up a small oblong piece of paper-thin beechwood. 'I've had a message from the garrison commander,' she said. 'What am I going to say to him about the man's arm you broke?'

Astinax was bald and genial at this time of the day, bald and threatening by evening. 'To Claudius Karus, my lady? You won't need to say much to him,' he said, facetiously.

She held back a laugh. 'I can't quite understand why he needs to pursue the matter,' she said, 'unless he's been told to, of course. Karus knows we don't allow bad behaviour. He's been here often enough.'

Ram, the shorter of the two giants, fended off an inquiring wasp. 'You'd better let one of us go with you, my lady. The streets are swarming with extra troops. I heard that the emperor himself is expected any day now, him and his son. The builders are preparing that big place on the side of the Stanegate for him and his retinue.'

'The emperor?' said Dania, staring at him. 'Are you sure?'

Ram, one would have thought, would not be too moved by the sight of a lovely woman after all he had suffered. He had been taken from his family in southern Britain, forced to be a gladiator and, excelling at that, had been granted his freedom. He had worked for Dania at the House of Women for the last three years and, so far, had shown not the slightest interest in the women themselves, and only Dania was able to thaw, one by one, the ice crystals that encased his heart. Unable to ignore the beautiful languid curves of her back under the long cotton tunic, he released his breath slowly as her green almond-shaped eyes opened wide with surprise. 'Yes,' he said. 'Septimus Severus, no less. We'll find out more today, and still more tonight. I'll come with you to see my lord Karus, since I know what happened and, if I keep my eyes peeled and my ears open, who knows what we might discover between us?'

Having picked up a good working knowledge of several languages during his time at Verulamium, Ram would be a useful escort in more ways than one. Dania looked down at her bare toes, aware of his singular protectiveness. 'I'd better go and put something on my feet then,' she said.

Ram swiped a hand around his chin. 'And I'd better go and have a shave in case I bump into the emperor himself.'

'And I'll hold the fort,' said Astinax, grinning through the gaps left by missing teeth. He wore the resilient and not unattractive expression of a battered man whose spirit was still intact.

'Thank you, Astinax. I don't suppose we'll be long.'

'What shall I do if your friend the lady Julia arrives?'

Pertly, Dania looked over her shoulder. 'If you can keep an eye on things at the same time, entertain her. The bath-house will be empty.'

'Hah!' said Ram, scathingly. 'He'll not get a word in edge-ways.'

'Good,' said Dania. 'So just listen. As a centurion's woman, she should know what's going on. Be nice to her, Astinax. Yes?'

The grin widened.

No Brigantian woman, let alone one of the Boar Hill tribe, would have needed to enquire too deeply into the reason for a personal visit of a Roman emperor at this time, for it was well known by now that the occupying Roman army were having a hard time of it in this far-flung northern outpost of the empire on the Wall. Ha-drian's Wall, they called it, begun by the Emperor Hadrian to control the flow of tribes and traffic, taxes, tribute and trade between the hill tribes on the southern side and the barbarian Caledonians on the northern side. The British hill tribes, the Briganti, had never split them-selves into two sections as neatly as the Wall would suggest, for some of them were scattered on the far side, too.

Over the last six years, the resistance against Roman au-thority had grown more successful than anyone could have foreseen; anyone except Dania herself and her brother Somer, now chieftain of Boar Hill. Had it not been for the amazing success of her venture, her people would still be in the sorry mess they'd been in when she left. But for her courage and foresight, the whole of the Brigantian fighting force would have remained ignorant of the Roman army's strengths and weaknesses, their movements from fort to fort and all the changes that enabled the hill tribes to strike, time and time again, like satanic fiends in the night, disabling, wounding and even thrashing them on more than one occasion.

Eventually, the Roman command had decided that more must be done to reverse the tide and, having acquired at last an emperor with a reputation for fearlessness, had sent more reinforcements than ever before from all parts of the Roman world to deal with the problem. The emperor Septimus Severus and his eldest son were to see to it personally, using the regional headquarters at Eboracum and Coria as the main supply base. Extra cohorts of troops were pouring almost daily into the town, hastily building new barracks, covering the surrounding fields with tents of hide in tidy rows, drilling the men well into the evening of each day, crowding the streets with their silver-scaled clanking bodies, demanding produce and 'requisitioning' horses and waggons. To Dania's annoyance, some had even made a nuisance of themselves at her house.

The House of Women, open only from late afternoon onwards, was always popular with those soldiers and citizens who could afford it. Never had the competition for admittance been so fierce, and never before had the inmates had such an opportunity to discover what the chieftain Somer and his Brigantian compatriots needed to know. Looking, sounding, and living as a freeborn but local citizen of Rome, Dania had taken great care in the preceding six years never to disclose her origins. Only two people had come with her from Boar Hill, one of whom was Etaine, her woman; the other was Bran, son of Brigg, who had been renamed Brannius. Romanised Briton by day and Briganti messenger by night, Brannius was now twenty years old, only two years younger than his half-sister and utterly devoted to her, tall, comely, and proud of his dual role.

He stood by her side as she concluded her ritual at the small shrine of Diana, where a painted figurine of the goddess of woodlands and hunters reminded them both of their beginnings. 'I feel some unease about this meeting,' Dania whispered to him, adjusting the beeswax candle in the alcove. 'I don't know why.'

'Don't be,' he whispered back.

Turning to share the personal nature of the advice, she touched his smooth chin with her knuckle and a smile that made him wish they were not related. 'We've come a long way, Bran, son of Brigg,' she said. 'I think we may have redeemed ourselves, after our six successful years. I'm sure you're right. What is there for us to fear?'

Bran could have explained, but now was not the time for that.

Six years ago they had been brought here to Coria to establish a small weaving shop, just as she had suggested. They had not been left penniless or ill equipped, but nor had they found that first year easy, for they could scarcely make the beautiful hooded cloaks of waterproof wool fast enough to keep up with the demand, and they had taken on two local women to help them.

The sudden eviction from close-knit family into the vast bewildering strangeness of town life had been even harder, especially for Dania who, as a chieftain's daughter, had expected to retain her high rank for the rest of her life. Now she was, if not exactly a nobody, an ordinary citizen subject to a host of restrictions far more irksome than any she'd been used to. Romanised British women, she discovered, did not enjoy the same status as hill-fort women, and the closeness that had sheltered her at Boar Hill had disappeared over-night. It was a terrible loss she had not anticipated when she had bargained for her life, for her parents and Somer had been her world to whom she had never needed to explain anything. Somer had stood up to protect her against Mog; he had been the one to arrange her new life. He was her hero, and it was to each other that they owed their existence. Daily, her scorn of the Roman invaders remained intact while she strived to rob them of every slip of the tongue that would help to build Somer's status as the most fearsome chieftain ever.

Bran's regular returns to the tribe with any information he could glean, always at night, soon made a difference to Somer's success, and results quickly began to show, causing consternation to the Roman command along the Wall. So lax had things grown at the forts in the vicinity that the garrison once lost an entire tent-carrying unit when they were ambushed and, soon after that, another two units were lost when a fort was set on fire during the long hours of winter darkness.

It was about this time that Dana, who had re-styled herself Dania in keeping with her new status, discovered that Etaine had regularly been sleeping with soldiers from the garrison for money, her matter-of-fact explanation being that it was an easier, quicker and more lucrative method of making ends meet than by standing at a loom all day and half the night. Since they both knew how to avoid conception, there had been little danger to Etaine, and when she brought in a young camp-follower one day who was in dire need of medical assistance, their lives began to take on an unexpected and most unusual dimension. Their reputation as healers of women's problems soon spread like a forest fire through the gossipy, nosy, close-knit town of Coria.

Yet, because their arrival on Weaver Street had been so carefully arranged and executed, Dania's apparent connections with the relatively new breed of Romanised Britons and her background story of well-bred relatives in Eboracum and Cateractonium seemed to satisfy even the most curious of neighbours. It was not thought remarkable that she should be an unmarried woman in business, or that she should employ local people to help with the weaving and, when she extended her property to include the shop next door, mostly on the earnings of Etaine and Jovina, it made sense to employ a tailor who could help to maintain a front behind which the other more personal services could continue in private.

In their third year, Dania bought the land behind the shops and built a large three-sided house of two storeys and a garden that sloped down to the Cor burn. More recruits applied to join the House of Women as a safe base from which to work where they would be treated respectfully. She applied for a licence and was given one. Dania vetted the women carefully for intelligence as well as beauty and, just as importantly, for their willingness to listen when their clients, mostly of officer rank, talked about their work either in bed, at the table, or in the luxurious baths. That willingness had to include the accurate passing-on of any information to Dania, for now all her household shared a common loyalty to the larger tribe of the Briganti. What their lovely mistress did with the information they did not ask, though they may have deduced something from the increasing irritation of their clients towards the local hill tribes, particularly the one situated on Boar Hill, hidden in the woodland twenty miles to the west of Coria.

The changes to the original modest business were also reflected in Dania herself, so much so that, on her secret visits to Boar Hill, she always reverted to the way she had looked when she left it as a defiant and hurt sixteen-year-old. In Coria, however, she was the lady Dania, tall and slender and as close to men's ideals of a goddess as it was possible to be. She had grown to be a radiantly lovely woman with enchanting green black-lashed eyes, the same rich black as her abundantly waving hair which, as a lady of quality, she amassed on top of her head, bound by cords and ribbons that almost, but not quite, kept it in check. She held her superb figure as if she'd had dancing lessons since childhood, capturing men's attention with the sway of her walk and the unconscious grace of her hands and arms. Adopting the Roman style of dressing, as most civilians were doing nowadays, the softly draped fine wools, gauzy linens and silks skimmed modestly but provocatively over her lovely breasts and narrow waist, her hips and long shapely legs. The swan-like neck that, in public, was always covered by a fine veil, was by evening exposed to reveal necklaces of gold, amber, jet and pearls.

Demanding a high standard from the women who worked for her, Dania's personal principles had placed her totally beyond the reach of men. Not once had she joined the ranks of those who served the wealthy officers on their nightly visits to the House of Women, who came by recommendation only. She refused to admit all and sundry, nor would they have been able to afford it. Dania herself none of them would have been able to afford, and, although once or twice she had allowed herself to become fond of a man, thankfully he had been posted before a situation could develop. She was mistress of the house, no more, no less.

One of their most frequent guests was the centurion Claudius Karus, whose generous and frequent offers she had never accepted, though he had always taken it well. As an officer, he had the advantages of better pay and the permission to marry, which his legionaries had not. But Karus preferred bachelorhood and his visits to the House of Women; and to his revealing grumbles about life on the Wall, Dania and the others listened with interest and sympathy before passing on the information, usually within the same night. Now, she fully expected that Claudius Karus had sent for her to prove his efficiency to someone while putting her usual discretion to the test in public. No, there was no reason for her to be concerned, except that the soldier whose arm had been broken might have decided on some kind of revenge.

They walked in single file through the busy streets of the town, the giant bare-legged Ram one pace ahead of Dania, and Brannius one pace behind, hailed from both sides by friends within the narrow confines of the street. Once in Dere Street, they were obliged to keep well out of the way of the marching boots and pack-bearing burly bodies of soldiers, heads encased in shining steel, spears bristling from the ranks like a monstrous hedgehog.

'Legionaries,' Brannius whispered. Dedicated, disciplined and very dangerous, they were the fighting machines that the men in their tribal family hoped to vanquish by more unorthodox methods than open warfare.

'Auxiliaries, not legionaries,' Ram contradicted him. 'Syrians, too. The worst sort. Not renowned for discipline. Horses...well, we have better ones than those in the local knacker's yard.'

'How many?' said Dania, noting the swarthy skins. Her words were masked by the clatter of hob-nailed sandals and hooves on the stone road.

'A cohort. Usually eight hundred. Mixed, half-infantry, half-cavalry. Come, that's the last of them. We can get across to the Stanegate now. Mind that muck.'

Stepping over the mounds of steaming manure, they crossed over into the wide main street lined with big stone-built granaries on one side and towering temples, soldiers' barracks and officers' houses on the other behind a high stone wall. All around them people jostled and swerved to avoid the piled and lumbering carts and solid groups of soldiers who strutted with helmets dangling like buckets from their arms. Turning left into a side street, they were even more enclosed by the military world of shouted commands and the crash and yell of men practising arms, the stamp of feet and the shrill blast of a bugle that sent shivers down Dania's spine. All about them was ordered, white and polished, monumental and regimented, typically Roman.

'We turn right through this archway,' said Ram who had

been in places like this before. 'My lord Karus's office will be somewhere down here.'

Twice they were challenged and allowed to pass before they reached the wooden door where a polished legionary stood on guard duty, his spear held across it, his eyes beneath the steel brow-band wandering with furtive curiosity over the three visitors. 'Your business?' he said to Ram, assessing the impressive bulk. Ram's knee-length tunic was the only garment he wore over a pair of short pants, and its short sleeves revealed arms like tree trunks bound by leather wrist-bands.

He placed himself in front of Dania, shielding her from the man's too-obvious scrutiny. 'My lady's business is with Centurion Claudius Karus,' he said. 'She is expected.'

The guard opened the door and spoke briefly to the man inside. White-robed officials carrying piles of wax tablets in their arms passed to and fro over the tiled floor, their sandals slapping, ahead of shaven-headed slaves. Fully armed soldiers clattered past in coloured tunics, belted and buckled with silver and leather, with dangling dagger-sheaths and scabbards, their faces studiously intent. From the shadows of the echoing hall, the large red fan-shaped crest of a centurion approached them, his expression hidden between the curving cheek-pieces that met under his chin.

'The lady Dania?' he said. 'My lord Karus will see you in here.' His stiff glance at Brannius and Ram suggested that they should be excluded, but Dania changed his mind before he spoke.

'My bodyguards always attend me,' she said, sweetly. 'My lord Karus knows them both.'

The centurion looked as if he was about to say something, but the door at the end of the hall opened and an officer beckoned them forward, and Dania was left with the strangely elusive sensation that there was more to this than a routine enquiry into a man's injury. They entered and the feeling was reinforced by the lack of greeting from Claudius Karus, for now he was rigidly poised in full armour behind an unknown officer, his usual welcoming smile stifled, his arms like ramrods, his blue and usually twinkling eyes registering little by the way of recognition. So, it seemed that Karus's office had been taken over, and she would have to fend for herself.

Resigned, Dania turned her attention to the profile of the officer responsible for Karus's unusual silence, a tall powerfully built man too engrossed in speaking to his clerk to acknowledge her arrival with Brannius and Ram. At first glance, she was unable to guess at his rank, though it was obviously a very superior one. His dark red tunic was carefully pleated, but it was covered from the hips upward by a moulded and embossed leather body-piece, to the chest of which were strapped three vertical rows of engraved silver discs that she knew to be awards for outstanding service. Upon each broad shoulder lay a silver torque in the shape of a laurel wreath, drawing her eyes briefly to the thick column of his neck. Leather flaps hung from his armour, almost covering his short sleeves, and the light from high windows caught upon his heavily muscled arms ornamented with wide gold armlets, more awards for valour and service. Tight leather breeches reached as far as mid-calf and showed him to be a cavalry officer, the bare skin below as bronzed and hairy as his arms.

As he slowly turned to her at last, she saw the face of a man of thirty years or so, though with the helmet covering so much of it, it was hard to tell. The huge black-and-white striped crest on his helmet rocked and steadied.

Dark eyes looked her over without giving anything away, though it was the slight backward pull of his shoulders that contradicted his seeming indifference. Dania could by now interpret most of the signals sent out by men. 'Who's this?' he said, curtly.

His voice was deep and not, she thought, of this country. And his manner was churlish, to say the least. Nettled, she glanced at Karus, thinking that he might unbend enough to introduce her. But when his eyes remained fixed on some distant object above the door, she returned her attention to the aggressive male and quickly decided that silence would be the best way to deal with him. The room was scattered with men, one of them with his arm in a sling and looking very ill at ease in full uniform.

When the officer received no immediate reply, he looked sharply at Karus. 'Well?' he barked. 'Is somebody going to tell me?'

'The lady Dania Rhiannon,' said Karus, tonelessly. 'The next on your list, my lord. The assault case. Owns two shops and a house on Weaver Street where the assault took place. Sir.'

'And these two?' the man barked again, setting the plume nodding.

'The lady's bodyguard and companion, my lord.'

'Which one's the husband and which the lover?'

Dania thought it was time to speak for herself. 'I'm sure you meant that as an insult, my lord, but, as insults go, it could have been much worse. This is Ram, a free man employed by me to protect the inmates of my house. Brannius is also freeborn, as I am. He is my half-brother and therefore could not possibly qualify as either husband or lover. Have you any more questions of a personal nature before we discuss the reason for our being here?'

The man's eyes narrowed and, for an instant, he appeared to be totally taken aback by her fluent reproof. Through a half-open door, sounds of shouting and a loud yelp cut through the room's uneasy silence, and then the crest waved violently as the man signalled for the door to be closed against the ensuing sounds of a scuffle. It did nothing to steady Dania's racing heartbeat. He looked down at a wooden tablet being shoved slowly across the table by the clerk's finger. 'You are here to answer a charge of assault upon a soldier in the Imperial Roman Army,' he said, sternly. 'You have a house on Weaver Street. Is that the house to which you invited the legionary Lucius Grappus? *Step forward!*' he yelled at the arm-sling. The injured man obeyed.

'I did not invite Lucius Grappus to my house,' Dania said. 'He invited himself.'

'Eh? That's not what I've been given to understand. But he *was* assaulted and he *does* have a broken arm, sustained on *your* property. So, how do you explain that?'

'He was *not* assaulted, he was ejected from my premises for unacceptable behaviour. His broken arm is his own fault. My two bodyguards have orders to—'

'What unacceptable behaviour, exactly?' The officer had not moved from the spot, but Dania felt his overpowering closeness and the strength of his hostility from where she stood. 'What was his offence?'

'He was drunk,' she said, not wishing to go into all the details.

'And…so? Is that something you can't handle at your house?'

'If you must know, he relieved himself into the pool. Some of my guests were in it at the time.' Now the officer moved at last, coming to stand before her to take a closer look. 'You have a *pool*? Do you mean you have *baths* at your premises? A bath-house? Is that what you're saying?'

'Yes,' she said, lifting her chin to look him in the eye. 'I have a bath-house. Is there some reason why I should not?'

He turned to glare at the injured man, whose expression-less face inside the helmet was, chameleon-like, taking on the same colour as his red tunic. Clearly, this was a detail he had omitted from his report. Though his superior kept up his visual attack upon the embarrassed soldier, his next question was aimed at Dania. 'So tell me, lady, exactly what kind of establishment do you keep on Weaver Street that has a bath-house where both men and women too, I take it, bathe together?'

She took a deep breath. 'It is a house that some of the men in this room have visited often enough,' she said, tiring of having to defend them when they were doing so little to back her up. 'It is a house of great charm and pleasure to which only men of impeccable manners and refinement are admitted. With money, naturally. Your Lucius Grappus does not fulfil any of those requirements. In fact, he then went on to vomit on my dining room floor and, if I'd had my way, he'd have had both arms broken. I had to have the cool pool scrubbed out, and my mosaic floor too.'

His eyes widened again. 'You have *mosaics*?'

'Yes. Don't you? You find that of more interest than the insulting behaviour of one of your men?' The snub would have been hard to ignore.

Like rival mastiffs, they faced each other down until the officer turned angrily away to snarl at the wretched arm-sling. 'Get out! I'll deal with you later. I can hardly fine a woman, whatever kind of house she runs, for objecting to scum like you. And *why*...' he rounded on the poker-faced Karus next '...was I not given all the facts, Centurion? This woman runs a brothel, no less. Does she pay the proper taxes?'

'I beg your pardon, Tribune Peregrinus,' said Karus. 'I expected to hear this case myself. Yes, she pays the appropriate tax. Sir.'

'Do you?' he said to Dania.

'My lord Karus has told you that I do. He collects it.'

'Does he, indeed?'

'You may examine my accounts whenever you wish, and my receipts. I'll have them sent to you. I have a trusted slave to do them. A Greek.'

'You have slaves?'

Trying not to show how ruffled she felt by his constant challenges, she swept him a pitying look from her emerald green eyes. 'You have been too long in the army, my lord,' she said. 'Perhaps you should see more of the world.' Making the slightest signal to Ram and Brannius, she made an exit of such velocity towards the door that the soldier there hardly had time to open it before her, 'I bid you good day' floated back into the room on the tip of her long diaphanous stola.

Expecting some kind of explosive intervention at any moment, the three of them felt something like bewilderment to find themselves so promptly and easily freed, with a silence dogging each hurried step. The bright light outside made them gulp and move on without a pause, the soft linen of Dania's deep plum-coloured tunic swirling round her ankles, its wide gold-embroidered border glinting in the sun. It was not until they were once more in the narrow side street that she slowed. 'Bran, my sandal's undone,' she whispered.

He took her wrist and drew her to a halt, dropping to a crouch to attend to her laces while Ram stood close, with his back to her.

Brannius straightened. 'You're shaking,' he said.

They walked more slowly. 'Thank you. Yes. Let's get home.'

'You did well, my lady,' said Ram, in front. 'I wonder who that bastard is. Tribune, Karus called him. First time we've had one of *them* up here since we came. Things must be hotting up.'

Brannius was cynical. 'Having sorted out the local barbarians,' he said, 'he'll be off back to Eboracum tomorrow to collect another silver gong. Job done. We'll not see him again.'

'Oh, you have *mosaics*,' Dania mimicked, 'and *baths*, and *slaves*…and you wear shoes, too? Whatever next? *Peasant!*'

'Did you recognise the accent, Ram?' said Brannius.

'It's familiar, but I can't place it. I'll find out. Leave it to me.'

Julia Fortunata's incessant chatter was the very last thing Dania wanted but, hearing the high-pitched squeals echoing through the entrance hall from the distant bath-house, she knew that the chance of picking up some of the latest information was too good to miss.

To her relief, Astinax was still at his post and still grinning at the outrageous invitation he had politely refused from the centurion's woman. He chuckled as his mistress approached. 'Etaine and the bath attendants are with her, and her woman, whatever her name is,' he said.

Dania's eyes laughed at him. 'I'm sure you know exactly what her name is,' she said. 'But I wish they'd go home to bathe instead of coming here. It takes up my morning.'

'But just think,' said Brannius, 'what juicy morsels you'd be missing. She has to tell it to someone, so it might as well be you.'

It was quite true, Dania thought as she kicked off her sandals and padded softly along the corridor towards the bath-house. The air here was humid, the tiled floors warm underfoot, and the squeals had subsided. Julia Fortunata was being massaged.

Dania breathed in deeply, pushing the recent unpleasant scene at the barracks to the back of her mind. It would return later, she was sure, to nag her with every offensive detail, reinforcing her belief that men were best kept at arm's length. 'Julia!' she called across the shimmering pool. 'Lovely to see you again. What's the news?' It was best to get her own questions in before Julia's.

A damp head of yellow bleached hair lifted from the white pillow, the plump face changing from a frown at her washed-off nail paint to one of relief. 'Darling!' she called. 'Come over here quickly. I *must* tell you about the most *amazing* man I've seen for years. He's…ooh…he's a *brute*!' She giggled, rolling her slightly prominent eyes while, above her, Etaine's hands glided smoothly over her shoulders, oiling and kneading the superfluous layers. Julia's black mascara had run during her time in the steam room, her flushed cheeks and large pouting mouth reminding Dania of a full-blown rose about to drop its petals. Julia had always been ready to drop her petals at the slightest invitation.

Inwardly, Dania groaned at the prospect of having to listen to yet another of Julia's finds who, since the start of the new arrivals, would be the latest object of her lust. 'Yes?' she said. 'You must tell me. Where's Titus gone off to?'

As mistress of the centurion Titus Flavius, Julia had the best of both worlds, the security of well-appointed married quarters close to the officers' barracks and the freedom to release herself if she was offered a better deal. Needless to say, she made it her business to keep looking and, if Titus Flavius had not been so blind to the wiles of this vivacious and amoral woman, he might have been more receptive to the not-so-subtle warnings of his fellow officers concerning her virtue. Titus had no need to visit the House of Women, but he had no objection to his mistress's friendship with the lady Dania while he was so often away on duty.

Julia's plump pink body wobbled under Etaine's hands, her mop of hair flopping down again. 'Oh, Titus has hardly been home since the new battalions started to arrive. His men have been up at the Wall for the last few days. They have to extend the fort there ready to house the new cavalry unit. He's never been so busy, Dania. I'm getting quite desperate.'

'Desperate for what?'

'For a man, silly. What else? Ouch! Etaine, be careful!'

'I beg your pardon, my lady. Is it tender there?'

'It's tender everywhere,' said Julia, petulantly, looking with some envy at Dania's approach and the plum-coloured gown that slithered to the floor. 'Where've you been?'

'To the commander's office. Nothing much.'

'Ooh! See anyone nice?'

'No. They're so wrapped up in armour and their own importance that you can hardly see them at all.'

'I don't know how you exist without a man, Dania.' Back on the subject, she set about giving her friend a full description of his height, build, limbs, apparent virility and, sadly, his marked indifference so far to her attempts at friendship. So now, she told Dania, she needed the full treatment: a massage, manicure and pedicure, hair removal, facial, and a promise from Dania to invite him here so that she could drop in, accidentally of course, at the same time.

'No,' said Dania, swishing her feet in the cooling pool. 'Out of the question.' She sat on the edge of the deep blue-tiled bath that would have been lined with white marble if she'd been able to afford it. She had had the room painted to look like a sunny garden with trees and birds on fences under a blue-painted sky with cotton-wool clouds, though the floor was tiled. Behind them was the rest of the bath complex where guests could sit in hot steam, be oiled and scraped, sponged down in warm water before being toned in the pool. There were bath-houses at most of the forts along the Wall, but none of them, so her guests said, compared to Dania's, where they could enjoy the company of women at the same time. For a price.

'Why not?' said Julia, seeing her well-laid plans go astray.

'You know why not. I have to make a living, and my girls don't need your kind of competition. If you want to meet your handsome brute, you'll have to invite him to dinner yourself, love.'

Julia giggled at the compliment. 'You're mean,' she simpered, hanging a limp arm over the edge of the couch.

And you, Dania thought, are self-indulgent and manipulative. 'Yes,' she said, 'I know. But to make up for my meanness, I'll do your eyebrows.' Anything rather than have her here in the evening drooling over her latest heart-throb, whoever he was. 'What's his name, this new man?'

'Er…Fabian Cornelius Something-or-other. They always have three names, don't they, and I can never remember them all.' Like Dania, Julia was a Romanised Briton, but from Londinium in the south.

Dania lowered herself into the water's silky embrace and felt the refreshing coolness steal upwards to her chin, comforting her after the anger of the morning and the unbelievable escape with not so much as a warning. Nor had there been an apology, but that would have been expecting too much from such a man. He had rattled her more than she wished to admit, for now she realised that his attempted insult had been to get her to speak for herself. And it had worked.

She pushed herself away from the side to lie upon the first surge of water and to feel the sensuous ripples flow over her skin. 'So they're expanding the fort up on the Wall, are they?' she said to Julia, recalling a waving black-and-white striped crest above a shining helmet with a guard as big as a shelf sticking out over the back of his neck. There had been a small mascot of a bird up there too, she was sure. A peregrine falcon, perhaps? Peregrinus? Was that what Karus had called him? Tribune Peregrinus? Well, she need not worry; no tribune would visit a house of women, for he would certainly have one of the best officer's houses at the fort where his wife and family would live also. Poor things.

Well before Julia's massage was finished, Dania stepped out of the pool like a water-goddess, dripping and sleek, her back turned away from the inquisitive eyes of her gossiping friend. Not even the two young bath attendants or Julia's slave were allowed a glimpse of Dania's back, for only Etaine and Brannius knew about the puckered scar on her left shoulder-blade like two crescents one inside the other. The two deadly tusks of the wild boar. The mark of the Boar Hill. She had not even seen it herself, but she remembered her mother's tears, and Etaine's too, and the malevolent fanatical gleam in the eyes of Mog, the chief Druid, as he prepared to flaw the perfection of her loveliness. Mog had gone, just before her father, and she had refused to attend his funeral.

But by some happy quirk of fate, the coolness that once had existed between Dania and Mona, her older sister, had changed to a more mature understanding after the news of Dania's injury and expulsion had reached her. Mona had married into a Caledonian tribe over on the northern side of the Wall, not too many miles away, but separated by the physical barrier that made contact difficult. Mona's childhood envy of her younger sister had grown worse in the early years of her marriage, for she had lost both family and freedom while Dania still had both. Then, after hearing of the harsh treatment meted out to Dania, and her near-escape from a terrible death, Mona's heart had softened, and she had sent messages of support.

She had two young children; her young husband had two concubines who also had children. She could not reach Dania at Coria, nor dare she try. Regularly, they had sent verbal messages by whatever means they could over the last six years, by travelling merchants, by local traders and anyone who was allowed to pass along Dere Street through the Wall at Portgate and back again. Eventually their communications began to contain certain coded information that Mona's adopted tribe and their neighbours found extremely useful in planning their swift attacks against the Roman presence. In the eyes of her family, Mona's esteem began to soar, for it was only she who could decode Dania's seemingly innocent messages. The only problem was the unreliable nature of those who carried them and the lapse of time between sending and receiving. It was time, Mona's warrior husband said, that the two sisters met.

'Leave it to me,' Ram had told Dania earlier. Sure enough, as soon as he'd locked the street gate behind Julia Fortunata and her slave, he came striding back to his mistress. She was standing alone in the deserted garden where the singing birds and droning bees sounded like heaven after that barrage of inane chatter. He loped down the white stone steps towards her, nimble-footed in spite of his bulk. 'I've made enquiries,' he said. 'That bastard's come to tighten up on things before the emperor arrives.'

'So he'll be returning to Eboracum after that?'

'No, he won't. He's the new commander of a top cavalry wing of five hundred known as the Ala II Peregrina. The Second Peregrine Cavalry Wing. It's to be housed up at Onnum on the Wall, next to Portgate. They're already enlarging the fort up there. Stables, new bath-house, the lot.'

'Yes, I heard about the enlargement. I take it he was testing the ropes this morning. And his family will be here in Coria, or at Eboracum?'

'No family. He's a career man, one of four tribunes come over with the emperor to command a double-strength auxiliary unit between them. No time for a wife, apparently. And he's from Gaul, like his men. Brilliant horsemen.'

Dania sat down on the stone bench, carefully arranging the folds of her loose tunic over her knees. She was aware of a sick feeling in the pit of her stomach. 'His name?' she said, recalling the earlier disquiet she had felt before their meeting. When it came, she found herself saying it under her breath in time to Ram's reply.

'Tribune Fabian Cornelius Peregrinus.'

'May the gods help us,' she whispered. It had been her wish to come to live here at Coria, to help her tribe in return for her life, and she had kept her word since then at great personal cost, ever fearful of being discovered. Now, the might of Rome and the emperor himself had come to punish them, and doubtless every northern tribe would be made to suffer. 'Warlords,' she said. 'They've come for vengeance, have they not, my friend?'

'Yes, my lady,' said Ram. 'Warlords. The price of success is seldom cheap. I should know.'

Chapter Two

The misgivings continued unabated and, though Dania put on a good show of unconcern for the rest of the day and the busy evening that followed, her natural composure failed to carry her through the night without several times keeping the full moon company, trying to equate the disturbing events of that morning with Julia's alluring picture of Fabian Cornelius Peregrinus. Either Julia was deluding herself or she, Dania, had caught him on a bad day. Whether he had the body of an athlete or not, Julia's description of him as a brute was the only one that could be verified for certain.

Her resolution to dismiss the matter from her mind, however, was to be countermanded by events which, if she had been thinking straight, would not have been so much beyond her control as they appeared to be. She had sent Brannius off to Boar Hill last night to acquaint her brother with the most recent developments, and he was not expected back before dawn tomorrow. The servants had already begun to clear up and set the place to rights after last night's guests when an early messenger arrived from the commander's office. His message was brief and to the point: the Tribune Peregrinus wanted to see her accounts and to interview the Greek slave who compiled them. At once.

Her offer had been an act of bravado; she had not expected him to accept it and, if she had stopped to think, she would not have mentioned the Greek slave Eneas, a beautiful and sensitive young man, not the best material to withstand the typical army interview. She recalled the noisy scuffle in the room next door and the tribune's dismissal of the aggression. Accusations of army-style beatings, bullying, bribery, theft and confiscation of goods were rife amongst the civilians of Coria, even from visiting merchants who tried to register complaints.

'I cannot send Eneas alone,' she said to Albiso, her steward. 'He'll be terrified. They'll make him say anything they want.'

Albiso's thoughtful air suited him well. He was a well-educated slave, intelligent and steadfast. His silver-blond hair was thinning now, but his figure was that of a younger man, tall, lithe and spare, his linen tunic and loose-girdled wide-sleeved tunica revealing sinewy legs and ankles above immaculate leather sandals. His rather drawn face creased as he spoke. 'I'll go with him, if you wish, my lady. Or I could send Ram or Astinax, if you prefer.'

'Tch!' Dania sighed and looked down at the basketful of rose petals, herbs and flowers in the basket before her. She had wanted to forget all that, and now the tribune was making sure she did not. 'Wouldn't you think,' she said, 'that they'd have enough to do without bothering about a civilian's accounts? They're obsessed with taxes, that's the trouble. Send Ram with Eneas and tell him to get a receipt for them. I want them back.'

Albiso bowed and disappeared.

It was the nones of May, the day of the month when all the household shrines were decorated with flowers for the gods, of which Dania favoured seven, no less, in the House of Women. Some were of Roman origin, some were typically British, while other gods were shared to cater for the mixture of clients and household. Everyone had his favourite. The goddess to whom Dania made her private offering on this day was Coventina, whose watery shrine was in a fountain at the far end of the well-tended garden where the stream rattled beneath sleepy oak trees and combed the water-weeds like green hair. Scattering her last handful of rose petals into the well, she watched them swirl and tip over the edge and slide downstream into the shadows. Eneas and Ram had been gone for hours.

She tried to occupy herself more than usual, conferring with the cooks about the special evening meal, meeting the women and gathering their news, treating a queue of patients from the town and dispensing herbal medication from her small surgery, bandaging a child's cut head. She soothed a feverish infant with a dab of honey on the end of her finger while giving way to a moment of sheer bliss as she heard the wee thing sigh upon her shoulder and smelt the warm aroma of its hair. It would never be for her as it was for other women, for she was to all intents and purposes a Roman citizen with the mark of the Boar Hill upon her, and what man of either persuasion would understand the paradox in that?

* * *

When the afternoon wore on and still there was no sign of
Eneas or Ram, she felt it was time for her to move matters
forward. Tying her hair up inside a pink turban that left a
quantity of glossy black curls to escape the crown like a pot
boiling over, she threw a faded pink cloak around her shoulders and set off for the commander's office at a pace similar
to that which she had used to escape it the day before. Her
gold-corded sandals and those of Etaine threw spurts of dust
up behind them, and greetings were barely acknowledged.

This time, no explanations were needed. They were not
challenged. It was as if they were expected. 'We can't be,'
Dania whispered to Etaine, who had smiled at the winks of
at least two centurions and a standard-bearer. She was older
by several years than her mistress, blonde, and timelessly
pretty, petite, yet with the stamina of ten women. 'He doesn't
know I'm coming. How *could* he know?'

The guard pulled back his spear and opened the door for
them, releasing a surge of colour into the metallic world of
breastplates and helmets and echoing acres of stone and tile.
A crested centurion would have intercepted the flurry of faded
pink and green stripes, the cream and blue, the floating silk
scarves that caught in the draught, but he was too late. She
knew which door to attack and how gently to push aside the
spear that guarded it, and how to hypnotise the helpless man
with one stare from the deep promising green of her black-
lashed eyes. In that critical moment they were through, with
the guard almost falling into the room behind them, stutter-
ing with apologies and dropping his spear with a clatter.

Only two men were there, resting their behinds on a table

with their backs to the door, bareheaded but wearing leather-bound link-mail over their tunics, their weaponry in a heap on the table behind them. The fair bare head of Karus was easily recognisable; that of his companion could be guessed at from the width of his shoulders and from the way he ignored the crash of the door as it hit the wall. It was Karus who turned to look over his shoulder, whose word caused the tribune to smile and to lazily stand to greet his visitors, and Dania was as sure then as she could be that her visit *was* expected. Equally disturbing was Centurion Claudius Karus's comradeship with his superior. It was not a state of affairs Dania approved of; it felt like a betrayal, though she had betrayed his confidences time and again.

The look that passed between the two men was clearly of the *I told you so* order. 'Ah,' said Tribune Peregrinus. 'The lady Dania. Karus, take the other lady with you as you go.'

Dania protested. 'No. Etaine stays.'

But Etaine's arm was in Karus's familiar hand, and she was far too sensible to argue with two Roman officers, and the door was closed to hoots of laughter from the hall that afflicted the shame-faced guard at the door, a new recruit.

Again, Dania and the tribune faced each other across the room with green-eyed indignation on one hand and the faintest air of self-satisfaction on the other. 'Where are they?' she demanded. 'My servants have been here long enough.'

'Safe,' he said. 'Perfectly safe. You can have them back.'

'Then why…why…?' It was not so easy, after all, to deliver the high-sounding words she had rehearsed all the way here. Speaking to an anonymous triangle of face clamped between metal cheekpieces was one thing, but now she could see the parts that fitted so well with Julia Fortunata's gushing description, the hard masculine good looks, the crinkly dark hair and the set of his perfect head on the powerful neck, the chin square and softly blue-shadowed. What upper-class re-finement there had been from the start had now been mellowed and moulded by years of soldiering, narrowing the dark eyes and concealing any latent softness behind a hard veneer of discipline. There would be no dealing with this warlord except in his own military terms, for now he would have no time for the niceties of civilian life, no sensitivity, no finer feelings except for brotherhood and Roman honour.

She held her ground as he came towards her, no less im-pressive in his serviceable working gear than in full trophy-laden armour. There was a distant aroma of horses about him, and she knew from the heathery scent overlaying it that he had been out on the moors until only a few moments ago. These were the signs she had learnt from the hill tribes, signs that others would miss.

'Why, my lady?' he said, in answer. 'A wager, that's all.'

'*What?*'

He leaned towards her, intrigued by the growing anger in her eyes. 'That I could make you march back into here as fast as you marched out yesterday.'

Outraged, but refusing to back away, she gave him stare for stare. 'I see,' she said, icily. 'So I was supposed to ask permis-sion to leave and then offer the appropriate salute. I believe I was right, Tribune Peregrinus. You *have* been too long in the army.'

'And I suspect that you, lady, have been too long without a husband. Perhaps that's why you manage a brothel instead, so that you can run through a few hopefuls first before you—'

He saw the retaliation flash in her green-fired eyes and his hand caught the blow meant for his head well before it connected.

But the fury caused by his quick response and his insult was not so expected, for now Dania fought him like the wild cats of Boar Hill and not at all as a well-bred Romanised lady would have done with pleas for release, and tears. She had been taught well by the other women how to drive attackers off screaming into the woodland, how to kick and knee and stamp, how to twist and bite, to head-butt, spit, gouge and scratch, but this was the first time she had ever put it into practice.

Beyond her reach, he allowed it to continue so far and no further, and there was scarcely a moment when he was not in control of the situation. After which he closed in upon her and, holding her hard against the wall, waited for her to run out of steam, fascinated by the astonishing transformation from self-possessed woman of the world to frenzied barbarian. The pink turban now lay some distance away, and the loosened torrent of black hair fell in an uncontrolled mane of waves over her face and shoulders, covering the tribune's hands like the softest caress of water, tangling into the small metal rings of his mail shirt.

But Dania was not to know how, in that moment of instinctive but profitless response to his jibe, she had unwittingly revealed what she had been practising for six years to conceal. Nor did she appreciate at the time how the depths of her fury had been directed not only at the insult but at the man himself who, since their first meeting, had begun to represent a real threat to her and her future. That he was to invade her life, one way or another, was to her a certainty, for never before had she lost a night's sleep in trying to reconstruct a man's image, even from parts she had not seen. He had laid a wager on her return and she had helped him to win it, stupidly, like a love-sick girl. This she did not begin to appreciate until later, by which time it was too late to reverse it.

Predictably, her strength waned against the hard war-toned muscle of his arms and the clamp of his legs and body, and she had no breath left to continue. Not even with Con the Silvertongue had she needed to fight to free herself, for then she had only to close her mind to what was happening to her body while mentally reciting the most complex formula for one of her weaving patterns. The event had always been over before the last throw of the shuttle. Now, when she was well aware of her physical dilemma, she found the tribune's face still uncomfortably close to hers, still watching the savage wildness in her eyes and the deep fearfulness behind the blazing emerald rage. A lesser man would have let her go and run for cover, but the tribune's initial interest had now taken a different turn along which he resolved to tread very carefully. He had never been one to quit when things got interesting.

'Steady…steady,' he said, softly. 'Stop fighting now.'

'Let me go,' she replied, breathlessly. 'Let me *go*! I'm not what you think.' She pushed at him again, though his grip remained as firm and punishing as before.

'I know,' he said. 'Calm down. Karus told me you're not to be bought, and I didn't quite believe him. But I wanted to know why. Now I think I can see. It's fear, isn't it? Eh?' Lowering his head to her level, he searched her eyes more closely to find her answer. 'You're afraid, aren't you? Is that why you're not for sale?'

'Your questions, my lord,' she panted, 'are as unwanted as

your insults.' Strands of hair across her lips lifted at each breath. 'I am no more afraid than any woman whose affairs are being probed without good reason. My business is well run, orderly, legal, and causes no offence to anyone, least of all to the army who benefit from both our services *and* our taxes. What *more* do you want? I have my own private reasons for remaining chaste, the most obvious of which is that it tends to intrigue clients who believe that the answer must lie in money.'

'And doesn't it?'

'We would not be having this conversation, my lord, if it did. I've told you, my reasons are personal, but you can believe what you wish. Most men who ask flatter themselves that they can change my mind, but they're soon paired off with one of the women, and that's the end of the matter. *Now* will you release me? You're hurting.' She pushed again in desperation.

'And do you try to tear these deluded flatterers limb from limb, too? Your life must be exhausting if it is so, lady.' Tribune Peregrinus had seen fear often enough to be able to recognise it, and he believed he was not mistaken in identifying the nature of the lady Dania's. Slackening his grip just enough to allow her to move, he felt her trembling for the first time, the shaking in her legs.

'No,' she said. 'I employ two men to do that. You've met one.'

'Ah, yes, the gladiator is with us now, and the Greek.'

'Where are they? You said they're safe?' Her eyes opened wide with concern, and the tribune understood completely how the young guard at the door must have felt, though he would not avoid punishment for it.

He drew her away into the room, keeping hold of her until she was seated on a stout wooden stool. 'Not only safe, but probably enjoying themselves, too. Your giant is showing my men a thing or two, and your charming Greek lad is helping my librarian with my boxes of files.'

'I see. And my accounts? I can have them back now?'

'Not until I've had a look through them. Tell me about your household, lady. Are you as concerned about all their welfare as you are about these two? And the women. How do you recruit them?' He sat opposite her with his bronzed arms along his thighs so he could watch the way her hair fell in rippling drifts off her shoulders. Her cloak had fallen away in the tussle, and now he could linger over the peachy flesh of her arms where it showed between the pins. Long graceful hands massaged her wrists, diverting his mind along dangerous paths.

Where did she recruit them? This was unsafe ground, for several of them had been mistresses of soldiers killed in action in distant parts, some were local runaways, one was Welsh, but all of them held in common their hatred of Roman domination and a desire for vengeance. To their upper-class clients, they were all perfectly integrated into the new culture and unscathed by the changes to their lives. They were good at deception on every level.

Dania pushed an armful of hair over her head and stretched her neck in an unconsciously graceful movement that was too preoccupied to be intentionally seductive. 'Some of them,' she said, glowering at him, 'came to me for help. I have some skills with herbs, simple remedies, not witchcraft. Women come to me with their children each day. Some of my women came to escape abuse from men. They were on the streets. I care for them well, and they are free to leave, but none of them do. Some are local, some from further afield. All of them are free women, not slaves, and all take money as the law allows. I don't let anyone walk in without an invitation or a recommendation, otherwise I would not know of their suitability.'

'Suitability to pay, you mean?'

'Wealth and manners. I don't accept boors at my table.'

'And Claudius Karus is a regular?'

'My lord Karus is a regular guest, as are many of your officers.'

'Then perhaps I ought to apply for an invitation.'

'On your record, my lord?' She looked away in disdain. 'I suggest you save yourself the embarrassment of a refusal.' She did not see his smile.

He stood up and went to retrieve the tangle of pink fabric that had been her turban, handing it to her and leaning against the table from where he could observe the re-binding of her hair. Criss-crossed with pink and gold ribbons, her superb breasts lifted as she wrestled with the mop, and the tribune shifted uneasily at the hot ache of desire stirring his loins. Soon she would become the elegant creature of yesterday, a woman so in control that she had refused to speak until he had provoked from her a well-deserved rebuke. In minutes, she was restored, and few would believe that she had just shown him a glimpse of her other, primitive side. He passed her the faded cloak that had fallen off, noticing how quickly she covered her shoulders with it. And now the original picture was complete, only the remainder of an angry flush and reddened wrists telling of what had happened between them.

In one sense, however, Dania's impromptu visit had the desired effect of releasing her servants who were required at home. They waited in a group in the great hall, Ram, Eneas and Etaine talking noisily to Claudius Karus until the appearance of the tribune with their mistress whose expression had lightened not a whit since her arrival. One look at Eneas's serenity soon changed that; he had not been maltreated, he had been fed, and he had enjoyed himself.

The bright blue eyes in Karus's good-natured rugged face sought Dania's for signs of forgiveness but, though understandable, his lack of support had stung her and she would not look at him. Like all centurions, he was tall, well built and very fit, yet it was not until she could see the two officers stand side by side that Dania could compare his healthy attractiveness with the disturbing virility of Tribune Peregrinus about which Julia had raved. Unwittingly, Dania had to accept that, this time, Julia had not exaggerated, though 'brute' was too fine a description.

She would have made her brief courtesies and left if the tribune had not insisted on asking Ram and Eneas about their time as his guests, then turned his attention to Etaine and his fellow officer. 'The lady Dania insists that I need someone to sponsor me if I want an invitation to the House of Women. Would you be willing to vouch for my good manners, Karus?' He looked at Etaine and smiled.

Karus bowed his curly head. 'Certainly I would, my lord,' he said.

Dania's look was meant to freeze him to the spot. 'I believe the tribune is jesting,' she said. 'He's sure to have invitations from all the officers' wives to meet their daughters. He'll not require our lowly company, I'm sure.'

'Not quite the same thing, twelve-year-old daughters,' said the tribune, looking wistfully over his shoulder.

The men laughed, and, when Etaine sent her a pleading look, Dania knew she could not hold out. 'Then we shall expect you both for dinner one evening,' she said, ready to bring this shambles to an end.

'Would this evening be convenient?' said the tribune.

Dania clenched her teeth, wondering why she was agreeing to this. 'Of course,' she replied. 'Today is the nones of May, the rose festival. You must wear either white or pink to match my scheme.'

The men's bellows of laughter turned several heads, but the manner of Dania's exit from the building was conducted at a more sedate pace than her entry, accompanied by two officers who suddenly saw a most agreeable end to the day.

But in the privacy of his office, the Tribune Fabian Cornelius Peregrinus carefully extricated a long black curling hair from the metal links upon his chest and held it up to the light. Stretching it to its limits, he let it spring back again before taking it to the charcoal brazier and watching it frizzle to nothing. 'So,' he whispered, 'you're not what I think you are, eh? Wrong, lady. I think you may well be what I think you are.'

Fabian looked up at the colourful statue of the god Mars above the doorway to the commander's house and nodded to him like an old friend. Halfway across the courtyard he was met by two shaven-headed young men who bowed and kept up with his long stride, having learnt to expect the disrobing to begin anywhere between here and his private rooms. The tribune's fingers were already pulling at his belt-buckle.

He had welcomed this assignment to Britain's furthest outpost after the difficult campaign in Gaul with the emperor's army. After the battle at Lyon, he had been singled out again, commended, and decorated with honours, and now he was prepared to take on what was little more than a series of insurrections, another outbreak of resistance to the Roman rule along the Wall. It was time, the Emperor Septimus Severus had told him, that these barbarians learned whose land this was. Severus was not known for his gentle persuasion in these matters.

'My lord,' said one of the slaves, catching the heavy belt and scabbard, 'the cook wishes to know…'

'Tell him I shall not be dining at home tonight,' said Fabian, 'and I may be late back, too. I'll have my wine in the bath-house, Ajax.'

'Yes, my lord. Will you wear a short tunic, or long?'

'A long white one with a purple stripe, and the dark green dalmatica over it. And some discreet gold, I think.' He paused to have his leather boots unlaced and removed while his mail shirt was pulled off over his head, then his linen tunic, calf-length leather breeches and brief underpants. Naked, he was everything that Julia Fortunata had guessed at and more, for she had no way of knowing about the panel of dark hair that ran from throat to navel and from shoulder to shoulder. Years of punishing training had developed his muscle-bound body and hardened the bulging arms and legs with sinews of steel, and the swell of his chest was evidence of the miles of daily running and swimming, the weapons' training and horse-riding in which he had revelled since the age of ten. Unlike most other military tribunes, he had been in the Roman army for fifteen years, a tribune for five of them, and this would probably be his last posting before achieving his ambition to be elected to the senate. There was no better way to the top, not for the son of a noble and wealthy family whose estates in Gaul could swallow up this northern wasteland in one easy bite.

Having invested heavily in his career, his father would be proud of him. He would understand the significance of a success on the edge of the empire, where his auxiliary Gallic cavalry troop would look to him alone for their victory. And although they were prepared for any kind of hardship, he himself had not expected to be so soon on the trail of something as alluring as the lady Dania. The emperor would be with them in less than a week, and there was no time to lose if he wanted to make an impression. He sang loudly on the way to the bath-house, a song that his soldiers sometimes sang about a maiden and a lusty satyr, leaving Ajax and Privatus in no doubt about the direction of his mind.

Two hours later, the centurion Claudius Karus came to escort him and, together, they rode up Dere Street under a rich pink sky that changed their white tunics into the prescribed colour, before they turned into the shadows of Weaver Street. Men came forward to lead the horses away to the stables, and the iron gate to the House of Women swung open.

The mistress of that house had had plenty of experience at putting a brave face on things, but this was very far from what she had wanted, or expected. If things had gone according to plan, she would have kept the tribune at a healthy distance for some considerable time. And Karus too, for that matter.

Etaine had other opinions. 'Look at it another way,' she advised, fixing the last plait into place on top of Dania's head, 'we've not had anyone of his rank here before, but that's not to say we won't be hearing something valuable, once we've softened him up. All the men talk about troop movements and conditions and who's off sick and whether there'll be a full moon for night patrols, and there are very few who can resist saying that bit more than they ought, especially if you sympathise with them.'

'Well, I shan't be sympathising with either of them.'

'Then you'll be wasting a good opportunity, my lady. There, now,' she said, holding up a polished bronze mirror, 'take a look at that. Is that what you had in mind?'

At last, Dania smiled, turning her head this way and that to catch the last of the daylight upon the ropes of tiny pearls and the fine gold net. 'Yes, thank you,' she said, reaching for a pair of long gold and coral earrings. 'I think we're going to have to be a bit careful now, though. That man intends to look through the accounts and, although they're in order and up to date, it shows that there's more to his interest than sampling our hospitality. As for needing good company, nothing will convince me he's short of that.'

Adjusting the earrings, she licked a finger and followed the arch of her eyebrows with it. Men were all alike in their needs, and very predictable. Young and not-so-young, handsome or plain, ambitious, poor or wealthy. Some of her clients were successful merchants rather than military men, eager to offer friendship and 'help' with the collection of taxes as a prelude to trading concessions. Business talk was not discouraged at Dania's table or in the bath-house, nor was it only signet rings that men accidently dropped into the water each evening.

'Whatever you do,' Dania said, 'don't ask him any questions.'

Etaine's gentian-blue eyes opened innocently. 'Oh?' she said. 'You think he may want to talk to me, do you?'

Dania was not deceived. She had seen Etaine's interest and expected that there might be some competition for the tribune's favours. 'You can leave Karus to one of the others tonight, if you wish. I think you deserve our noble guest. Jovina will be happy to step into your shoes.'

Apart from Etaine, Jovina had been with them the longest. From Italy, she had followed her common-law soldier husband to Britain where he had subsequently been executed as a punishment to a rowdy battalion of mutineers. Her ensuing hate for the Roman military was put to good use at the House of Women, for her strong point was a knowledge of languages, and many a careless word from a Gaul, a Batavian, a Thracian or an Iberian had been picked up by Jovina's pretty ears.

'Yes,' said Etaine, 'Jovina and Flavia Augusta too, I dare say.'

'Then we shall be a lively party,' Dania said, smiling. Flavia Augusta was a southern Italian from Calabria who had bought her own freedom from slavery, not an easy thing to do. A wild handful, the men called her. 'And Candida?'

'Candida and Bronwen, Valetta and Ceri. Seven of us. That's a full house, so it's going to be a bit of a squash.'

Dania's usual practice was to have the table in the dining room laid with an assortment of cold dishes from which guests could refresh themselves at any time during the evening. Men and women would lounge, three to a couch, along three sides of the low table, though Dania always sat in a cushioned basket chair so as not to be too close to either her guests or her employees. Tonight, however, she had prepared a small dinner party for the festival of the roses to which more food and the very best wines had hurriedly been added, as well as more cushions to the couches. More glasses, more pewter plates, red Samian ware from Gaul and the big bronze serving dish that none of the women could carry. The guests would bring their own napkins, knives and slippers, but of Dania's collection of silver spoons, not one had ever been stolen.

Thoughtfully, she weighed in one hand the two heavy armlets of finely twisted gold strands, wide enough to conceal the shadowy fingerprints on her wrists, and of recognisable Brigantian workmanship. She could explain the armlets away as a gift or a purchase, but perhaps it would be best not to invite any comment on this of all evenings. To Mog's prediction, the anklet had been sawn off some years ago and fitted with a hinge so that she could wear it whenever she visited Boar Hill, just to prove him wrong. But he was no longer there to see, and it would be madness to let it be seen here in Coria. 'My gold bracelets,' she said. 'All of them, I think.'

'All of them, mistress?' Etaine watched her shake them into position, but the light was fading and only Dania could see, and still feel, the blueprint of the tribune's astonishing strength. 'Your ivory comb, too?'

'No,' Dania said, rising. 'I don't want to look like a char-
ioteer's horse in battle array. I shall go and check on things
before the arrivals. I wish Bran was here. He's so good at
times like this.' What Julia Fortunata would say when she discovered who had been to dine was the least of her concerns.

It was the unflappable Albiso who sensed Dania's nervous-
ness as he escorted her through the rooms to inspect every
last detail. Having dissuaded her from entering the busy
kitchen to ask the cooks yet again if they understood her
lengthy instructions, he followed her towards the dining room
and was rewarded with a more relaxed smile.

'Albiso, I don't know what I'd do without you. It's…beau-
tiful.' Dania revolved, slowly taking in the swags of pink
roses looping across the pink-panelled walls, the trails of ivy
festooning the lampstands and table. Bowls of roses had been
placed in every corner, and petals scattered the dishes that
held the cold first course on pewter, green glass, black and
red earthenware. Purposely, she had chosen foods for their
colour, pinkish oysters and prawns in a pink fishy sauce,
green endive and white radish salads, green olives, tiny hard-
boiled quails' eggs in nests of pine kernels with herbs and
honey; these were some of the co-ordinating appetisers.

The couches, too, had been covered with white, green and
pink blankets and tasselled cushions that echoed the soft
mellow tones of the mosaic floor, and now with the sun's last
rays flooding into the room from the garden beyond, the
effect was enticing and seductive. She sniffed, holding a
knuckle beneath her nose. 'Thank you,' she whispered. 'It
can't possibly go wrong now, can it?'

'It will be talked about for weeks and remembered for years,' Albiso assured her, prophetically, 'and your reputation as a perfect hostess will be unequalled, my lady.' Albiso had been her best investment since her arrival at Coria, his experience with an upper-class Romanised family in the east of the country having begun as a third-generation slave. In far-flung Coria, he and Dania had found a need of each other that exceeded the usual master-servant relationship; in exchange for her trust and protection, he had offered her his vast knowledge of Roman manners and house-management. 'Better light the lamps then,' he said.

'The rooms are all tidy?'

'Spotless, my lady.'

That was one area in which she had needed no help, having enforced a rule that the women's rooms leading off the corridors on the ground floor should at all times be kept clean, attractive and comfortable. Her own uncomfortable days of lovemaking would be hard to forget.

'Shall I leave the guest list with you?' said Albiso.

'No, I know who's coming.' She had invited seven to coincide with the day of the festival, but now there would be nine, and that was not a good omen. Unthinking, she probed for the umpteenth time with her fingertips between the gold bracelets for the still-aching bruises, and was surprised how the memory made her heart thud in response, reminding her of the threatening pressure of the tribune's body against hers and his uncanny perception of her fear that was more than simple rage. He would assume, naturally, that her fear was of men in general in which case, she thought, her best method of defence would be to pair him off with Etaine, whose methods of getting men to talk were highly effective. Even a tribune would not be immune to her.

Barefooted young men in white tunics filed past her into the dining room while Etaine led her six friends into the entrance hall, each woman robed in tones of pink and holding a garland of sweet-smelling herbs to place around the neck of the guests. Their chatter gave way to smiles at the approach of the first group of men in dazzling white ankle-length tunics, followed by more who drifted slowly across the courtyard like wind-blown may-blossom, trying to disguise their eagerness behind animated men-talk.

At the verandah steps Ram and Astinax bowed, assessing the physique of each male as they had learnt so well how to do, but concealing their verdict behind punch-toughened masks. Moments later, the last two guests emerged to join the gently whirling pool of colour and the cadences of laughter and, though their training had also taught them how to keep their thoughts hidden, neither of them could prevent the admiration showing through their eyes at the first seemingly artless greeting. Of the two, only Karus knew how, this time, Dania had truly excelled herself.

As if to represent every part of the rose except its petals, Dania's silken gown flowed and blended in tones of green as she walked towards them. Cross-bands of gold and pink ribbons outlined her waist and breasts, and a length of green gauzy silk was tied casually round her hips to drape down one side. A pink rose upon one shoulder nestled into the veil swathing her neck and shoulders, its purpose best known to herself and Etaine, but which might have been mistaken for a desire not to compete for attention. She gave no thought to the possibility that she would have outshone the best of them, even in rough homespun.

To the tribune she held out a hand for him to kiss, as she knew some of the Gauls did, with a smile that did not quite reach her eyes. This is business, she appeared to be saying, not the beginning of a friendship. 'You are most welcome,' she said, contradicting her thoughts.

Two dark eyes smiled back at her before making a detour over her perfect coiffure that suggested he was comparing it to an earlier, more natural arrangement. The touch of his lips upon her knuckles, so different from his first unmannerly greeting, was as gentle as a moth's wing. 'I am honoured, my lady,' he said, holding on to her fingers until she returned her eyes to his.

Confused and disturbed by what she saw there, she took refuge in her greeting to Karus, a cool peck to both cheeks with the same professional smile. Behind them, there was laughter at the usual ritual of changing from outdoor sandals into slippers, the obstacles of bending bodies, swinging garlands and wobbling guests, always a source of hilarity at the House of Women. She placed garlands around their necks and could see that the tribune was already impressed not only by the guests' faultless dress and the loveliness of the women, but also by the sumptuousness and exquisite taste about which the fourteen-year-old Lepida had chattered all the way home. Clearly, it surpassed anything Fabian Cornelius Peregrinus had expected, whatever that was.

There was the usual exchange of gifts: Fabian had brought a small package of peppercorns tied with a ribbon, a rare and expensive spice for most citizens. Later, he was to discover that, to Dania's cook, it was not as rare as all that. Karus offered her a tiny blue glass perfume-bottle with a stopper as big as a pea, and she accepted them both with genuine delight.

Soft shadows in the evening light, weaving figures of white and pink, glowing lamps on tall iron stands, shining reflections, patterns underfoot and the flickering wicks before the flower-covered wall-shrines made a kaleidoscope of colour that danced to the distant sound of pipes, flutes and tambours, cymbals and castanets. Already eased by their welcome, the men were led towards the dining room from which could be seen a troupe of musicians in the garden beyond, ducking and dancing beneath lanterns hanging from the trees.

'I prefer the women to introduce themselves,' said Dania to Fabian, walking between him and Karus and rescuing her hand at last. 'I find it works better that way. But I *will* introduce you to the guests, once we're seated. If I do it now, the meal will be delayed and that, you know, drives a woman mad.' It was her attempt at lightness that began to melt the fine dusting of frost.

She led the two of them round the back of one couch to the centre position. 'The place of honour is yours, Tribune Peregrinus. Will you take the one next to it, my lord Karus?'

'Still angry?' Karus whispered to her.

'Yes,' she replied, smiling.

'I had no choice.'

'So you thought I'd better have none either. Now I don't have enough women.'

'I'll go without.'

'Thank you.' She didn't want to tell him that that had

already been decided. Bowing their thanks, the men lay diagonally across the couches, resting their left elbows on the large tubular cushions. The first man to be introduced to the tribune on his right hand was already half-known to him as Vitalis, the pharmacist-doctor from the garrison hospital at Vindolanda who came often to talk with Dania as much as to take advantage of the other pleasures.

But by now there were other men known to Tribune Peregrinus: two handsome British centurions and a Frankish decurion, a seasoned Italian standard-bearer and a much younger Iberian adjutant who could talk the hind leg off a donkey. The only guest he had not already met was Metto Lentus, a leather merchant and owner of the large tannery at Cateractonium, which supplied the garrisons along the Wall with every sort of leather, fur and parchment. On his visits to Coria, he would always call at the House of Women, paying in kind rather than coin. It was a trade that benefited both, especially the shop of Dania's excellent tailor.

Around the table, the atmosphere was instantly cordial and, even though the guest of honour was amongst subordinates, his easy conversational manner showed that, out of uniform, he was one of them at heart. There was laughter and teasing, the women sitting alongside the men to help them to the food, moving from place to place to keep the chatter rattling along like a well-mannered stream. Talk ceased during Bronwen's reading of one of Sappho's poems, her Welsh lilt as enticing as the words. Jugglers threw goose eggs in the air to the accompaniment of tabor and cymbal and the occasional shriek of alarm, and two of the women danced to a slow exotic melody on the pan-pipes and cythera, making the men chew on their lips and tap fingers on the polished oak table. Two more sang a love-duet of haunting sadness while Dania plucked at a lyre, and, towards the end of the third course, the acrobats began their performance. Slaves soundlessly replaced the roast barnacle-goose, the salmon and the rissoles of lamb in rosemary with the 'third tables' of fruits and tiny cakes, anise and caraway seeds, topping up the wine and mead in each silver goblet.

From her basket chair on the open fourth side of the table, Dania rinsed her fingers in the rose-petalled water-bowl and moved her chair back into the shadows, well satisfied and curious to see who was more engrossed in their partner than in the acrobats. But as if on a string, her gaze was slowly drawn towards the far side of the table where the eyes of one man were exerting a magnetism to put an end to all the unsuccessful evasions she had tried earlier. He was not watching the amazing contortions of the troupe, nor was he responding to Etaine's hand upon his shoulder, but his steady contemplation held Dania's eyes in a grip as real as his previous one upon her wrists and, though she blinked and tried to look away, she was obliged to read the message she had learnt to interpret in so many languages, both silent and spoken. The soft steady beat of the tabor faded, only to be caught in a different and private part of her body, leaving her breathless and apprehensive.

She closed her eyes at last and looked away, drawing the green veil closer around her neck to cover the burning sensation that stole into her cheeks. Her guests and the women were occupied and, above the tribune's back, Karus was carefully removing Etaine's hand with a shake of his head. This was the time when Dania could leave them, allowing hands to go where they pleased.

Taking a last sip of her watered Rhenish wine, she rose as smoothly as a shadow, praying that the man's interest would be diverted to something within his reach, but feeling it still upon her as she left the room filled by soft laughter and music. Her heartbeats drowned out the applause, and the soft draught of pursuing feet sent rose petals swirling around the hems of their gowns.

Chapter Three

It was Dania's way to leave the table for a spell to allow her guests the chance to do the same, if they wished. In the large entrance hall lit by oil lamps, she would recline upon one of the couches and watch from a shadowy recess to monitor the progress of her hopes. Her tabby cat would usually join her there, but tonight there had been fish on the menu and she was joined instead by the man who had made no bones about following her so promptly from the table.

She was not best pleased. The idea of having to engage in any kind of conversation with him irked her and, knowing that this was her duty as a hostess did nothing to make the burden lighter. At home on Boar Hill no one would ask a man his identity or business until after he had partaken of their food, but this was not the Roman way. So why did she fear she was in for a grilling?

Doing her utmost to control the thudding in her chest, she watched through half-closed eyes devoid of welcome as the tribune's gold-bordered robe settled next to hers, noting how the wide sleeves revealed strong wrists that angled down to the inside of his thighs. A heavy gold ring flashed on his left hand, the badge of equestrian rank, and the white under-tunic of finest linen and silk showed a narrow purple stripe as if it were of no real consequence. The Romans, she knew, lived by such tokens. Following the long legs down to the crossed ankles, she noted the briefest of leather sandals and was suddenly reminded that her own feet were bare. She pulled them carefully beneath her pale green hem.

'You left yours beneath your chair,' he said, quietly.

His hands were still relaxed and, as her eyes moved slowly upwards to reach his face, he shifted his body to face her, placing his arm along the low back of the couch. She felt trapped and already at a disadvantage.

'And you have left Etaine with Claudius Karus,' she said. 'A pity. She was so looking forward to spending time in your company, my lord.'

'Does that apply to you also, my lady?'

'I take it you prefer an honest answer?'

'That is what I would expect from you, certainly.'

'Then, no, it does not apply to me too. I think I should go and invite the physician Vitalis to join us. He speaks the most profound good sense, I find.'

'I hope you'll hold out a little longer. At this moment, there is only one person whose company I want.'

'Oh, then I'm sorry for it. The last two hours must have been difficult for you.'

'You know that's not what I meant.'

'Do I?'

'Yes, you do. The meal was a great success, the food and

conversation of the very best, your skills as a hostess without equal, the women all beautiful and good company, but…'

'Flavia Augusta would suit you well, I think.'

'…but I prefer the one who tells me…'

'And Ceri, too. I saw her looking long at you.'

'…who tells me she's not available. Is she still of the same mind, I wonder?'

'I should not waste your time asking her, if I were you.' When he did not immediately reply, she turned to look over her shoulder and, anticipating an expression of resignation, at least, was disconcerted to find that his eyes, black with hunger, were caressing the nape of her neck and then her mouth until they came to rest in the cool greenness of hers. She tried to hide her concern, but she knew he had seen it. 'Tribune Peregrinus,' she said, as a prelude.

'My friends know me as Fabian.'

'Tribune Peregrinus, I am sorry if you have forgotten what I said when we met this afternoon. I thought I had made the situation clear. I *am* unavailable not only to you but to anyone, and that is not about to change. Now, do you mind if we talk about something else? I think we've worn *that* subject out, and I've nothing more to add.'

'Where is your half-brother tonight?'

Her shoulders tensed under the too-abrupt change of direction and, for a numbing moment that seemed like an hour, she could not remember what to say. When she did, she was aware of its desperate ring. 'Er…he's out. Seeing a young lady in Coria. He has his own life,' she added, lamely. Unconsciously, her hand strayed again to the bruises beneath the gold bracelets, probing, waking herself to the danger. Lying had not grown any easier even after years of practice, and many times recently she had felt that her two different lives at Coria and Boar Hill were about to submerge her beneath their never-ending deceit. She must swing the conversation into deeper channels.

'How do you find the cold up here in the north?' she said. 'My weavers and tailors make excellent cloaks and breeches for all seasons. Made to measure. Any colour. Fur-lined, dec-orated or plain, long or short, hooded for riding. Your troops are cavalry, so I understand?'

Fabian smiled, leaning forward to lay his forearms along his thighs and looking back at her with the lamplight playing upon each chiselled plane of his face, on the healthy tan of his skin and muscled cheeks, on the varied brown tones of his crinkly hair that fitted like a neat dark cap. 'Yes,' he said. 'It's certainly cooler up here. I dare say we shall all be needing cloaks if the summer is as short as they say, and the mists as thick. At the moment, the men are keeping warm by extending the accommodation. They can't live in tents for ever.'

'Oh?' Dania said, keeping the interest level low. 'Accom-modation on the Wall, you mean? Or here at Coria?'

'Up on the Wall, for one. The builders and engineers are in charge of that. But that won't be enough for my own five hundred horses and men.'

'So what will you do, stable them in billets?' She knew there was no possibility of that. The Roman army were stick-lers for having everything under their direct command, not scattered all over town.

'No, we're about to rebuild another place about half a mile away along the Stanegate. What did they call it…?'

'The River Fort? You're rebuilding *that*?' She stared, struggling to disguise her interest at the news. The River Fort had once been built of timber by the early Roman military before the Wall was erected. But the site they chose was occupied by Dania's ancestors at the time, a minor detail of no importance to the invaders who burned the settlement to the ground, including the splendid chieftain's house, slaughtering the protestors, abusing the women, and sending the rest off to eager Roman slave merchants. Those who managed to escape went north into the woodland to a place they named Boar Hill. Just over a hundred years ago, the hill tribe revenged themselves and their ancestors by setting fire to the River Fort one night with such devastating efficiency that it was never repaired, but left to die back into the ground, since when they said the place was accursed, a place of ravens, crows and wolves.

'Karus and I went over to have a look at it this afternoon,' said Fabian. 'It's a good site, between the river and the Stanegate. It should take only a week or two to make it habitable, with plenty of timber around. I think we should have men on the job from tomorrow.'

Dania could hardly believe what she was hearing. Talking so soon? This was almost too good to be true. How much easier would it be to glean information if they were to become friends instead of opponents? The thought was dismissed as soon as it appeared. The man was far too dangerous. He would not be satisfied with a mere friendship, and one small step down that road would inevitably lead to disaster. But now she held information that Somer could make good use of, which she could not send by Brannius for he would be on his way home at this very moment. She would either have to send one of the men, or go herself.

By her side, the tribune was studying the mosaic floor between his feet, his powerful shoulders hunched, his head turning from side to side. 'Dido and Aeneas?' he said. 'You know the story, then?'

'Yes, believe it or not, my lord, I do. It was designed for me, not chosen from the mosaic artist's pattern-book.' She was uncomfortably aware of the boast, but humility would cut little ice with this man.

He turned to look at her with the same quizzical expression. 'Why,' he said, softly, 'when it's so very tragic?'

'Life is,' she whispered, before she could find a lie to offer.

Had she been a man, whether on his side or hers, she might have been able to say, *Life is heroic, and death even more so. Revenge and honour, fighting and dying are all that matter. Love is a woman's business, not a warrior's, and Aeneas had no choice but to go.* But she had long since stopped believing that the glorious afterlife had more going for it than this one, and if it was as full of her battle-crazed ancestors as they said it was, without any real proof, then she would rather stay in this world with all its shortcomings. The gods had dealt kindly with her, placing her in relative safety, but while the men were indulging in their lust for blood and honour, even fighting amongst themselves, it was the women who suffered most. She knew. She saw it every morning in the sad little crowd who came to her gates, whose sagas of woe and mental trauma were far more difficult to treat than coughs and infections. For them, life was a tragedy every bit as heartbreaking as that of the wealthy queen Dido, who was probably weak, anyway.

Two intertwined couples, Etaine and Karus amongst them, sauntered into the entrance hall to recline on two of the couches between the shrines to continue their whispered conversations with an intimacy Dania did not want to be a party to. She stood, her slight hesitation indicating to Fabian that he should do the same, a message he understood with gratifying promptness. They passed through the dining room on their way to the verandah overlooking the garden, allowing Dania a glimpse of her friend the physician who was happily engrossed in a three-cornered group with the vivacious chatterbox Valetta and the leather merchant. It occurred to Dania that her companion might take the hint and rejoin the company, but instead he took hold of her elbow and manoeuvred her firmly towards the wide open doors and the shallow steps that led down to the formal pathways where flowerbeds doubled as a herb garden.

To resist would have drawn attention to them both; to pretend duties elsewhere would have been an unthinkable snub to an honoured guest; and to remonstrate, even *sotto voce*, would have made very little difference if his grip was anything to go by. She tried it, just to prove her point. 'My lord,' she whispered, admitting to just the merest hint of insincerity in the protest. Here she was, being led towards the darkest corner of the garden by the most handsome and superior officer any of them had ever seen, her bare feet tripping alongside his while her body shook like a virgin, part-excited, part-annoyed, and very much aware that each step was taking her deeper into danger. She *must* put a stop to it. Now. 'My lord…no…I cannot leave my guests yet,' she hissed.

Beyond the splashing fountain and the low box hedges, the

lawn sloped gently down towards the grove of oak trees beneath which Coventina's Well was lit by a single lantern. Low stone walls surrounding it channelled water into a stream, and it was upon one of these walls that Fabian seated her, brushing off the mossy bits, but keeping hold of her as he sat, much too close to allay any of her concerns.

'Now,' he said, turning to face her, 'let's hear it, my lady. What's so tragic? What is this reticence all about? Why are you not married? Are you widowed, is that it? Who are your family? Where are you from? I can find no record of your citizenship in my office.'

Something moved alarmingly under her ribcage, and she shrugged, angrily. 'Would a simple yes do? Or perhaps a no?' she said.

She felt his sighing half-laugh upon her cheek and, from the house, the sounds of music were carried on the night air cleft by the wings of moths and the squeak of bats. There was a man's shout, and a distant bugle-call from the barracks. 'Try again,' he said, 'if you will.'

Lifting the gauze veil from her neck, she draped it over her head and wound the ends more securely around her, hoping to show him that she had no intention of revealing herself to him. 'Tribune Peregrinus,' she said, 'do you suppose such enquiries would be better suited to your tribunal at the garrison than here in my garden? I have no objection to my guests talking business, if that's what they want, but I've been preparing this event for some days and I had hoped to get more out of it than two muddy feet and a recital of my credentials. I could fetch my lyre and sing them to you?'

It was too dark for her to receive enough warning of his

purpose, for she had not believed that any guest, however high-ranking, would ignore her declared intent to remain masterless. But he was quick, and it was clear by his hold upon her that he knew exactly which way to swing her backwards so that she had to cling to him to keep her balance, though he held her secure. With her head cushioned firmly against his shoulder, there was no defence she could devise that would not result in her falling over backwards into the stream.

'Ah,' he said against her mouth, 'but I remember what it takes to make you compliant. As an honoured guest I have no wish to overstep the mark, my lady, but it would be a pity if all you got from this wonderful evening were two muddy feet. And I *do* need to know more about you.'

The first thing he apparently needed to know was only a breath away from his taunting words, and though he had given her time to anticipate something similar to Con the Silver-tongue's over-excited puppy-dog enthusiasm, what she experienced in that first moment of contact kept her mind focussed on the unbelievable difference between a bungler and a past master.

Her visual world tipped backwards into the starry sky and she was held, helpless to right herself, while the tribune's discoveries began, and she began to see that perhaps she should not have assumed that all lovemaking was the same until she had more to go on. The fear and anger were still there, but for those few incredible first kisses they had to take a back seat. Even when he paused, her struggles could not be taken too seriously and, when he continued, her mouth was ready and tingling with anticipation, her hands peaceful against his back and shoulder. When at last he gave her a chance to speak, her mind was in turmoil, her words emerging sideways, staggering like a drunk out of an inn.

'Not…not that…no, my lord…mustn't happen…please.'

'You're married, then? Or grieving for your man? Tell me which.' If the experience had shaken him too, he gave no sign of it.

'This is…is unfair. You have no right to ask, and you *have* overstepped the mark, sir. I could call my guards and have you thrown out.'

His lips teased hers, and there was a smile behind his words. 'Yes, you could do that. But you won't because you're curious now, aren't you? And I believe you'll allow me back, by and by, to remind you. Is that not so, my beauty?'

'No, indeed it is not so,' she snarled, struggling more fiercely. His humiliating observations were too near the mark. She was not only curious, but amazed and tempted beyond caution to sample it again. 'It is *not* so, my lord. I cannot afford to take a lover…*ever!*' *And if I did, it would not be one of your kind. A citizen of Rome.* 'I refuse to tell you any more than that. You will have to understand that even a man of equestrian rank must learn to take no for an answer. Now let me up. You are spoiling my evening.' Her angry words had begun to falter and shake as impending danger and strange emotions fought within her and, when he delayed on the edge of a decision, her fears surfaced like a geyser under pressure. Her struggles became more frantic, putting them both in danger of a fall.

'All right…all right…I can hear you!' He brought her upright, catching her flailing arms by the wrists, not in the least put out by her attack. 'Hush, now, that's enough.

Hark…what's that? What's happening?' He turned aside to look towards the house where dark figures could be seen moving quickly across the lamplit rooms. Voices called from the verandah.

'Tribune…Tribune Fabian…come quickly, my lord!'

He loosened her wrists and in one bound was halfway across the garden, sprinting with his long robe screwed up in one hand, leaving Dania reeling on the wall of Coventina's Well with her heart pounding shockwaves through her arms.

The urge to stay alone in the solitude of the garden, pulsing with the re-awakened demands of her body, almost overcame the discipline of a lifetime. Almost, but not quite. Using all the foul names she could remember to describe her honoured and insolent guest, she held her face between her cool hands until her breathing had returned to normal, then followed him at a more leisurely pace along the path, observing the sudden exodus from the house at a safe distance.

'What on earth's going on?' she said, picking up a clod of soil from someone's shoe. The last white tunic disappeared across the courtyard as she spoke.

Astinax and Ram were laughing. 'Early night,' one of them said.

The women stood about or sat in groups, their lovely faces registering bemusement but no real alarm, their toes nudging idly at the rose petals. It was not the first time this had happened. Etaine came forward, stifling a yawn. 'It's a raid,' she said. 'Two soldiers came rushing down from the fort up on the Wall. I think it's serious.' She placed a finger against her lips before Dania could respond, warning her that Metto the merchant and Jovina were crossing the dining room behind her to the door that led to the women's quarters. Metto was in luck.

Etaine waited for the door to close before she continued. 'The military had to go,' she said, frowning at the two guards' levity. 'There'll be no takings tonight.'

'We can manage,' said Dania. 'Did they say who's involved?'

'They didn't seem too sure. One said the Caledonii, the other said Brigantii but, whoever they are, they've torched the roof that's just been put on the new cavalry block and barracks, and they've killed— Oh…ye gods…look who's here!' She peered over Dania's shoulder into the garden where a cloaked figure came bounding out of the shadows and up the verandah steps, his face smeared with dirt, sweat and blood. *'Bran!'* she called, like a mother.

Dania pressed a palm against her midriff as relief turned somersaults inside her. Brannius's return from Boar Hill was always at night through the oak grove at the back of the house to avoid any accidental meeting with clients. This time, the secrecy was even more necessary, but he had not stopped to change his raiment in the stable as he usually did before entering the House of Women, and at once Dania's recent fright found an easy target.

'What in the name of the gods,' she hissed at him like an angry gander, 'are you thinking of, coming in here dressed like *that*? Don't you know…?' She pointed towards the entrance where Astinax and Ram still hovered.

'I *saw* them,' Brannius said, his voice still hoarse with yelling. He was not his usual energetic self, but hurt and exhausted, his dark hair plastered over his forehead like a dirty rag, his cloak sliding off his shoulders to bare a sweating torso scored by the slashes of blades. 'I saw your guests, Dana,' he repeated, letting her take his cloak. 'I waited till they'd gone. I actually followed the two messengers part of the way from the Wall to here.'

'You were there? At Onnum?' Etaine said. 'In the fighting?'

The women gathered closer to hear. 'Yes, I was part of the raid. My lord Somer decided to act on the information straight away instead of waiting till there were more men up there. Besides, there's a moon tonight again. He allowed me to go with them, this once.' He sank down upon the nearest pristine couch and lay back into the swansdown cushions, closing his eyes. His long chequered wool breeches low-belted on his slender hips made an incongruously muddy sight amongst the rose petals and pink-robed women. Even so, there were several pairs of eyes that missed no detail of his manly apparatus.

Dania sat beside him in the hope of more. 'Was it successful?' she said. 'Were any of our men hurt…killed? Tell me the truth, Bran.'

Without moving or opening his eyes, he droned tonelessly on the brink of sleep, 'Yes, it was successful, Dana. We raided the fort at sundown just as their builders had stopped work and gone into the fort. We set fire to the timbers, the scaffolding, the platforms, and some of their men were caught before they could arm themselves. It was slaughter. But there are more of them than we thought, and we had to make a run for it back into the woods. They thought we'd gone for good. We waited till they were settled down again, then we attacked a second time. We lost a few men, but they lost more. It was good, Dana. Somer yelled at me to go home and tell you, so I did…and here…I am.' Lacking training, he was too tired to breathe.

Dania could see that it would be useless to ask him for more details. Carefully, the two giants carried him to the bath-house and then to his bed while the pink-robed women carried leftovers from the kitchen back to the dining room where they occupied the still warm couches. Dania sat with them, but apart, blocking out their chatter and quite unable to hold back thoughts that advanced like a landslide, filling her mind and churning up her carefully regulated emotions. Her fears about the tribune's menace had so far been borne out, but he had also shown himself to be just as foolish as the rest of them when it came to spilling valuable information. It had been on just that kind of idle talk that the fort at Onnum had been attacked tonight, and men's lives lost. Given the choice, she hoped the man would be too occupied to visit again but, if he did, could she afford to antagonise him when his loose tongue would be of so much value to Somer and to her sister Mona's family?

Etaine came to join her, closing the verandah doors against the cool night air and stooping to examine the glass perfume-bottle on the small table. Smiling, she unpinned the squashed pink rose from Dania's shoulder and laid it next to Karus's gift. 'And there's the difference,' she said, regarding them. 'At least Karus can understand the word no. That's what rank can do, you see.'

Dania had no illusions about what had happened. He had even admitted it. Having learnt how to make her respond, he had found her weakest point and was using it against her. No doubt he would have done the same to any woman. 'Sit with me,' she said, 'and don't ask what happened.'

Pulling up a stool by the side of Dania's chair, Etaine placed another cushion behind Dania's head. 'Put your head back and tell me,' she said. 'We could all see who he wanted, love.' Etaine could be motherly to her mistress, too.

'It won't do, Ettie,' Dania whispered, stretching her neck like a swan upon the cushion. 'I was a fool to think he would behave like a gentleman, or that I could manage him. Next time, if there is one, I shall keep someone with me.'

'Well of course there'll be a next time, and you're going to have to deal with it. He'll get the message eventually, I suppose, and maybe he'll take one of us, but I wouldn't bet on it. Still, it would be a pity if we lost him altogether. He'd make a better friend than an enemy, that's for certain.'

That was exactly the conclusion Dania had reached. 'He makes my hackles rise,' she said. 'I dislike him. I don't want him here. Arrogant…insolent…!'

'Don't worry,' Etaine smiled, knowingly. 'Tonight's little setback will keep them busy for a while. You know what they're like when this kind of thing happens. Why not take a day off?'

'To Boar Hill? You've been reading my mind. Want to come?'

'Yes. When?'

'Tomorrow, as soon as Bran's recovered. We'll take Ram too.'

'Er…no. Astinax.'

Slowly, Dania unfurled herself like a fern frond and turned

her green gaze upon the woman she had known since child-hood. 'Astinax?' she said. 'You and he…?'

'Mm-m,' said Etaine, blushing prettily, 'but he doesn't know yet.'

'What about Karus?'

'A woman has to look to the future,' she said, without emotion.

More than any woman of her acquaintance, she knew that Dania would empathise with that sentiment. That was what had been uppermost in her mind too when she had pleaded to be sent to Coria six years ago. Her future. Naturally, the men of Boar Hill believed that to be expelled from the heart of their incredibly clannish family was a fate potentially worse than death itself, but Etaine knew different. She was in a better position than most to watch her mistress's growing sensitivity, her concerns at the eternal feuding within the set-tlement, their preoccupation with petty insults and revenge of the maddest sort, and the conflicts even between the local tribes, if there was nothing else to do. Their opposition to the Roman oppression she could understand. The invaders had been over here for generations, growing more proud and dominating with each new governor, but Dania's role as spy and informer, though successful, did not come naturally to her. Etaine witnessed her mistress's best years slipping fruit-lessly away along with her unfulfilled yearning for mother-hood and, secondary to that, for a loving relationship with a loyal man. That was the price of freedom, which had not con-cerned her when she was sixteen.

Etaine had experienced, as all the women had, Dania's poorly concealed unease at the tribune's visit and, given his position and apparent determination, it seemed more than likely that he would pursue her, despite her objections. She heard the door open during the night and guessed the reason for the sleeplessness. She went to wrap a shawl around Dania's shoulders, trapping inside the plait of hair as thick as a man's wrist. 'You're thinking of what's happened?' she said. 'Or of what might happen?'

'Both,' said Dania, without moving. 'It's all right, love. There's nothing in it. It was only a kiss, nothing more. Only marginally better than Con's.' She caught Etaine's smile in the moonlight and knew the lie would not be believed.

By the light of a small oil lamp, the dining room was eerily pinkish-brown and still heady with perfume, incense and roses, and Dania was lying on the couch where the tribune had reclined to eat his dinner. That in itself was significant, Etaine thought. 'I'd say that there may not be anything in it yet,' she said, 'but that there *could* be, if you were careful.'

'No. You know I could never be involved with anyone, least of all with one of *them*. You yourself can see no future with Karus.'

Etaine ignored the reference to the centurion. She saw no future in any relationship, whether Roman or not, with a man who was in love with another woman and who called her by the wrong name when they were in bed together thinking that, because he was paying for it, it didn't matter. 'I was thinking of the short term,' she said. 'The tribune could be useful to us.'

'He could also be a liability. He was asking me about my citizenship and my family. I expect he sees me as a blackmail victim, eventually.'

'Silly. There's no law that says everyone must be a Roman citizen before they can run a licensed brothel. Those other two brothels in Coria where the rabble go are run by local women. If it concerns him, tell him that you've applied for citizenship. As for your family, say they *were* in Cataractonium and Eboracum until the last of them died six years ago and left you some money, that's all. Bran and I will say the same. You never had much contact with them, so you don't know any more than that. The only thing you have to decide is how to deal with him.'

'I know what Somer will say,' Dania whispered.

'What?'

'Kill him.'

'Oh…well, that's a man's way, love. We can do better than that.'

'Perhaps. But at what price, Ettie?' Being still unsettled and fearful, she was thinking more of the personal heartache than the political repercussions.

'The Tribune Peregrinus, my lady,' said Albiso, thinking that his business must be mighty important for him to be visiting Dania again so soon when there was the aftermath of a raid to be dealt with. He bowed and poured wine into two silver goblets, turning the handle of the matching water jug towards her before withdrawing just slowly enough to catch the visitor's first words.

'Dania Rhiannon, I have come to apologise for last night.'

Now pull the other leg, thought Albiso, closing the door quietly.

Dania was even more astonished and not a little disconcerted to be visited at this hour. Her guest wore a short white tunic, edged with red and strapped with silver-ornamented leather, a pair of dark leather trousers and a deeply fringed cloak fastened upon his right shoulder. Someone, somewhere, she thought, must be holding his plumed helmet. Then she wished she had been wearing something more becoming.

Accepting the usual salute to both cheeks while trying not to be too aware of the aroma of cleanliness, she waved an arm in the direction of a couch. His lips had lingered just a fraction longer than they ought for the sake of courtesy. 'There is no need, my lord,' she said, trying to regulate her breathing. 'I quite understand the situation. I trust you all returned safely. Any losses?'

She poured water into the wine and handed one of the goblets to him, seating herself with her back to the light to hide the effects of her sleeplessness. Why should she care? she asked herself.

'Heavier on our side than theirs, I'm afraid,' said Fabian, taking a sip and studying the chased goblets. Hares and hounds, as usual. 'We took one prisoner and we shall get something out of him before the day's out.' *Before we kill him.* 'But there will be an immediate counter-attack, of course.' He stared into his wine, tipping the reflection this way and that. 'I also came to say that the centurion and I will be occupied for the next few nights, and to thank you in person for your hospitality. I hope I did not lose your approval, my lady?'

She knew what he referred to, yet saw no reason to pursue the matter. Better to make light of it. 'We enjoyed your company,' she said, keeping it general. 'So it's night raids for you, is it?'

'I fear so.' His intent gaze and the slight play of a smile around his mouth spoke of other things he would rather be doing at night. With her. 'I don't suppose…? No,' he said, smiling at his change of mind. 'You were angry, I recall.'

'Better not to suppose, my lord,' said Dania, crossly. 'My stand on mixing business with pleasure is as firm as ever and you will be welcomed here, if you should wish it, as a client. Nothing more.'

'You are still angry. Why?'

'Because you insist on pursuing—' She caught herself just in time.

'Yes? Pursuing?'

'Something I would rather forget.'

'Except that you have not forgotten it, have you?'

'It will be of little use, my lord, for you to visit the House of Women unless you intend to patronise our facilities. This is not an inn, and I have neither the time nor the inclination to entertain you whenever you have nowhere else to go. I thought you understood that.'

If he understood, he was keeping it to himself. Smiling, he tossed the remaining wine down in one gulp and stood up in the kind of easy bound that emphasised his superb fitness. 'Mmm, that's a good vintage,' he said, wiping his mouth with the back of his hand. It was a curiously ungentlemanly gesture, but typically soldier-like, a fascinating mix of gentility and coarseness that intrigued her.

He came to stand before her. 'Your time and your inclination, lady, are immaterial. I *shall* be visiting again and you had better start calling yourself a facility, for that is what I shall be coming for.' He leaned down before she could move, placing his hands on each side of her thighs so that his face was only a breath away from hers. 'Think about it,' he whispered. As if she had not been doing.

'I do not need to, Tribune,' she snapped, holding her head back. 'Nor did you lose my approval when there was no approval to lose. I bid you good day. Albiso will see you out.'

'And in again,' he said. 'Be prepared, eh?' He straightened, catching at her elbows to draw her up. 'Dania Rhiannon,' he said, releasing her.

'Tribune Peregrinus,' she said, because she could find no riposte before he walked away, exchanging a few words with Ram and Astinax as he cleared the courtyard in a dozen fast paces.

'What did he say?' she demanded. 'Did he tell you…?'

'Yes,' said Astinax. 'It's Boar Hill they'll be heading for tonight. Are you ready for off, m'lady? We can't waste any more time.'

'It's not *me* who's wasting time, it's Bran. Go and get him, will you, Ram? Bring the horses round. Where's Etaine? Where are my saddlebags? Isn't *anybody* ready? Oh, *do* come along!'

Behind her back, Ram did a mincing side-step, ducking and covering his head with one arm from an invisible blow while grinning at Astinax.

It was not far, though for Dania's party of four who knew the hazardous route up through the thickly wooded and rocky hillsides, the journey did not present the same difficulties as it would to a Roman army in the dark. It was this kind of terrain that gave Boar Hill an advantage, for Roman army tactics favoured more open warfare instead of the terrifying hit-and-run methods used by the northern hill tribes. When the rivers were high, the tribe's tendency was to raid towards the east, which is what they had done last night at Onnum, the Roman fort on the Wall two miles above Coria. Acting on Brannius's information, Somer had reacted with typical immediacy, trusting implicitly in Dania's contacts.

At the first shout from his guards perched high up on the earth ramparts surrounding the settlement, his white head appeared at the thatched porch of the chieftain's great hall. *'What?'* he yelled.

Men ran along the platform inside the timber palisade, already shooting the bolts to open the heavy gates. 'Your sister, my lord. Shall we let her in?' They grinned, anticipating his response.

'Silly sods!' he yelled back, passing his spear to a man behind him.

Each time she visited, perhaps once on each of the four festivals, there were changes to be seen, a finger or two on the height of a child, a new torque on a young nobleman, a pregnancy, a death, other changes too slight to identify with certainty. But in her six years' absence, Dania had never seen Boar Hill immediately after a raid until now, and although she had once been used to the sight of severed heads pinned around the door of her father's hall, of terrible wounds and the mutilated bodies of enemies, those six years of respite had begun mercifully to cloud her memory and to fill it instead with the finer things of life. Every visit to her family brought back memories of her happy childhood, a place of barefoot freedom, an escape from responsibility. Here, she was as unfettered as the wind. But after two days or so, her returns to Coria came as another kind of welcome to the real world. The duration of her visits became shorter now, especially after her mother, Rhiannon, went to live with Mona on the far side of the Wall. She needed to help her extended family, she had said, and Somer had accepted the excuse.

It was not something Dania could hide. Somer understood. He had even expected it to happen. Though she always wore the clothes kept specially for the purpose, Brannius had told his half-brother how they dressed in Coria and had seen how the younger women were greedy for every detail while the older ones scowled and scratched, muttering about the disgrace. A brothel, they said. Only Romans would see the need for such a ridiculous and unnecessary institution, they said. Dania must have lost her wits. Then Somer had shut them up by reminding them to whom the menfolk owed their victories.

They came seeping out of their round-houses, carrying infants, smiling, running to meet the quartet. But Somer was there first, running to lift her down from the pony, to enclose her in a bear hug and to keep her in the circle of his bandaged arm while greeting the others with a smile. There was a secret one for Etaine, for it was she who had taught the young Somer what a chieftain's son needed to know about how best to win a woman.

He chortled in Dania's ear, still elated. 'Well done, sister. That was some victory we had last night. Come inside and hear. Morning Star is feeding our newest lad. You've come to share our triumph? Sacrifices later, then a feast to end all feasts.'

'Somer, there'll be no feasts tonight.'

'Eh? Why not? You've seen signs?'

'No. Listen. I have urgent news. It came only this morning.'

He let go of her suddenly to stand in front of her, watching her eyes for signs of foreboding. 'Three ravens flying together? Ducks refusing to lay?'

'No, not that. Let's go inside. Bring the saddlebags, Astinax.'

She never entered the hall without recalling the events of that dreadful day, but today the large warm-smelling cavern was colourful with new hangings and furs spilling from benches. A loom taller than a man leaned into one corner, tended by two maids who lured a pattern downwards from the upper bar. A wee bairn tottered towards her with a drooling smile, trusting everything that moved, and Dania scooped him up with his tiny clinging hands upon the neck of her cloak, pulling the heavy gold pin towards his mouth.

Through the fire's blue smoke she smiled at Somer's lovely young wife, Morning Star, who suckled a new babe at her breast. She was the sister of Mona's husband, and the exchange had been a rare love match as well as an expediency, and now she looked up to smile shyly, first at her husband and then at the visitors. Dania felt an ache tugging at her womb.

Seated on a cushioned stool, she told Somer what the tribune Peregrinus had said about a counter-attack that night. They must prepare immediately, she told him as the saddlebags were emptied of stone jars of Italian wines that the local tribes envied, bolts of cloth from across the sea, amber beads for the women, and costly spices, Roman things that they despised yet could not get enough of.

Still euphoric with success, Somer was not inclined to be hurried. Plenty of time, he said. There was something she should know, too. 'Con the Silvertongue is missing. We think he was killed in the second attack, but we were not able to go and look for him. He's one of five we lost.'

A chill stole through Dania's bones like another winter of her life gone, freezing the hair along her arms. 'Could they have taken him prisoner?' she said, remembering what Fabian had said. Con would have preferred death to that.

'That would be shame indeed. I cannot think it. He would never let himself be taken. Not Con.' He sighed and looked away, and there seemed no more to be said. He had done his best to hide any bitterness. He had given Con a large share of the decision-making, for Dania's ex-husband was only weak where women were concerned. After her departure, he had married again and begun to raise a family and, if his behaviour tended towards the unpredictable at times, at least he had caused no trouble under Somer's leadership.

'I must go and speak to his wife,' said Dania. 'Perhaps I may be able to find out more. I shall try. But there's something else you should know, brother.' She told him of the enemy's plans to rebuild the ruined fort where their ancestors once lived. Predictably, he was horrified. His roar frightened the little ones, and it was some time before they could calm them down.

He wanted to know who had told her. Dania had wanted to refrain from mentioning the new tribune again, but, knowing that Brannius would have spoken of the initial skirmish at the garrison, then been here at Boar Hill during the next phase, only she could tell it at first hand. Omitting the personal moments, she felt obliged to tell Somer how he came to dinner, a revelation that earned a half-smile from Etaine.

Somer's hawk-eyes caught the look. Like Dania and Brannius, he was dark with straight black eyebrows and a handsome swooping moustache like the reversed horns of a prize steer. He wore his hair in the warrior fashion, rinsed through with lime-saturated water to whiten and stiffen it into spikes like a flight of arrows. Dania had never asked his wife what damage the hair-style did to their intimate moments, and Con had never indulged in it, perhaps for the same reason. In their own way, the men here were as proud of their appearance as the Roman men.

Somer was also mindful of the sacrifice imposed upon his sister by Mog the Druid that prevented her from fulfilling her natural role as wife and mother. A member of the Boar Hill tribe, posing as a Romanised Briton, would instantly be suspected of treachery. It was a secret she would never reveal to any man. But Somer had the ruthless streak that any chieftain must cultivate if he wanted to keep his position, even where his own family was concerned, and he had little doubt that his sister's efforts to conceal her identity from the enemy would be sufficient to make a risk worth the taking. And Etaine's half-smile and Dania's responding blush warned him that something had happened.

Dania watched an old woman in the shadows kneel down to begin grinding flour on a saddle-shaped stone quern, her knees creaking almost as loud as the corn-seeds. 'It was the good food that loosened the tribune's tongue,' she said, smiling at Etaine through the heat of the fire.

'When do they plan to rebuild the old fort?' Somer demanded.

'Very soon,' said Brannius. 'Perhaps when we've fought off tonight's raid we should go and upset them before they get too many men on the job. It's no more than a night's work.' Already he was counting himself among the warriors.

'We will. By the gods, we will. He talks then, does he, this tribune? Is it only food that makes him careless or is it just plain arrogance, I wonder? Did he use the women?'

Was there a trace of envy in his questions?

'No, brother,' Dania said, quietly. 'None of them did. They had to rush up to Onnum to catch the Boar Hill tribe. Not quite the end to their evening they'd been looking forward to.'

Laughter was inevitable, and a little coarseness too, but when Somer stood up and signalled Dania to do the same, she passed her warm gurgling little armful over to Etaine and followed him. Outside, there were hounds everywhere, sniffing and licking up the puddles of blood around the porch. Between the houses, men repaired broken chariots and weapons, and the hammering in the forge rang across the practising blasts of a tall carnyx that reared like a bronze serpent from the trumpeter's lips. Somer was not responding to the urgent news she had brought with her.

Linking her hand into his arm, she walked with him up the earth ramp to the palisade where the platform served as a seat. From that viewpoint, they could see the extent of the settlement and the clusters of conical thatches, the workshops and granaries, the washing drying on the roofs, the tethered goats, the roaming pigs and geese. By nightfall, she thought, this peaceful scene would be one of chaos, burning thatches, screaming women and howling men. 'Somer,' she said, firmly, 'they'll be raiding *tonight*. I came especially to tell you this.'

He patted her hand. 'We'll be ready. But they don't favour night attacks as we do,' he reminded her. 'They don't know the land well enough for that. They'd have enough of a problem finding us by day, so I'd be surprised if they try it in the dark, love. Oh, I know they can probably see our smoke from the Wall and beyond, but they don't know how to get their clumsy weapons up here.' He patted her hand again, 'But you must start back at sunset, even so.'

'Yes,' she said, unable to explain the sense of relief that came because he had been the one to suggest it. 'Yes, I suppose we'd better.'

'This tribune,' he said. 'What else do I need to know about him? Is he ready for retirement? A last posting, do you think?'

Wanting to talk about him, yet not wanting to, she tried to keep her answer prosaic. 'Oh, probably not. He's not as old as all that. Perhaps a few summers more than you.'

Somer had twenty-six. 'I see,' he said. 'And he's interested in you? Personally, I mean.' It was an idle question. Who would not be?

'Oh, no, of course he isn't,' she said, rather too quickly. 'I think he's far more interested in getting results before the emperor's party arrives. He's even got Karus on the hop. By this time next week they'll have limewashed everything.'

'And if it moves, they'll salute it?'

'Something like that.' They laughed, but Dania knew there was more to come.

'Could you get more out of him if you took him to bed?'

She looked sharply at him, but what had been intended as a glancing rebuke for his mistake was held instead by a look that told her it was no mere jest. 'What are you saying?' she said, frowning, 'You *know* I can't.'

'You said he was not particularly interested in any of the women. Did that include Etaine?'

Again, the envy. 'Yes.'

'Did she try?'

'Yes, I believe so.'

'Did he say he was interested in you?'

'Oh…Somer, really! This is neither here nor there.'

'*Did* he?'

She looked at his green and red check breeches and the heavy bronze armlets over a maze of swirling blue tattoos. 'Well…yes. But I told him I was not available. Policy, I said. Where is all this leading?'

'And does he believe you?'

It was some moments before she finished her search for a suitable reply. 'He'll have to, won't he? I'm not in that game, Somer. I can't afford to be. It's too dangerous. I don't like the man. Typical officer type. Full of himself. And he's a Roman, anyway.'

'From Rome?'

'No, from Gaul. They have the best cavalry. He leads one of the special Gaulish units of five hundred auxiliaries. And it doesn't matter where he's from, I don't want him.'

'That's not the point, is it? If we want good first-hand information, we have to give him what *he* wants.'

'*We?*' She sat bolt upright, bristling with indignation.

'Who's *we*? I'll find out what I can, whenever I can, but I refuse to get any more intimate with him than—'

'Than you have already? So that's what the blush was about.'

'You're jumping to conclusions, Somer. I've told you, I'll not put myself or my household into more danger than we are. We're in *daily* danger, brother. You cannot ask me to go further than that. It would put us even more at risk if he found out where I'm from. Can't you see that?'

'Then you take care he doesn't find out. If it's the mark you're concerned about, keep it covered, keep the light off it, keep his hands off it.'

'Enough! I've had my fill of this business. There will be *no* exceptions.'

Her brother's voice took on a severity that she supposed must have come with the issuing of orders and the yelling in battle. 'This business,' he snapped, 'isn't something we can pull out of when we've had enough, Dana. Last night, I allowed Bran to join us because he needs the experience. He was scared witless but he did it, and came back with his first head. Con the Silvertongue's new wife gave birth to their child last night and she had to make a sacrifice too, as the other women did. What you're doing at Coria is indispensable, make no mistake, but we still need every acorn cup of help if we're to stay on top. You have a rare gift, Dana. You could capture any man you choose. And you have the knowledge to prevent any fruit of your union as I know you did with Con. You must use it.' His tone softened as he heard the echo of his own ranting. 'He's only a man, Dana, and you're not a virgin. You know what to do. I don't suppose Con ever paid the slightest attention to your back, did he?'

The hairs along her arms prickled and a sickness churned inside her, heavy like a bad meal. Never had she expected to hear such a suggestion from Somer, of all people, the one whose protection had never wavered for an instant, even in the face of the chief Druid. Now he was not only withdrawing his support, but asking her to launch herself into an act of the utmost danger, for such folly would undo them all, not only her.

'Somer, I can scarce believe I am not dreaming. You know I will do anything to help Boar Hill's survival, *your* survival. I have always worked to that end. It was my reason for going to Coria. Have you forgot? It's no good talking blithely of me not being virginal and him being only a man, nor could you compare him to Con, either. Of *course* Con didn't make love to my back. He didn't make love to any part of me, if you must know, but that's not to say a Roman wouldn't. It's nonsense, Somer. Sheer nonsense. You must see that.'

'Well, then,' said her brother, doggedly, 'give him just enough to make him come back for more and pay you well in information. Ask him where—'

'It's not like that,' she said, tersely. 'We don't ask. Not specifically.'

'What do you do, then?'

'We wait, and listen, and sympathise. We soften them up, bathe them and feed them. Let them do the talking.'

'And massage?'

'Yes, that too.'

'So offer to massage him for a start, eh?' He placed a large tattooed hand over hers and could not help noticing how quiet she had become.

'Somer,' she said, 'I had not thought that you of all people would suggest I loan my body out to the enemy. Those who work at the House of Women do so voluntarily because that's what they were doing anyway, and they have always accepted that I have a different role to play. Now you want me to perform these services against my will, accepting one man of high rank while trying to fend off all the others who will see it as a change of policy. Have you any advice on how I might do that? Karus, for instance? How do I explain it to him and retain his good will at the same time? I wonder what our father would have said to this idea.'

'Needs must, Dana. This is war. We have to use any weapon we've been given. You live in comfort. This is not an impossible price to pay, and you're clever enough to know how to stay undercover. You'll find a way to do it.'

'No, brother. I shall not find a way to do it. It is an impossible, foolish, unnecessary price to pay for information. He's a tribune, for pity's sake. Tribunes don't get drunk. They're not the soft idiots you seem to think they are. Tell me what we're supposed to do when he discovers who's passing on his plans, *if* I manage to hear any. He's clever, Somer, not one of your eager young novices.'

'You up sticks in the night and come back to live at Boar Hill. This is your home. We can even start building houses for you all, if you wish.'

The proposition, delivered too glibly, did not ring true, like so much of what he had just said. 'My home is *not* here, Somer,' she said, standing up and moving away from him. 'It's in Coria.' It was the first time she had felt it, and the sentiment took her by surprise after all the years of clinging to a simple lifestyle, to her old status, and to a certain adulation that her visits always caused. But Somer was hardening, becoming ruthless and careless of life. Her life. The risk was too great.

He stood up, reaching her in one stride to view the scene of familiar domesticity before them, to hear the squeal of children and to feel the moorland breeze catch at their clothes. 'Rubbish,' he said. 'You'd never leave Boar Hill for good, Dana. It's in your blood.'

'You can talk to me of blood, Somer, after what you've just been saying? Would you have suggested such a thing six years ago when I was branded to prevent me consorting with the enemy? That *was* the reason I suffered, wasn't it? Or have I got it wrong, as I've got you wrong too?'

'You haven't got me wrong, Dana. I mean what I say. Things have changed and you're required to make a sacrifice, that's all.'

'*Another* one? May the gods help me. Whatever next?'

'Do it, Dana.'

'I will not. You cannot insist.'

'I can, and I do. I order it. You may not disobey me.'

'Somer…please. We are kin.'

'Then you should trust me, as you always have.'

'As I always used to do,' she whispered, turning away. The sun had disappeared behind a mass of dark clouds and a chill wind whipped at her loose hair, blowing it across her face. Her feet were cold and bare and the wool of her tunic scratched her skin, prickling her like teasels. 'I'll go and have a word with Con's wife… widow,' she said, half-dreading that she would see what she would never be able to have. She would feel barren and out of place, and she would be asked to explain why her chieftain brother was not out looking for Con the Silver-tongue and returning him to his new family. And, for once, she would not have a defence ready for Somer's new-found tyranny.

Chapter Four

⟨⟨⟨✦⟩⟩⟩

The days that followed Dania's short visit to Boar Hill were, in many ways, just as disturbing as those before it, for now she could see more clearly than ever that Somer was not the only one to have changed. She had, too. Even Etaine and Brannius noticed the change in him, though the one to suffer the harshest pangs was Con the Silvertongue's young wife who had just given birth to a girl. Everyone knew Somer's opinion that Boar Hill had no more room for female children. It was males they wanted, boys who would grow into warriors.

The distraught woman was inconsolable at the news that her husband would not return and now, she told Dania and Etaine, she would not be allowed to keep the babe, her third girl. Somer would not have been so determined, she sobbed, if Con had been here to protect her. In one night, her life was shattered.

Dania had pleaded with Somer to be lenient, in this case. Was it really necessary to leave the wee creature all alone in the forest simply because it was a girl? Would he have insisted if Con had been there? It was her second clash with him that day. She had seen the set of his mind: he was growing more and more like their father Brigg, fanatically jealous of his position. He had told Dania to mind her business, that others had been exposed that year already and doubtless there would be more. It was a fact of life, and Con's wife was no different from the rest. Anyway, she had two lasses already.

Racked by guilt at her own helplessness, she had wept for Con's wife, offering to take her and her children to Coria. But Somer would not allow it. There was no reason, he said, why she should not bear sons to another man while she was still fertile. It was at such times that Dania was relieved to have a home of her own to return to, though her inability to help cut deep into her conscience and she could find little sympathy for Bran's hurt pride when, instead of receiving Somer's praise for his part in last night's raid, he had been denied his request to take part in next night's raid also.

'Your place is with Dana,' Somer had roared at him. 'You go to Coria and protect *her*, fool! And see that you do!'

That had re-directed Bran's mind quite sharply towards his duties, but it also reminded Dania to have a quiet word with him about divided loyalties, and they had left soon afterwards with the bitter taste of inhumanity in at least two mouths. While she and Etaine were doing all they could to sustain life, Somer was bent on doing the opposite.

The next uneventful week at the House of Women was not matched by what was happening on Boar Hill, however. Somer's success took a sudden battering, and it was the ex-gladiator Ram who brought the news to Dania after one of his newly implemented coaching sessions at the garrison. The tribune had invited him to instruct groups of his men in the finer points of sword-fighting and Dania had approved, since it was guaranteed to yield some clues about the enemy's future plans. Two days after the visit to Boar Hill, Ram broke the disturbing news that there had been no attack on the expected night, but that Somer had suffered a heavy defeat at the River Fort, where their ancestors' old haunt was being rebuilt to house some of the new cavalry units.

Dania placed the water jug on the gravel path and stood upright to face Ram, giving him all her attention. She had been pouring warm water on the rose-bush roots to encourage them to bloom. 'How many?' she said.

'Difficult to say exactly,' said Ram. 'There were about four-hundred-and-eighty men there, waiting in ambush for Somer's men. He would have stood little chance in that situation. He was lucky not to have been wiped out altogether, but it was pitch dark by then and they were not pursued when they retreated. Apparently the loss was heavy. Very heavy.'

'But my brother is alive?'

'Yes, I believe so. They'd have said, if they'd got the leader.'

'So they were prepared for the River Fort to be attacked, then? How did they know that?'

'No telling,' said Ram, wiping a huge ham-like hand around his bald head. 'They can usually work these things out for themselves, you know, and they have their scouts. They must have expected there'd be some resistance. I can tell you something else interesting, though. They're holding a captive at the garrison taken during that raid up on the Wall on the night of your dinner party.'

'Yes, I heard from Fabian Peregrinus that they were holding someone. Have you discovered who it is?'

'Only that he's a big chap with red hair, but that could apply to almost all of them, I suppose. Do you think it might be Con the Silvertongue?' He watched her face pale visibly, but he himself had visited Boar Hill on very few occasions and was still not familiar with Somer's noblemen, nor did he know of Dania's early relationships. To Ram, Con was just another warrior.

Etaine took Dania's hand and held on to it, trying to divert the invasive chill that crept over her arms while the implications tumbled crazily through her mind. Con's shame. Somer's assumptions of his death. The appalling fate that awaited captives. But most of all, Con's desolate wife. Now more than ever, it was up to her, Dania, to put aside her own personal fears and do something to effect Con's release. Did captives ever escape from the Romans?

She gave instructions to make offerings at every shrine in the house. Her own favoured goddess, Coventina, mother of life, became the recipient of a small wooden model of an infant, where the clear spring water held it lovingly.

Brannius had just returned from the commander's office bearing Dania's account scrolls, and he had confirmed her worst fears. He had seen one of the centurions strutting about wearing Con's heavy gold torque around his neck as a trophy, and the young man's face was white with rage as he strode across the entrance hall, hardly able to remember that he had a message to deliver.

'I don't want to see the bastard when he comes here,' he yelled in Dania's direction.

'What are you talking about?' Dania said, catching at his arm as he headed towards the bath-house. 'Come back here!'

Brannius stopped, glaring like a rebellious child.

'What do you mean, *when he comes*?' she yelled, confronting him. 'When *who* comes?'

'He's coming here this evening,' he said. 'That bloody tribune asks if you'll *be pleased* to receive him.'

On two counts, Dania was enraged, and she saw no reason to contain herself. Before Brannius could guess at the effect of his words, his head was knocked sideways by a stunning blow from his half-sister, his expression registering complete surprise laced with respect. She had never done that before. Pride prevented him from comforting the four white fingerprints.

'Do not *ever* forget to deliver a message again,' she spat at him. 'Do you understand me?'

'Yes, my lady.'

'Was there more?'

'The tribune said he may be late. That's all.'

'Then you may go. As for not seeing him, you will offer him the same courtesies as we do to all our guests. That's what they're paying us for. If you cannot do that, you may leave the House of Women. I shan't prevent you. But if you choose to stay, you must accept every change without comment. The last thing I need at this time is other people's personal problems. I have enough of my own to deal with. Is that clear?'

'Yes, my lady. Forgive me.'

'I do. And stay clear of that bath-house. I'm going there myself. Send Etaine to me, then take those scrolls upstairs to Eneas. He needs them.'

'Yes.' He looked aside, shamed by his temporary weakness. 'It was Con's best torque,' he whispered. 'I watched the smith fashion it.'

'Yes, and his captors are going to take more than his torque from him if we are impolite to their officers, Bran. The rules are changing and you'll have to try to keep up.'

Brannius turned his big hazel eyes upon her, puzzled by her new approach. 'You'll be entertaining the tribune, Dana? Alone?'

'I'll have to find out what he's coming for first, won't I?' she said, knowing that he was coming for her.

She was sure she had overreacted.

'Won't do him any harm, love,' soothed Etaine. 'He'd have got more than a clout over the ears if he'd stayed with Somer. You were right to discipline him.'

'I'm scared, Ettie.'

'Shh…shh. Come and lie down and I'll massage your back. The tribune's only a man, love.'

But that was what Somer had said, and that had been no help, either.

By the time the tribune arrived, leaving his two slaves to wait outside on the verandah, it was almost midnight and Dania had stopped expecting him, though her nerves were still as taut as lute strings. She had fidgeted with the flower arrangement, placed a jewel in her hair and taken it out again, re-wrapped the long sash around her hips several times, changed it from peach to violet and, as the evening grew cooler, had spoiled the whole effect with a soft wool and silk shawl wrapped around her shoulders over the simple unbleached linen robe. Her hair had already begun to slip in wayward spirals towards her neck, her sandals long since discarded.

The tabby cat took one last swipe at her hand and fled.

'The Tribune Fabian Cornelius Peregrinus, my lady,' said Albiso.

This time, the steward was denied even a preliminary greeting as he poured the wine for, although he took his time over it, there was nothing to be overheard, nor could he make head or tail of the guest's immobility. Or of his mistress's. He relieved the tribune of his fringed red cloak, draped it over one arm, bowed and withdrew, his lips pursed in disappointment.

Dania stood to receive her guest as he moved forward into the soft circle of light from the two remaining lamps, showing her again what she feared, his strong features and firm mouth, the dark brows casting his eyes into shadow, though somehow she knew both their journey and their message. She sensed again the compelling power of his masculinity, his commanding presence, the persistence she had not managed to dent since their last uncomfortable meeting, his damned good looks. How she wished they had not been enemies.

She saw that for him, as for her, the day had been a long and busy one and that, whatever his reason for coming here, it was not for the kind of merry company she had provided before, nor was it to offer her the same kind of antics as those that concluded it. The house was peaceful, the women all privately occupied, the servants invisible. Her hand shook as she offered him a glass goblet, forgetting to water the wine. Forgetting to greet him.

'Dania Rhiannon,' he whispered, accepting the drink.

'Fabian Peregrinus.' She brushed a sticky palm down her robe, hoping he would not notice, but thinking it unlikely when she was noticing every detail of his immaculate dress. His loose-sleeved tunic of startling white was edged with narrow scarlet braids that she was sure would denote his rank. Unusually, though perhaps it was different for Gauls, he wore long white breeches, the bottoms of which ended in feet that tucked into his ankle-high sandals. A ring-buckled leather belt sat low on his slim hips, its end encased in ornate silver.

'No weapons, you see,' he said. 'I am defenceless.'

Her eyes reached his, telling him much the same thing. Her mouth was dry. After a false start, she managed a kind of welcome. 'Tribune Peregrinus, it's long past the hour when… er…the women are—' she glanced towards the door to the apartments, annoyed by her own lack of assurance '—and I am, as you see, not at my best at this time of the night. Is there something…?' *Release Con the Silvertongue. Send him home to his wife before it's too late. Then go, and release me from this obligation.*

He took a sip of the wine, unwatered, watching her over the rim of the glass, replacing it on the table with irritating slowness. 'My lady,' he said, 'do you think we might begin again?' When her eyes searched as if to find the beginning, he saw that she had missed his meaning. 'No,' he said. 'I mean from the *very* beginning. We started badly. I was uncivil. You had every right to be angry and you *were* correct, I have been too long in the army with not enough opportunity to polish my manners. I took advantage of you last time we met and, instead of commending myself to you, which is what I intended, I fear I've done quite the opposite. There will be no repetition of that, believe me. My behaviour was unacceptable. Please forgive me. Can you believe that I would rather be friends, my lady? That all I want is the pleasure of your company?'

'All?' she whispered. 'Really?'

His mouth quirked at the corners. 'Inaccurate. No, not quite all.'

'But I have already explained—'

'Yes, several times. I had hoped you might be a little curious.'

She turned away from him to hide her trembling, feeling that they were already on the path she had marked out, yet travelling too fast. 'I've been far too busy, my lord, to feel anything like curiosity. Indeed, judging by the volley of questions you fired at me last time we met, I'd say that the curiosity was entirely your own. I'm not sure that I'm ready for another grilling.'

'And if I promise to ask you no more questions? If I say that you may ask me any personal questions you wish?'

Such as, where is Con? Have you harmed him? 'Tribune, do you ever take no for an answer? From a woman, I mean. No, how foolish of me. I don't suppose for one moment that any woman has ever given you the remotest no, has she?' She turned to look at him over her shoulder and saw that he was not laughing as she thought he would, self-consciously agreeing with her.

'My memory of other women has deserted me, lady. You have been at least a dozen different women since we met:

proud and silent, then scathing, fierce, tempestuous, afraid
and panic-stricken, self-possessed and elegant, a perfect
hostess, entertaining and witty, musical, scholarly—'

'Stop! You have over-run the dozen, my lord.'

'I could go on.'

'Please don't. The subject is wearing a little thin. If you
have not understood me by now, I'm afraid there's not much
I can do about it. I meant what I said. What you have in mind
is not what I do.'

His reply was surprisingly gentle as he held out a hand to
her, as he would to feed a bird. 'Lady, you are trembling. Is
the idea so very abhorrent to you? You have nothing to fear
from me. I would not boast of it. No one else need know.'

Even if she had not already decided, his new tenderness
might well have swayed her, though she knew the venture to
be fraught with dangers and almost certain heartache. This
man was obviously experienced in casual relationships, a
cool predator without a heart to speak of, whereas she was
vulnerable and emotional with a sad lack of seduction techniques and a growing revulsion for deceit.

He insisted, touching her hand with his fingertips. 'I have
seen what lies beneath the façade, remember. You will not
need to fight me as you did then. This is not about conflict
or domination, but about mutual comfort, and much as I
admire the women who work here, my needs are of another
kind. I could never use their services while there is one who
has all I want, everything I dream of, beauty and grace, charm
and wit. And courage. You would be an asset to any man,
Dania Rhiannon. You are wasted here in this backwater. You
ought to be mistress of a great household. You ought to be in

my bed and at my side, as my woman. You were made for loving and motherhood, my lady, not for watching from the sidelines as others pair off. And I believe you have not found a man with enough dogged persistence to take you, until now. And I don't intend to accept no for an answer.'

He had maintained his brief contact with her, no grabbing or invading like the first time, yet that touch of his fingertips with the beguiling sentiments she had never heard before from any man acted upon her like a drug, toppling her headlong into capitulation. She had little doubt that others would have heard similar compliments from him before they yielded, but the sweetness of the delivery was so new to her that she could overlook that minor flaw. After all, he would not realise how cleverly she was about to use him.

It was time to take him further, though the possibility of pleasing Somer was not as attractive as it once had been. She took a deep breath. 'I think…' she whispered, watching her thumb advance upon his brown skin.

'Yes?'

'I think there may be a small service I could render, if you agree. Without obligation, you understand? Merely a gesture.'

'Whatever you wish.'

She took hold of his hand and enjoyed the warm grasp of his fingers as the first slow step was taken. 'But I must ask you first to remove your shoes. The floor may still be wet.'

It was well past midnight, but the tiled floors of the bathhouse were still warm as she led the tribune past the disrobing room, through the warm and hot rooms towards the cool pool area where the massage bench was covered by a clean white towel. The water reflected dumpling-shaped clouds from the ceiling in a darkly mysterious mirror of water that rippled in the glow of one cresset-lamp left burning for safety. The garden scenes on the walls were now like distant hedge-rows across a field with shadows dancing upon every surface.

'Your clothes,' she said. 'You may leave them over on the bench by the wall. The attendants have retired for the night. Do you need more light?'

'No, I can manage. And you, my lady?'

'I shall wait till you're ready, then you may lie down on the towel over there. I shall go and get the oil.' Removing her shawl, she tossed it aside.

'Ah, I see.' Then he understood.

Moments later she returned with a small glass of clear oil and a pile of towels, with another tied around her waist. Fabian Peregrinus was lying on his face with his forehead resting upon his strong arms as if he was asleep with a smile of satisfaction playing around his mouth. He was completely naked.

Dania had massaged the women many times, but she had never before performed the service for a man, not even her ex-husband and, although the contours of the male back were familiar to her, this particular specimen was quite exceptional, even by the standards of Boar Hill. Superbly fit, toned to perfection, the tanned skin bulged with muscle and sinew, the paler skin below his waist resembling a brief pair of pants over his neat oval buttocks. Dark hair dusted his long legs, and the width of his shoulders spanned the bench almost beyond her reach.

Now, my beautiful stallion, you shall have a mauling like the one you gave me, but here there will be no retaliation and no interruptions.

She moistened her hands and, pouring a drop into the valley of his spine, began to cover him with a fine film of almond oil, using long slow sweeps that brought deep moans of pleasure from his throat. As she had expected. 'Ideally, we should have music,' she murmured.

'Will you answer me just one question?'

'It depends,' she said, digging her thumbs into his neck muscles.

'Do you often perform this service for your clients?'

'Why do you need to know that?'

'So that I can gloat, if I'm the exception.'

'Then you may gloat. But speak of this to another soul and it will be the end of a very short friendship and the beginning of a perpetual enmity.'

'You have my word on it. I am honoured.'

And I will make you sing like a lark for this honour, my noble lord. 'You are also hard work. Women are smaller and much softer than this.'

'Then your reward shall be accordingly greater.'

'What reward?'

'What would you like?'

Information. 'I'll let you know if I think of something.'

In silence, she worked on his back, moving downwards over buttocks, thighs and calves, sparing him little by way of gentleness. In an attempt to reach the far side of him, she leaned on him with her hips instead of going round to the other side of the bench, ruthlessly lending him the warmth of her body, enjoying the feel of him under her fingers with alternate gentleness and vigour. She did not intend him to fall asleep.

She placed a towel across his hips. 'Turn over, if you please.'

He obliged with a groan while she held the towel in place to spare her own modesty rather than his. But the sight of his hair-covered chest made her pause and think how to tackle it, this being an area that generally received no attention from a masseuse to one of her own kind.

'Is there anything you cannot do well, my lady?' he said.

She began on his shoulders and arms. 'Plenty. And there are some things that I *will* not do.'

'For example?'

'Questions!' she reminded him, sternly.

'Sorry.'

Perhaps because he heard a warning in that, he interested himself in the folds of her loosened gown as she bent over him, and the way her hair had begun to fall like a veil of crazy corkscrews. She did nothing to adjust her robe, nor did she try to prevent her hair from occasionally touching his skin and, when again she had to reach the far side of him, there were moments when she let her weight lean on him in the most provocative and unprofessional manner. Eventually, she sighed. 'Wait. I need the footstool.'

She took it round to his other side where, well above him, she was able to lean down and knead him, shamelessly revealing the voluptuous cleft between her breasts and caring not a whit about the tight fabric that strained across them. Moving downwards, she allowed him to see the smooth pear shape of her hips and waist, knowing that the lamplight was shining through the robe, teasing him but making him suffer the thoroughness of her hands.

She attended to his feet and toes without once looking at his face, then his wrists and fingers. This, however, caused a temporary hiatus when he caught her hand and brought it up near his face to examine the wrist where last week's bruises were now faint dabs of green upon her skin. Then he released her, and she continued without a word being spoken, and whether he was attempting to remind her of something or whether it was mere curiosity she was not able to tell.

She stood back and wiped her hands upon the towel as she removed it from her waist. 'Not the very best of massages, I'm afraid, but the best I can manage at this time of night. Can you stand?'

In one fluid move, he swung himself upright and wrapped himself in the bench-towel. 'If that was not your very best, my lady, I look forward to your next invitation with some impatience. That was the most memorable massage I've ever had. Thank you.'

'You're welcome to take a dip, if you wish.'

'Will you join me?'

She had already begun to move out of reach, collecting the towels as she went. 'Yes, in the dining room for refreshments. Then you must go.' She heard the splash as she walked away into the dark corridor where at last she was able to raise one fist above her head like a victor. Her wide grin spread into a gasp of silent laughter. *'Bene!* Now *you* have a sleepless night, my lord,' she whispered.

Fabian Peregrinus emerged to find Dania snuggled into her wide basket chair with her legs tucked sideways beneath her and the shawl covering everything that he had hoped to see more of, except her bare feet. In their absence, the low square table had been laid with an array of delicacies, imported almonds, olives and dates, local hazelnuts and walnuts, pieces of curd cheese on fried bread and small slices of sausage, dried apple rings and oat biscuits.

'Local mead,' she said, handing him a goblet. 'It doesn't improve by being watered down. Will you take a couch?'

His hair shone like polished jet, and he had about him the cold fresh look of a man exhilarated by exercise and water. But Fabian had his own ideas about where he would sit and, taking up the other basket chair in one hand, he threw its cushion on to a couch and placed it firmly next to hers. 'Last time we ate together,' he said, sitting down, 'you sat as far away from me as you could. I'm making up for it.'

'As I recall, you made up for it that night.'

His unashamedly wide smile did not accord with his earlier apology, and Dania wished she had not mentioned it.

He reached for the plate of dates and passed it to her. 'Dania Rhiannon,' he said. 'I am fascinated by your family name. Am I allowed to ask its origin?'

'I have taken my mother's name,' she said. 'It's Welsh. It means goddess.' She took a date and nibbled it, ready to veto any more enquiries.

'Very appropriate. So your mother is from Wales.'

Expecting him at any moment to ask about Brannius, she was relieved when he began to talk about the mosaic floor-pattern of zodiac signs, about the problems of mural-painting in damp climates, about the frescoes in his native Gaul and the emperor's talented wife and their sons who were due to arrive within the next day or two. And when the lamp-wick began to send up smoke signals, she was reminded of the time she had just spent in conversation with the man she had expected to drop at least one expensive piece of gossip for her to catch.

'I must leave you to your sleep, my lady,' he said. 'I have to take more men up to the Wall tomorrow. There are some parts that must be repaired before my lord Severus arrives or there'll be questions.'

'Up at Onnum, you mean?' Dania rang a small silver hand-bell.

'Yes, and further west. The problem is that the rubble they used for the infill on the original has disappeared and now it's hard to find enough, so we're going to have to make some parts of the Wall narrower.' He stood, allowing Albiso to place the red cloak around his shoulders. 'Troops are always vulnerable while there's repairing going on, that's the trouble. There are so few troops up there at the moment and so many unarmed people about clearing the site and supplying materials. Let's just hope we can get it finished before the local half-naked barbarians get themselves organised again. We beat them soundly the other night, though. Did you hear?'

'Yes, I heard,' Dania said, tipping the cat off her knee. 'News of that kind spreads quickly in Coria.'

'Ye…es,' he drawled. 'I suppose you must hear of our successes as soon as anybody in a place such as this.'

'Men do tend to talk of their successes in a place such as this, my lord,' she said, smiling impishly and offering him her hand. 'It's to be expected.'

He took the hand and raised it with a smile, realising what he had said. He touched her knuckles with his lips, but he held her eyes with a look that spoke of more intimate farewells. 'I hope soon to do the same, my lady. I hope you will receive me when I come again. You said that you would think of a suitable reward. Have you thought of something?' He kept hold of her hand.

The idea of selling her time to this man, to any man, had never once occurred to her, nor did it now. 'No, my lord, I have not. I don't accept rewards for entertaining my friends in private. Shall we not mention it again?'

'Forgive me. I meant no offence. I didn't want you to think I was taking you for granted.'

'You have not taken me at all, Tribune.'

Not yet, his eyes were saying. 'You *will* receive me again? Soon?'

'Certainly. At last I've managed to find a side of you I think I could get to like.'

Her *double entendre* made him grin. 'May I ask which side?'

'Questions again. Go home, Tribune. Your slaves will be weary.'

'Incomparable woman.' He bowed formally. 'Dania Rhiannon.'

'Fabian Peregrinus,' she said.

But it was not her own heady triumph that remained in her mind longest that night, nor was it the careless information he had let slip, nor even the feel of his superb body under her hands. It was the easy grasp of his fingers upon her wrist that she could still feel hours later, an innocuous gesture that reinforced the fact that, even lying on his back, he was able to halt her fantasy of being in control. Then she began to wonder exactly what she had let herself in for and, if he was as careless with his plans as he appeared to be, how had he achieved so many honours and become a tribune? Surely it was not simply a question of wealth, land and connections? It was time to investigate further.

Losing no time in sleep, Dania woke Brannius and sent him up to Boar Hill with the message for Somer. From the tribune's own mouth, she told him. Unarmed men. Not enough armed men on duty. Gaps in the Wall west of Onnum. Timber and food supplies to demolish *en route*. And most important, Con the Silvertongue as captive. Confirmed. Make sure his wife receives the news.

At dawn, dressed in dull functional working clothes like local women, with baskets on their arms, she and Etaine and two of the youngest maids walked up Dere Street towards the Portgate, the place where the road passed through the guarded Wall on its way north. To the early traffic lumbering over the stone cobbles in heavy carts and waggons, the four women were taken for herb and mushroom pickers in the long dewy grass, the hem of their brown tunics and cloaks already darkened with wet. Thinking of pretty Etaine's recent smiles, Astinax had wanted to go with them for their safety, but Dania had pointed out that his unique form would attract too much attention, which she wanted to avoid. It was merely to survey the progress of the repairs at the fort, she told him. And she needed the walk.

It was only two miles from Coria but uphill most of the way, some of it very steep, and more than once they overtook resting ox-teams that had passed them earlier. Woodland and

moorland covered the hills where water gushed down deep
gullies, past boulders and outcrops of heather, cotton-grass
and spiky sedges. And all the way there, Dania and her com-
panions watched the densest forest over to the left for signs,
which they knew to be a waste of time for, if the Boar Hill
tribe did not wish to be seen, they would not be. When they
raided, they made a din like witches in Hades. An occasional
bird-call would make them look up from their herb-gathering, thinking that it might be them, but there was nothing to
note except how the supply waggons of which the tribune had
spoken were not much in evidence. Soon, lit by the sun from
their right, the great Wall appeared on the horizon, a giant intimidating offensive barrier across their land.

The thudding tramp of hobnailed boots approached from
behind, taking them unawares and sending them skittering
into the deep scratchy heather to wait for the solid wall of uni-
formed soldiers to rattle past with the sun winking on their
helmets. Despite the steep hill, their pace did not slacken even
though their back-packs looked cripplingly heavy, and such
was their number that Dania was not only puzzled but concerned, too. Was this the few troops about which the tribune
was so concerned?

The women sat on a boulder to watch at least four hundred
men pass by, with still more coming up behind them. Next,
a massive troop of cavalry rode past on horses considerably
larger than those bred in these parts. Speechless, they
watched, horrified by the sheer number of men armed with
spears, javelins and swords, their shields slung below their
saddles, moving like a scaled creature along the road. The
clatter was deafening.

The standard-bearer at the head of the infantry did not, however, lead the men through the Wall at Portgate but instead wheeled round to the right, following the line of the masonry up to Onnum. Bristling with spears, the line of soldiers covered the half-mile up to the fort known locally as The Rock where the large complex of barracks had been damaged by fire only a week ago. At that point, the men were swallowed into the fort that stood high and forbidding on the skyline while lower down on Dere Street, the cavalry were still passing Dania's huddled group. Beyond them, the Wall rose to a height greater than that of two tall men, dwarfing everything in the vicinity.

Alongside the mounted men, several officers moved restlessly back and forth, their plumes and crests easy to spot from a distance. Etaine grasped Dania's arm, alerting her to one rider on a large-boned dapple-grey stallion, an officer who wore a white tunic, the striped black-and-white crest on his helmet looking like a giant magpie. His face was almost concealed by the curving cheek-pieces, but from one shoulder billowed a fringed scarlet cloak, revealing body armour of shining overlapping plates.

'Do you see him?' said Etaine. 'Cover your face, quickly!'

But Dania had already singled him out. 'May the gods defend us,' she whispered, petrified by fear. 'My message to Somer was wrong. They *do* have troops. What's happened, Ettie?'

'He changed his mind, love. Or somebody changed it for him.'

'Or I misunderstood what he was saying.'

They scrabbled further away up the hillside, blending with the heather. 'But if Somer launches an attack today they'll cut him to pieces. Even if he gets help from the neighbouring tribes,' said Dania.

'They *always* get help from the neighbours,' Etaine reminded her. 'Look, let's go further up to those rocks. If we try to go back down to Coria we shall not know what's happening and if we go on up to Portgate we'll be stuck there.' She looked along the road and saw that the last of the waggoners had gone, with no more to be seen. 'They've closed the gates,' she said. 'They're expecting trouble. I think I should run up to Boar Hill and warn Somer.'

But it was too late. Etaine's expression had changed to one of horror as she looked towards the steep wooded slope beyond which the settlement was well hidden. Her hand tightened over Dania's arm. 'It's no good. Come…quickly. Up here! It's them! I can see…look…through those trees yonder. Too late…too late! Oh, hurry up, you two!' She scrambled and they followed. 'Hide behind this rock. Hide!' Dark against the rough terrain, they threw themselves behind a boulder, panting with fright as the ground rumbled and shook beneath the pounding hooves of galloping horses and the leaping run of hundreds of tattooed spear-waving men hell-bent on revenge. Like a carpet, they swarmed across the rough ground towards the Roman army who, as one large machine, turned to face them.

'Somer!' Dania howled through her fingers. 'Go back! Go back!'

While the sun rose up higher for a better view, what happened in the next few hours was something that would be for ever etched on Dania's memory, for although she had witnessed fighting since her childhood, she had never seen a battle on this scale involving men of her own kin. The scene at the River Fort a few days ago was now being repeated, this time in daylight and on a grander scale and, at the end of it, the carnage was immense and very one-sided.

Nevertheless, Dania and her maids were not allowed to stay to the end, for they had been sought by Brannius, Astinax and Ram, who had run all the way from Coria to find them. It had taken Ram only a few moments to convince Brannius, on his return to the House of Women at dawn, that a victory for Somer was by no means certain. Ram had been to the barracks to begin his training session and had seen the cavalry passing along Dere Street on their way to the Wall. But Dania and her friends had been gone some time and Somer intended to attack today, Bran said.

The three men had donned long cloaks and followed the cavalry at a distance, searching the landscape for their herb-gathering mistress. Having found them shaking and helpless, they had hustled them away downhill to Coria while the howls and shrieks of the Briganti tribesmen echoed off the Wall, sending ravens and buzzards wheeling above them to wait for easy pickings.

At the House of Women they waited for news, though it was to find out who was left alive rather than to confirm who had won. Crowds flocked up the hillside to watch the battle, returning in relays at mid-day with varied accounts, few of which were exaggerated. The Roman army lost a handful of men and some took injuries, but the Brigantii lost dozens before they were chased back into the forests, their chariots and pride in tatters and some of their best men in chains.

Chapter Five

Ram said it was sheer coincidence, that's all.

Dania insisted it was her fault. She should have listened more carefully when the tribune said he was taking men up to the Wall.

Astinax said that military tribunes didn't take their precious cavalry anywhere unless it was to show them off or to lead them into a fight. They let decurions do the chores.

Nevertheless, Dania was adamant that if she'd not misinterpreted what he said, none of this would have happened. She did not dare throw in the excuse that it had been late at night and that she had been more aware of how he was saying it than of what he was saying. She sent Brannius back up to Boar Hill immediately to find out if her brother was still alive.

Etaine suspected she had been trying too hard to find something worth reporting.

Astinax wondered why she thought it required a cohort of infantry and five hundred cavalry to repair a wall, but if she wanted to blame herself, that was her privilege. On the other hand, he secretly doubted that Tribune Bloody Peregrinus would do anything without a very good reason.

And so, for Dania at least, the dreadful day alternated between thoughts of abandoning the role of informer and of wreaking every kind of personal revenge on the careless informant. She also thought it would have helped if she'd been in less doubt about which was which.

Between discussing what was happening two miles to the north of them and making use of the herbs gathered that morning, Dania tended the queue of women and children who came to visit her surgery on Weaver Street, which in turn helped to reinforce the certainty that she could never pull up her roots from Coria and flee to Somer's protection. These women needed her. They had no one else to turn to. And how long would Boar Hill remain safe? Sorting and spreading the herbs out to dry, infusing others, chopping roots and leaves, applying poultices and giving instructions helped to take her mind off other problems. Having bathed and laid upon the place where Fabian Peregrinus had laid last night, she welcomed the peaceful evening and the guests who came with it to the House of Women, though Brannius's failure to return caused her some concern.

Coria was not allowed to settle down after that. The news that the Emperor Septimus Severus and his eldest son were on their way spread through the market place early the next morning, switching people's interest from gory battle to showy pageant with the fickleness of children. Julia Fortunata, always ready for a show of any sort, breezed into

Dania's tailor's shop while she was examining a new batch of ladies' cloaks with deep embroidered borders and, rather than suffer her friend's usual attempts to wheedle a gift, Dania led her out into the street.

The usual traffic lined the route through the centre of town with faces more curious than enthusiastic. Emperors in the north were as rare as thunderbolts, and this would be something to tell the grandchildren about. Severus, Julia told Dania with an air of being in the know, intended to visit first the shrines, then to inspect the headquarters and barracks, and then he was to host a feast at his new home near the river. How did she know that? 'Why, from Titus Flavius, of course,' she said. 'Who else?' As the centurion's mistress, she had been hoping for an invitation, but it was not to be.

She pouted her very large lips, which she was good at, and let herself be swept along with the crowd, consoled by the stares and sly glances at the diaphanous linen across her generous bosom. 'Because it's only for the men,' she said. 'The empress has stayed behind in Eboracum with their youngest son, so Severus won't have his lady. It's a shame. I wanted another chance to see the *gorgeous* tribune again. Just wait till you see him, Dania. I expect he'll prefer blondes, though. They do, you know.' She tossed her bleached ringlets.

'Yes,' said Dania. 'I'm sure you're right. What's he like?'

'Tribune Fabian What's-his-name?'

'No, the emperor. Did Titus tell you?'

Julia would rather have talked about the tribune. 'Titus has never seen him,' she said, 'but he knows he's African and dark-skinned. *Very* peculiar to have a Roman emperor who's dark-skinned. He's heard about his reputation, too.'

'For what?'

'Cruelty. Apparently he's quite without mercy to captives. He did the most atrocious things to those he conquered in Gaul. Even some of the Romans objected, and that's saying something. His son is no better, either. He's nicknamed Caracalla because he prefers that type of cloak so much. Perhaps he feels the cold. Perhaps you should send him one of yours.' She grinned slyly at Dania's stony face, suspecting that she would do no such thing. 'You know, like they named Caligula after the boots he wore.'

But Julia's words had sent a chill to creep around Dania's bones in spite of the warm May sunshine. These were details she would rather not have heard. Con was brave, but no man deserved an undignified death, nor was his wife in a fit state to know how he had suffered. Surely there was something she could do to free him, something to make the tribune forget his loyalties, to act against his principles, twist himself around her little finger?

As soon as Julia found a group of friends she knew, Dania excused herself and returned to the shop on the pretext that she had forgotten to tell the tailor something important. She could not tell Julia how she feared and longed to see the man whose body she knew so intimately and whose touch was still doing strange things to her heartbeats, after two days. But he would be with the emperor tonight, and she would have no chance to twist him round anything.

As darkness fell, Brannius returned at last to say that Somer was alive but very angry. It was, she thought, a predictable response.

The House of Women was busy that night with officers and

influential guests who had come from the emperor's feast with loosened tongues and news fresh from Eboracum. At last, when the gossip became so detailed, Dania called in Eneas to record it on his wax tablets to avoid any more disastrous mistakes. Since the arrival of Eneas, she had learned to read, but her writing was still in its early stages and, apart from lending her greeting and name to a letter, labelling her medications and making the occasional list, she was content to leave the rest to her scholarly accountant.

While the guests came and went so frequently during the evening, there was little chance for her to succumb to the worries that hung like bats at the back of her mind. Regular customers brought new acquaintances from the emperor's retinue, the money flowed in, laughter and music filled the house, and the shadiest and most secluded nooks in the garden hummed like a beehive to the whisper of confidences. Dania was sorry when the men began to ask for their shoes, for then her concerns would return and she would have to find a way of resolving them, and wait.

After the departure of the guests, her last act at night was to visit each of the shrines in the entrance hall and to commune with the deities, offering them libations in return for favours according to their capacities. To one after the other she murmured a request, to Diana, to Epona, Cybele and Cernunnos, who cared for women in childbirth, and then to Brighid, the northern deity revered by the Brigantii. It was while she was speaking to Brighid that Albiso approached, his expression politely blank.

'Yes, Albiso?'

'The Tribune Fabian Peregrinus is here, my lady. He asks

if you will receive him.' The shock in her eyes confirmed that this was unexpected. 'I can tell him you've retired, if you wish,' he whispered.

It was, of course, a formality. The shrines could be seen from the entrance and the lamp in Brighid's alcove was lighting up Dania's face. There was no question of a refusal. She nodded. 'Let him come in,' she said.

'Will you require food, my lady?'

'No, thank you. Show him in, then leave us.'

Albiso bowed and went to take the red cloak although, as usual, Fabian was on the move and the steward had to sidestep like a startled crab.

'Dania Rhiannon,' said the tribune. 'I apologise for the late hour…' he glanced at the dumpy domestic figure of Brighid '…and for interrupting you.'

Each time she saw him he was dressed differently, this time in the formal toga favoured by the emperor for functions, long, white and voluminous, bordered along one edge by a narrow purple stripe. Dania noticed that the long end thrown over his left shoulder was knotted around his waist, presumably to leave his hands free. It was a typical soldierly thing to do.

'I did not expect you,' she said. 'The emperor's feast?'

Now that he was here, the disturbing negative thoughts of the day had begun to recede, making it difficult for her to remember the details of the grudges she had been harbouring against him. He must, she thought, have been by far the most handsome man at Severus's grand new house that evening, and suddenly the idea of there being no women present did not displease her. Even so, she wished it had not been so very late; she was an early bird by nature and she had been ready for bed some time ago.

'Yes, the emperor's feast,' he said. 'I could not get away earlier. He wanted to talk.' He glanced again at the shrine. 'Have I met this lady?'

'Brighid. Goddess of therapy and healing. Inspiration. Poetry. You will know her better as Minerva, I suppose. But I have one more to attend, if you don't mind waiting a moment. Over here.' She had been saving Venus till last for a dialogue about the difference between desire and love, hoping for some clarification.

The bronze statuette was overtly sensual, naked except for carelessly applied drapery not meant to conceal much. Caught in a graceful dancing pose, she held an apple, and her long tresses tumbled daintily on to her small breasts. She was very lovely, tall and lissome. And barefoot.

Fabian stood close behind her to examine the figure. 'In most essentials,' he said in Dania's ear, 'except perhaps for the rather undersized breasts, I'd say she's quite a good likeness of another goddess I know. I would have to make a more detailed comparison, of course. She appears to lack a navel, for one thing. That can't be right. Don't goddesses have navels?'

A ripple of excitement shivered her upper arms. 'This is very indelicate talk, my lord,' she said, trying to hide her smile. 'I would not wish to offend her by it.'

He moved closer and she felt the warmth of him as he placed his hands upon her waist, spreading his fingers wide to cover her ribs. And while he held her so, she knew he would feel her trembling even though the decision had been taken, the journey already begun. She placed her own hands over his, but he diverted her fear towards the figure that she had only ever looked at with a woman's eyes.

'Slender, but not as slender as this,' he whispered, moving his hands slowly downwards, 'and not as curved over here. Nor does she possess that same languid grace…' the hands moved over her stomach, then upwards '…nor are her breasts as beautiful as these.' His mouth was on her neck as he spoke, and she caught the scent of the cool night on his hair and skin. 'And she probably thinks as I do that it's time we paid her our homage in private. Come now, is it time to put your fears aside? I'll not hurt thee, lass. Is that what concerns you?'

She gasped as his hands moved up to cup her breasts so gently, melting something within her body. She shook her head.

'What is it, then? You're not a virgin?'

'No,' she whispered, stretching her neck under his soft lips.

He lifted his head to look round. 'Which is your room?' he said.

Do it. Go on, do it. Somer says you must. We need more information. 'I can't,' she said, turning inside his arms ready to struggle out of them.

He swooped, tipping her backwards and sweeping her off the floor, hoisting her high into his arms as he swung her round. 'Which one?' he said.

'Through the dining room…to the left…that door.' There was no more to be said. His arms were like iron girders, and he knew how to nudge her door open with hardly a break in his stride.

Beneath the light of a single lamp, Eneas sat at her table making fair copies of lists from a stack of writing tablets. He leapt up as Fabian entered with Dania, immediately gathering up the nearest pile and his stylus, closing the door quietly behind him.

The room was spacious and handsomely furnished with a large low scroll-ended couch that served as night and day-bed. The single lamp sent a dim glow that barely reached the mound of pale bed linen, furs and tasselled cushions and the white linen shift that had been laid ready for her. Long shadows washed across the high oaken shutters that kept out the night and, on the tiled floor, a large white sheepskin looked good enough to wear.

The panic that rose in Dania's mind began to abate before the tender invasion, dismissing fears of discovery and deceit, and bringing her senses to a different level of awareness. He had been right about the curiosity, though only she knew how that was changing to longing and desire, and some anger that he was the wrong man, the one she could not afford to want. The enemy.

But his knowing hands were skilful and surprisingly sensitive, for a soldier, and instead of telling her what he wanted, he told her instead what she wanted to hear, suspecting that she might not have heard it for some time. He was not to know that she had *never* heard such things before, nor had she ever been made love to. Con had had no time for preliminaries.

'You're a wild creature,' he whispered, gentling her with his hand soft upon her throat, 'an exquisite rare thing that won't let a man near her. Why, my lass? Why? Did no one tame you? Was it not good for you? Bad handling, was it? Hush…now, let me teach you, you with the hair like midnight and eyes like gemstones. Are you quiet now, my beauty? Eh?' His voice was deep with an inbuilt caress so different from his first commanding bark, the words spoken so close to her skin that she could feel them. 'Goddess,' he whispered. 'Dania Rhiannon.'

He took time to kiss her thoroughly, so that she was able to sense his hunger through even the most teasing brush of his lips that at first puzzled her, not having experienced such a thing before. When he persevered, she responded, tasting his mouth with nibbles that she soon discovered would kindle kisses of a deeper sort that left her moaning and aching for some kind of release. He recognised her softening. 'Stay where you are,' he whispered.

She felt the lurch of the soft padding beneath her as he stood to unwind his toga with arms flailing, throwing the heavy yardage over the end of the bed. He bent to remove his brief pants and he was as she'd seen him before, slender and long-legged below, wide and powerful above with arms as thick as tree branches. But now there was a more urgent signal that warned her once more to think of the terrible danger she was in.

Anticipating her last attempt at escape, he captured her again before she could evade him. 'No, lass! No…no!' he said. 'You cannot be for ever running from it. I've promised I'll not harm you.' Freed from his restraining garment, he knelt over her to untie her sash, hauling it from under her like a rope. 'There,' he said, 'that's a start. Now, we shall do as your lovely Venus does.' So saying, he began to slide her robe off one shoulder.

But again, the warning of danger loosed its power into her arms. For six years she had kept her secret close: she must not reveal it now. Catching at his hands, she held them in a grip he could not ignore. 'No…no!' she gasped. 'You must not! I cannot…cannot do this!'

'Hush, lass…all right. I'm going too fast for you. I should have known. It's all right. We'll take it slowly…we have all night.' Patiently, he pulled her into his arms as relief washed over her, leaving her giddy and confused.

'Will you stop if I ask you to?' she said, shakily.

'I can stop as long as you want me to. Till dawn, anyway.'

'That's not quite what I meant.'

'Will I stop? Ah, I see. Will I *stop*, if you ask me?' He grinned, caressing her arm. 'Well, of course I will, my beauty. Having got this far with you I'm not going to do anything you don't want me to. Just give me the chance to show you. To persuade you. I can, you know.'

He was more persuasive than she could have imagined, and skilled in the art of the slow seduction that was a long way from his presumptuous assault out there in the garden. Here, he was tenderly careful as she warmed to him, and when her hands reached up to caress his neck, he took advantage of her raised arms to explore her breasts and to draw deep sighs of rapture into his lengthening kisses. They were firm and full, and Fabian encountered no resistance when he gently drew her robe down over them so that she could feel his hand upon her bare skin, the soft rake of his fingers across her erect nipples.

He found the little ties that held the top edges of her sleeves together along her arms and pulled them loose, keeping her lips occupied so that she would not notice. Soon, she was bared to the waist, her breasts eager for his hand and mouth, her body awash with cravings for more of him. His hand moved on down, drawing her robe with it, meeting with no obstructions as it searched, tenderly.

Delving her fingers deep into the close cap of his hair, Dania felt her womb awaken at the warm tug of his mouth upon her nipple and her legs spread of their own accord, ready to enclose him more willingly than ever they had done for her former partner. Sneakily, as if to offer her one more chance to come to her senses, a picture wormed its way into her mind of a black-and-white striped crest upon a shining helmet, far removed from the soft sensuous stuff in which her fingers were now buried. Alerted by the message, she twisted away, nipping her teeth into his upper arm. It was hard and muscular and she could do no more than startle him, but it was enough to initiate a tussle between them that lasted only moments and which, in her case, was quite inadequate to best him. By the time it was over it was too late to recall the omen, and she was spread under him in a carpet of her loosened hair while he was pushing against her where she had sworn no man would ever go. She could hold out no longer. She wanted him, welcomed him.

Her cry of surrender and acceptance signalled the end of her exile and the beginning of a new life; freedom and captivity merged into one.

'Easy, my beauty,' he whispered, entering her. 'Am I hurting?'

'No,' she said. 'I cannot believe this.'

'Believe it. It's happening. At last I have you, woman.'

'It's not like…'

'Like what?'

'Not what I expected.'

'What did you expect?'

'To feel nothing. But I do…feel everything…every part of you in every part of me. It's the most…amazing thing… oh, Fabian… go on…go on…'

He smiled, plying her with all his considerable skills, able to guess at least one reason for her antipathy to the idea. For all she knew about lovemaking, he thought, she might as well be a virgin.

Dania fully expected him to finish pleasuring her well before the usual time-span of her weaving pattern, but this time the sensations pervading her body did not encourage any thought-wandering, nor did Fabian show any signs of stopping. She felt his arm slide beneath her waist to lift her hips on to a cushion, another caring gesture that gave them both more comfort and deeper contact, and she sent a fleeting prayer to Venus to make this last long enough to be remembered.

'Tell me if you want me to stop.'

'No…no, go on,' she said, grasping his arms. 'Please go on.' She heard his laugh of relief as he stooped to kiss her, and knew then with fearful clarity that, although there was for her an ulterior motive behind this capitulation, her heart was not as unmoved as it was supposed to be and that, if all had been equal between them, this commanding lover would have been a prize to aim for. She sent another fleeting message to Venus to keep her heart safe from him, suspecting that it was already too late to be of much use.

For the span of at least five complicated weaving formulae, ecstasy flooded her world way beyond the boundaries of her experience, beguiling and leading her through a variety of paces completely new and designed to provoke wordless responses, wild and primitive. There had been only one pace with Con, requiring no commitment from her. This time, her body performed in time to some distant mind music, exciting

Fabian, whose admiration of her flawless body increased his fervour. From the start, they were a perfect partnership, he the master, she the willing pupil, quick-learning and imaginative.

At last, generating a new layer of excitement that grew from somewhere deep inside, his powerful plunging rhythm became a current of energy that pulsed and surged like a tide upon her shore, and she cried out as the wave crashed over her and carried her along, beyond all control. Fiercely he followed, holding her hard against him as the wave buffeted their lungs, taking their breath away, holding it tantalisingly beyond their reach.

He groaned into her neck, slowed and pulsed again, then stopped. Exhausted and bewildered, Dania enfolded him, cradling his moist shoulders against her. 'Venus!' she whispered.

'What in the name of the gods did you say to her?' he panted.

She smiled and patted his shoulder. 'Questions...no questions.'

Half-covered by a jumble of furs and fabrics, they overlapped each other against a pile of cushions and, by the dim light of a distant lamp, sipped from a shared beaker of weak ale brewed locally by a grateful client. At first there was no chatter between them, both of them still gently tumbling through space, both readjusting their thoughts about the other, wanting to know more but reluctant to break the spell and not sure whether knowing would be a good thing.

Lying in the crook of his arm, she passed him the beaker and returned her hand to his chest to smooth the silky hair and to follow its course down beneath the linen cover.

With a hiccup, he slammed the beaker down on the side-table and made a grab for her hand. 'To do that to a man when he's drinking is most unfair!' he laughed, coughing.

'I wanted to see how far down it goes,' she said, demurely.

'You could have seen the other night, if you'd wanted to, witch.'

'I didn't want to be nosy.'

'Well, I'll show you in a moment, if you can contain yourself.'

'I can contain myself, Tribune.'

He rolled on to her, pushing her head into the black tangle of her hair. 'You cannot contain yourself, woman,' he scoffed. 'It took me all my time to hold you down. Wild creature. By the gods, what you'll be like when you've had more practice I can scarce imagine. I shall want to be there. So tell me, what was all the fear about? Eh?'

She tried to turn her head away. 'Don't spoil it, please,' she said. Fabian could wait; she could not. 'It's irrelevant now. Tell me about the emperor. Was he impressed?'

He pulled her up, gathering a fistful of her hair into his hand and twisting it into a coil. 'Severus? Oh, I think he's impressed, but he wouldn't say as much. He's not an easy man to please.'

Goose pimples ran along her arms, and she hitched the white fox fur well up over her shoulder. 'So do you have ways of softening him up?'

He made a sound that was not quite laughter. 'I've worked with him before,' he said. 'I know his ways. I know what he likes.'

'What *does* he like? Women?'

'No, he's been happily married to his second wife for a long time.'

'What then? Feasting, obviously.'

'That, and sport. Fighting sport, I mean. Blood sports.'

'Not an intellectual, then?'

'Neither him nor Caracalla, his eldest. They like nothing better than man-to-man contests. The bloodier the better. We're putting on some games for them tomorrow before we get down to the serious work. The men deserve it, too.'

'Open to the public?'

'Oh, yes, they'll want to see the fun. We'll use the parade ground as a stadium. My lord Severus and Caracalla want the captives to be pitted against each other to the death. Personally, I think we could put them to better use than that, but it's not my decision. He thinks it will be a popular move. I have my reservations.'

A tight ball of fear worked its way to the base of Dania's chest, pushing against her heart to unsettle its beat. *Con to fight to the death for a Roman emperor's enjoyment?* 'Don't you have any say in the matter?' she asked over the pulse that drummed in her throat. 'Do they all have to die that way?'

'Well, they won't perform as well as trained gladiators, of course, but if that's what the emperor wants, that's what he'll get. Seems a bit of a waste to me. There's one big red-haired brute amongst them who may put up a good show. He has tattoos on his chest like two half-circles, one inside the other. He's from the local Boar Hill tribe who we caught on that raid the night of your dinner party. Remember?' He pulled her closer into his arms, smiling down at her face, but unable to see the dread in the greenness of her eyes, or the constriction in her throat that almost stopped her words.

'What's his name?' she whispered. It was a question too far.

He appeared not to notice. 'No idea. He only speaks his own language, and no one is likely to offer to interpret for him. Now, my lady. Shall we return our attention to more… er…interesting matters?'

'Like where your furry stripe ends?'

'That, for a start.'

'And what for a finish?'

'Who knows?' he said, peeling back the fox fur. 'Probably not too far from the beginning.'

'This is all very confusing, my lord.'

'Then allow me to explain.'

She did, but try as she might to dismiss the shocking news from her mind for the next hour, her personal ties to Con the Silvertongue were too strong for her not to care about the inhuman manner of his death. To die with a sword in his hand would not displease him, but to fight in captivity for the enemy's pleasure would be a disgrace that his Boar Hill kin would take badly. What it would do to his wife she could not bear to think. Dania herself had not loved Con as his wife did, but nor had she hated him. Nor could she switch her emotions on and off to coincide with the tribune's needs. Her lovemaking was passive and heart-breakingly unfulfilled.

'Do you want me to stop, lass?'

'Yes… I'm sorry. It's been a long day.'

'Shh…no need to say sorry. You need to sleep. I understand.'

'Yes. Just hold me. Don't go.'

Tenderly, he held her in his arms until she slept.

The clamour of early morning sounds and the piercing blast of the cornum from the barracks carried Dania's dreams into the real world where daylight sneaked through the gap in the shutters and a clutter of bed linen adorned her couch in most unusual disarray. She rolled over, staring at the discarded sash and crumpled robe, the ruffled covers and the cushions on the floor, recalling the events that had put them there, events of great consequence, and probably life-changing.

Her hand stole downwards to comfort the tenderness there and to still the flutter of excitement. Life-changing.

Life-changing? Great gods...help me! Venus, what have you done?

It was what she had *not* done that mattered.

Throwing the warm covers away as if they burned her, she leapt out of bed and across to the basin of water over by the wall to perform the first, and probably the most useless, protest against the threat of conception. The table shook and towels fell as she washed vigorously between her legs, trying to think of an antidote to the night's passionate encounter, but remembering only preventions rather than remedies. She had broken the women's cardinal rule about safety. She, the mistress of the place, was a complete beginner. She had brought it upon herself and now her punishment would be several weeks of anxiety, at the very least.

Churning inside with conflicting emotions and the beginning of a sickening worry, she sat on the bed and placed one hand on the dent in the pillow where his head had rested. Dragging it slowly towards her, she held it beneath her nose to breathe in the lingering scent of him then, little by little, she lowered it to cover her womb, to hold its warmth close to her body, rocking gently as tears gathered along her lashes. 'Venus help me,' she whispered. 'This is your doing.'

The memory of his lovemaking and her own amazing discoveries kept pace alongside her predicament, the energetic bulk of him above her, his careful weight, the extreme gentleness he had used to indulge and gratify her needs, even that of sleep at the end. Could any lover be more exciting, more caring, more masterful? Though he had refused to accept any more delays, it had seemed at times as if the experience was more for her than for him, though he could not have known that the information she drew from him would turn out to be so bitter, so unacceptable. Had her sacrifice been worth that? Just to know sooner rather than later of Con's terrible fate? Would the price of future information prove to be too expensive after all?

She wiped her tears on the pillow and threw it aside. Something must be done. If this was to be Con the Silvertongue's last day on earth, it rested with her to do something to spare his dignity. Apart from Astinax, the only one who would know about such things was Ram. She went to open the shutters, letting a flood of colour wash across the room and chase away the clouds in her mind.

Ram and Astinax came to her in the secluded garden at the back of the house where silver spiders' webs stretched across the trellises and shimmered with dew-soaked sunlight, where pigeons clattered around the dove-cote, crooning love songs.

Ram was dressed, ready for his morning visit to the barracks, his arms and legs protected by bronze guards, his skin shining like polished wood. Though quietly embittered, he was careful of his appearance, and today his short tunic was spotless, his back and front encased in shining bronze plates, his wide-brimmed metal helmet tucked beneath one Herculean arm. A short broadsword swung from one hip, a dagger clung to the other, and Dania knew them both to be razor-sharp and quicker than a blink, despite Ram's immensity. His daily session with the soldiers was a two-edged sword, boosting his sense of pride in his teaching but reminding him of his losses and of those who had caused them. With Dania, his gentle courtesy was unfailing, his battle-worn face showing little more than steadfastness and pain, anger and wariness. To her, his pale blue eyes were more readable than to most, and now their wandering admitted that her news of Con's forthcoming ordeal was not news to him. He had even told Astinax.

It had cost Dania dear to get that information, and she was far from pleased. 'What's going on?' she snapped. 'I'm supposed to *know* such things.'

'We didn't *want* you to know,' said Astinax. 'It does you no good, my lady. Etaine told me what this Con the Silvertongue once was to you. It was bound to upset you. Ram and I agreed between us that you shouldn't be told.'

'So Etaine knows about this too?' She frowned.

'No, my lady, she doesn't. Only us, and you. How did you find out? Was it the tribune?' They had both seen him enter, and leave at dawn.

'I *asked* him,' she said. 'And it didn't come cheap. Don't

blame me. It's a chance to find out what's happening. I couldn't turn it down. I know the risks.' She turned away, colouring.

'Nobody blames you, my lady,' said Ram. 'But don't underestimate that man. He's no fool. If he spills information, it's because he wants you to know. You must not put your trust in him. The men at the barracks are in awe of him and his own men think he's a god. Beware.'

Dania was confident. 'Oh, I have his measure,' she said. 'He only wants what they all want, and he naturally wants what I told him he couldn't have, that's all. What possible reason could he have for telling me about Con's fate? Does he think Con is a special case? Does he think the emperor is saving something particularly brutal for him?' She saw the evasion in their eyes. 'Oh, *surely* not. Surely he wouldn't... *would* he?' Her hand settled on Ram's brawny arm and met the hard resistance of bronze, and she understood by their wary exchange of glances that the two men still knew more than she did. 'Tell me,' she commanded. 'You *must*!'

It was Ram who spoke. 'The men I've been working with these last few mornings have requested that I should fight him, my lady. As an exhibition.'

'You? *You* fight with Con? Kill him, you mean?'

Ram's voice held a cool matter-of-factness that had no doubt contributed to his excellence in the arena. 'I may not refuse, my lady. They believe I'm now on their side and I've purposely given them no cause to think otherwise. To decline would immediately invite their distrust. I must do it. But think on it,' he continued, reasonably, 'I shall not let him suffer, as another man would do. When I see he's beaten I shall dispatch him quickly, with mercy. He doesn't know me, so he won't give me away. It will be better this way than any other.'

Except for her eyes, round and filled with horror, Dania's face was covered by her hands. 'What if he should kill you, Ram?' she said through her fingers.

'He won't.'

'How can you be so sure? He's very strong.'

'He will have only his own sword. Nothing else. No protection. He's not used to wearing armour, anyway. It would hinder him.'

'Not even a shield?'

'No.'

Already she was trembling uncontrollably, but at this revelation she was sickened. 'That's inhuman…*barbaric*!' she hissed. 'They don't mean him to win, do they? He won't stand a chance. He has a wife and three children, Ram, and Somer will take the new one from her. Oh, may the gods help them all. And you, Ram. I would not have wanted this weight to rest on you, of all people.'

'The contest begins soon, my lady. Ours will be the last. I must go.'

'Oh, Ram, what can I say to you? Can no one be bribed?'

'Too late. The emperor has agreed to it. And besides, they'd rather have their sport and win their bets than take bribes.' He knew without being invited what she would do, and his arms opened for her like a brother's, to embrace her against the hard breastplate that would soon be spattered with Con's life-blood.

'Do it quickly, Ram,' she pleaded. 'Don't let him suffer. Oh, may the gods be with you both.' Reluctantly, she let him go, though she kept his hand in hers until the last moment. 'Will you go with him, Astinax?'

'I shall go,' he replied. 'Don't worry, Ram will give him a clean death and he'll die with his sword in his hand. Go in, my lady. You're shivering.'

Still she hesitated. 'I know you must go, but come back here as soon as it's over. Bring Ram back, Astinax. He'll have wounds, and I shall tend them myself. Don't let them…' Her voice faded as she wiped an angry tear away. 'Go, both of you,' she croaked. 'May the gods be with you, all three.'

Etaine came down the path as the men left. She stopped to embrace them, then hurried to take her mistress in her arms until her shaking began to subside. 'Here, take my cloak,' she said, placing it around Dania's shoulders. 'Tell me what's happening. Is something going on?' For her small size, Etaine was tough and resilient of mind, though even she could not help quaking at Ram's terrible task. Remember his background, was what she advised. 'Don't forget that he's a Briton, too,' she said, 'with training in both styles, tribal and Roman. Ram knows what Con will do, you know, the usual shouting of insults, the roaring and leaping to scare the opponent, the grimacing. And he's added more tattoos since you and he lived together. It won't last long,' she finished, sadly. 'It can't, can it? Do you want to talk about last night?'

'I need your advice, Ettie. There's a problem,' Dania said.

They heard the roaring begin while they attended the women who stopped their chatter to listen with obvious resentment. The news had spread quickly, and their menfolk had gone to watch and to cheer on those to whom many were related, one way or another. Their mood was not as equable as the military believed it to be at the tormenting of their fellow countrymen for the emperor's sport, and many of them were downright angry and ready to make trouble, even in the lion's den. There was not one of the women in Dania's surgery who failed to notice how the colour drained from her face, how her hand shook. It was mid-day when the last patient departed, laying a warm comforting hand upon Dania's arm as she left, as all the others had done.

Leaving the clearing-up to the two young assistants, Dania and Etaine hurried back to the House of Women, desperate for news from the barracks. A crescendo of roaring was carried on the breeze over the rooftops, then another and another until the air was filled with a howl that rose and fell like a swarm of wasps. Icy fingers crawled over Dania's skin to the distant din of men's blood-lust, and she knew that although she should be used to it by now, she was not and never would be.

Only a short time later, Astinax led a crowd of soldiers across the courtyard at the House of Women, running at a trot and bearing a stretcher between them, their faces twisted with the effort. More followed on behind to take over the burden, for it was a very heavy one and no one had the extra strength of victory. Astinax shook his head at Dania's silent enquiry.

Then she saw the bloodstained covering and Ram's sweat-soaked face, the deathly pallor and closed eyes and, while she struggled to hang on to her disbelief, she could not hold back a wail of despair. 'No…no…' she cried. 'He's not…no, he *can't* be! In the name of the gods, what's happened?'

The men laid the stretcher on the table in the dining room where water and sponges and every kind of repairing aid had been made ready, and it was Astinax who carefully peeled back the cover to show her the gaping wound made by Con's sword-thrust that he knew full well Ram could have avoided if he had wanted to. Drained, shocked beyond belief, he knelt down to arrange Ram's blood-soaked neckerchief as if it mattered to the half-naked body. 'It's all right, my good friend. We're proud of you. You did well in this,' he said.

Ram's eyelids twitched and opened wearily, his pale eyes searching for someone in particular.

'I'm here,' said Dania, taking his hand between both of hers. 'You're home, Ram. My hero.' She forced herself to smile for him, dripping tears on to his hand.

The gladiator's whisper was barely audible in the silent room. 'Where is he?' he said. 'Did he…?'

'He escaped,' said Astinax, on the verge of tears. 'The crowd took him. He got away.' With so many Roman ears listening, there was a limit to what could be said.

But Ram understood that, and was careful not to show either relief or pleasure before the last light faded from his eyes and he took Dania's look of gratitude with him on the next stage of his journey. It was Astinax who drew his eyelids down like shutters against the pain while Dania still made one last effort to hold him back with her pleading. 'Ram, don't go. Please don't go.'

'He's gone back home, my lady,' Astinax told her, and neither she nor Etaine were sure whether he referred to Ram or to Con. Or to them both.

That night, the House of Women was closed to everyone.

Chapter Six

One of those on whom Dania had always been able to rely at times like this was Brannius, her half-brother, whose late return from Boar Hill he had not even attempted to explain. Now she was obliged to exert her authority to get him to stay in Coria long enough to help with Ram's burial that night.

'What are you *thinking* of?' she snapped, wearily. 'Of *course* you must help. How can you go before we've laid Ram to rest? Does his sacrifice mean nothing to you?'

'It was quite unnecessary, my lady,' Brannius replied stiffly, glowering at her from beneath a thick mop of dark hair. Like her, he was barefoot, and had already donned his chequered breeches beneath his tunic, half-Celt, half-Roman, and full of anger at the turn of events since the tribune's arrival. Unlike his sister, Brannius was less careful how he showed it. 'And I have a mind to tell my lord Somer that it was unnecessary, too. Maybe he should also be told of one or two other unnecessary sacrifices going on at the House of Women while I'm about it.'

'Spare me the innuendo, Bran. What is it exactly that you think our brother ought to be told that will help his situation?'

'I think you already know, my lady.' He folded his arms and leaned against the open door of her room, his lithe frame haloed by the last light from across the garden. 'Would you want him to know how you sacrificed yourself to the enemy? A man with the blood of our kin still warm on his hands? Was the night a long one for you to bear in his arms?'

Dania's pallor showed little change in the deepening gloom, and Brannius did not see the hurt that almost veiled the anger in her eyes. Yes, it had been hard, but not in the way an innocent stripling of twenty years would understand. 'Get out!' she whispered. 'Go to Somer and find out if Con is there. If he's not, tell him what happened. Tell him I've obeyed his instructions. And this time, honour us with a prompt return. Go. We'll manage Ram's last rites without your help. The gods may understand you, even if the rest of us don't. May the gods aid you,' she murmured to the slammed door.

There was a new bitterness between them that neither of them had the heart to try to salve with explanations, and Dania wondered whether she ought to have taken Bran more into her confidence at the beginning or whether Somer would explain to him what he had ordered her to do. Her grievances against the tribune mounted: this was all his doing, Ram's violent death in particular.

She had never been one for tears, but now she buried her head in her hands and howled like a child for the loss of her beloved Ram, knowing how she had been his idol, the only person he had loved in a loveless world. With her, he had always shown the opposite face to that which the gladiator showed, caring, tender, utterly steadfast and solicitous in all his duties, dependable as a rock. For her alone he had shown rare flashes of feeling too deeply private for words.

Rocking and sobbing out of control, Dania let the waves of anguish blind her to everything except the blackest despair of loss and the love that Ram had held for her. She had treated him with a woman's respect and compassion lost to him for years when others had demanded only brute force. She had restored to him his self-respect and had seen the first signs of a growing humour. She had taught him to begin a new life and had then stood by while he went out and lost it, for her sake. For Con's wife's sake, and for the family that Ram himself had lost years ago. He had given his life for a family he had known only through her. She would have been distressed, and he could not have borne to see it, to know that he had been the cause. Would there ever be another man such as this?

Etaine came on soft feet to hold her, to shed tears of her own upon Dania's linen tunic and to lay a basket of white blooms at her feet. 'Here, see,' she said, 'this is to make a wreath for him. He will be waiting for it. He must have known how we loved him. Make it, dear one. Make it beautiful for him.'

They had all hoped for a private funeral, but Ram had far too many admirers for it to be kept secret. However, the crowd that escorted the white-draped bier halfway up Dere Street by the light of flaming torches consisted mostly of men from the garrison, his other friends being too fearful of their safety to appear away from their homes.

Since the incident at the barracks, soldiers had been swarming like ants through the streets, searching every shop and house, molesting innocent people and causing havoc in their attempt to find Con the Silvertongue. Ram's personal friends would have preferred a daytime ceremony conducted after their own fashion with a dignified Druid to help him into the Otherworld rather than a gaggle of noisy professional wailers, the blast of horns and pipes.

They gave Ram his armour and his weapons, and his favourite joint of lamb for the journey, the best mead in plenty, and all his personal jewellery of which, as a native Briton, he was very proud. Later, in private, his loved ones spoke to his favourite god, Cernunnos with the ram-headed snakes, sending many tears with the invocations and the scent of burning juniper.

With so much to be done that day, Dania had given no thought to her most personal problem, the one for which she had sought Etaine's advice. The seeds of the hemp plant she'd been given to chew lay forgotten at the bottom of her girdle-pouch, and when Etaine handed her a beaker to drink before sleeping, she took it from her with thanks more polite than enthusiastic, for she knew it to be a fresh brew of the bitter-tasting rue. Several times she stared down into the mirrored surface, willing herself to lift it up further, arguing that it must be done even while her body cried out to be left alone to do what *it* had to do.

The drink was still there at dawn the next morning, to be tipped into the bowl of roses on an impulse that Dania couldn't begin to explain.

Astinax came to her with the latest news. 'It's no more than we expected,' he told her, wiping a hand over his bald head. 'The Emperor Severus has a reputation for—'

'Yes, I know of his vicious reputation,' Dania said, inviting him to sit on a very solid bench with lion's legs. 'But to starve good honourable men, taken at random, family men, and lads, is *unspeakably* savage, Astinax. You say he'll not feed them till Con is found?'

'Till someone produces him alive they'll get neither food nor water. The town is under siege, my lady. No one dares to go out on the streets for fear of being arrested. It's time the military got a hold on their men instead of wasting ours. They're a disgrace, those foreign rabble. Rampaging like wild beasts. I've locked the gate and barred the two shops. There'll be no trading while people are too scared to move.'

'Thank the gods you're here,' she whispered, thinking of Ram's solid presence. 'Is Bran not back yet?'

'No, but it's early. He'll be on his way.'

'I've lost his support, you know. He blames me. I blame myself.' Her gaze wandered, almost guiltily assessing what she had gained compared to the losses of those who had depended on her for accurate information. For their safety. In the new day's light, her room was as green and leafy as the trees outside, bordered and panelled, scattered with foliage and birds and the soft outlines of dancing figures that had typified her mood at the time, but which now seemed to mock her fears with indecent revelry.

Astinax picked up the large shapely tassel that hung between his legs from the cushion, shaking his head at its flopping silkiness. As usual, he was blunt to the point of coarseness. 'Then you're wrong, m'lady,' he said, 'and Bran's wrong, too. You're not responsible for what's happened recently, and he knows nothing about what a woman like you needs. All he's thinking about is why he can't bed you himself instead of the tribune.' He shook the tassel and dropped it. 'Being your half-brother doesn't stop him wanting you, or from being jealous when somebody else manages it. It would have made no difference *who* it was.' He looked hard at her as if he'd just berated a soldier for dropping his shield.

It had not once occurred to Dania to see it from that angle, and the idea brought a flush to her cheeks even while she held his eyes. 'Bran, wanting *me*?'

Astinax leaned his giant frame backwards, grasping his great thighs with ham-sized hands. 'By the gods, woman, how can you manage a place like this and not see that every man who claps eyes on you is going to want you in his bed? Eh? Of *course* he does. That's what's been bugging him.'

'Then it would be best…perhaps…if he went back to Boar Hill.'

'He's got a mighty chip on his shoulder. It won't matter where he is, he'll make a nuisance of himself now.'

'Until I get rid of the tribune?'

'And how do you propose doing that when he's just had a taste of what he wants? Poison?'

'Astinax!'

'Aye, well. Pardon my bluntness, but getting information from the tribune is more important than what young Bran thinks about it. And our dear old Ram was right, you know. You shouldn't assume that the tribune is thinking with his prick. He's not as daft as that or he'd not be where he is.'

'So what do I do now?' she whispered. 'Carry on playing the game in the hope that I can win something that matters, or kill him before anyone discovers he once stayed here all night?'

Astinax stood up, posing no threat to his mistress despite the revelation that had not excluded even himself. He smiled as if her idea could not be taken too seriously. 'Well, for one thing, you're forgetting that he has a household who'll know exactly where he was on any particular night, especially since his slaves go with him, so you'd have to kill them too. For another, I wouldn't like to suggest how you might manage it where hundreds of others have failed. And if *you've* thought of it, you can be sure he'll have done the same. And just think of the reprisals the emperor might dream up over the murder of his favoured tribune.'

'Favoured?'

'Oh, yes. There are four or five other young bucks with equine status but he's the senior one they all listen to. He'll be a senator in Rome one of these days. He's ambitious, that one. Just think carefully before you take him on. Or take him off, for that matter.'

The door opened. 'Take who off?' said Etaine.

'Tribune Peregrinus,' said Dania.

Etaine closed the door quietly and stood with her back to it, aware that the light tone she had prepared was inappropriate. No one was smiling. 'You're thinking of…*murder*?' she whispered, looking from Dania to Astinax and back again.

'No,' said Dania, sighing. 'I'm thinking *murderously*. Not quite the same thing.'

'Oh. I came to tell you that Bran has just arrived. He refuses to change his clothes.'

The sigh deepened to a groan. 'Bad news, then. I might have known it. But I wish he'd see how he's putting us all in such danger by his stupidity. Tell him to come in here, Ettie.'

'D'ye want me to leave?' said Astinax.

'No, sit down again, if you will. I prefer you to stay. You too, Ettie. And send for Albiso. I feel the need of some support.'

Brannius entered, barefoot and soundless on the tiled floor, his feet stained with dirt and his hair wild with the damp morning air, his expression just as rancorous as it had been on leaving but now darkened by fatigue and the menace of further repercussions. If he was surprised by the unexpected audience he disguised it well, hardly waiting for Albiso to close the door before he began. 'It's as I thought,' he announced with a hint of drama.

Dania sat with her long legs curled beneath her, settling into the green and pink cushions of her couch and pulling the folds of her woollen wrap further over her shoulders. Since they had last met, things had changed. 'Welcome back, Bran,' she said, softly. 'We'll trade what you thought for the facts, shall we?'

Bran had the wit to recognise his half-sister's restraint. 'The facts,' he said, challenged already. 'Right. Well, the facts are these. You'll be glad to know that Con the Silver-tongue managed to reach Boar Hill. The gods only know how with so many hunting him but, well…you know Con.'

'Yes, I know Con,' Dania agreed. 'Will you sit? You must be tired.'

Having expected another stern reprimand for not leaving his Boar Hill clothes in the stable, he was already beginning to feel that his sartorial statement was going for nothing. He looked around him with an obvious distaste at the sumptuous colours and soft silky furnishings, the elegance and shining surfaces, deciding on his own kind of rebuke by ignoring the invitation. 'He didn't stay,' he said. 'There was an almighty row. He's sworn vengeance on my lord Somer.'

'Are you going to tell this backwards, lad?' said Astinax, brusquely. 'Why did he not stay after all?'

For an instant, Brannius looked chastened. 'Because he expected to find his wife and bairns where he'd left them, I suppose,' he said tightly, lowering his voice. 'They were not there. Fled. All gone while the men were away fighting. My lord Somer doesn't know where they've gone and, if the women know, they're not saying. Con blames our brother, my lady, for threatening his wife with the exposure of the babe.'

'How did Con know about that?' said Etaine.

'Sounds as if the women told him,' said Brannius, 'and the prisoners, before they were—' he scowled at Dania '—massacred.'

'Which we regret,' she replied, wondering how much more merciful the punishment would have been if Roman soldiers had been captured by the hill tribes instead. Different, certainly, but equally vicious.

'Con went into a rage,' Brannius continued. 'He tore his hut to pieces, took all his gear on a cart, threatened Somer with revenge and then, before they could stop him, grabbed my lord's foster-son Dias, and made off with him.'

If he had planned to make a stir amongst his stony audience, he had chosen the most effective news to achieve it. '*Dias?* He stole Dias, the fosterling? May the gods help them…him…all of them. Could they not catch him?' they asked.

Ten-year-old Dias was Somer's nephew, placed with the Boar Hill tribe by Somer's sister Mona and her husband to be fostered until he became a man at the age of fourteen.

During his seven years away from home, he might not speak to his father nor sit in his company, and the bond that grew between the fosterling and his adopted family was sacred and even stronger than natural ties. For a foster-child to be stolen was to gather the deepest shame upon the careless family.

'No,' said Brannius, 'there were not enough able men left to chase him, and the women had been told to stay out of the way. No one knows where they've gone. In Coria there's a price on his head. Did you know?'

Astinax robbed him of a second impact. 'Yes,' he said, 'it's the price of men's starvation. You won't be expected to pay that, lad. You'll be quite safe.'

'So will you!' Brannius snapped at him, sick of his disrespect. 'My lord Somer says you're to close this place down and return to Boar Hill immediately. I'm to take you all back with me. Along with one extra.' His eyes glittered.

Astinax met Dania's glance across a beam of sunlight, reading the name that tormented Brannius. Dania clutched at her arms beneath the woollen wrap. 'An extra? You mean the tribune, I suppose?' Like Astinax, she sought to rob him of the pleasure of saying it.

It was not quite accurate. 'The tribune's *head*, my lady.'

'Same thing,' said Astinax, dismissively.

'That's absurd,' said Dania, aware of her own hypocrisy.

'Ridiculous,' said Albiso. 'What good will that do now?'

'It will avenge my lord Somer's honour, and the lady Dania's,' said Brannius. 'I wonder you need to be told, Albiso.'

'I don't need my honour avenging, thank you,' Dania said. 'And I'm sure those are not my brother's sentiments either, are they?'

'They are, my lady. Our brother is shamed to have his own sister so personally connected to a Roman tribune. Yes, I told him. Why would I not? And this is why he demands your return to Boar Hill. He reminds you of his offer.'

Well, the chieftain's memory has suddenly become so selective that he can recall only what is convenient to him and no more. Honour, indeed. That was not a word that bothered him overmuch when we last spoke of this.

'What offer?' said Albiso. 'I never heard of any offer.'

Dania swung her legs down to sit erect and very still, keeping her mind strictly on course to follow each change as it happened, to stay on her feet as the rug was pulled from under them. 'My brother offered us all a place at Boar Hill if things became too difficult for us here in Coria. He seems to think that the time has come.' She took a deep breath. 'But you may as well know, all of you, that I shall not be accepting Somer's offer. I shall not be leaving Coria now or at any time in the future. This is my home, and to desert it would give away everything I've worked for. The rest of you are free to go, if you wish, as I'm sure Bran will do.'

'Hah!' His bark was cynical, though now Dania understood the reason. 'What a surprise, my lady. I wonder what else it is that keeps you here.'

'Keep wondering then, Bran.' Dania's restraint snapped at last, though she had half-expected the taunt. 'And while you're about it, you might also wonder why my brother should be so keen to invite a cartload of women to live at Boar Hill when he has no room for a wee girl-child small enough to fit inside your saddle-bag. Does he think I'm blind not to see through his wiles, I wonder? Does he think we don't know the price attractive young women are fetching on the slave-market these days? Perhaps we know better than he does. Think again, brother, then keep your misguided thoughts to yourself before they choke you. As for the tribune, I can deal with that problem myself, I thank you. I'm not the foolish woman you and Somer seem to take me for. The tribune wanted *me* only, and I wanted up-to-date news and I got it, and I shall get more, but if you want to add your own fancies to that, I can't stop you. Think what you like. I don't owe you an explanation, and, if I gave you one, you'd not understand it. Your heart has been with Somer at Boar Hill for this last year, Bran, so you may as well go to him. I'm not coming with you. Tell him that from me.'

'Bene!' said Albiso, with admiration. 'Well said, lady. I hope you'll allow me to stay with you and take care of things.'

'Me too,' said Astinax. 'I'm going nowhere. I also have your sister to look after, lad, now you've found more prestigious things to do.'

Brannius was stung. He drew himself up to his full height, though he was still a good head shorter than Astinax. 'And exactly how will you get this precious information to Boar Hill, my lady?' he said.

Dania's look was quizzical. 'How would Somer get *any* information, precious or not, if I were not here?' she said with maddening calmness. 'We haven't forgotten the route, Bran. We *can* manage without you.'

Brannius didn't much like the sound of that. 'Hah! Citizens of Coria tramping up Boar Hill with a unit of Roman infantry in their wake?'

'No, it hasn't come to that yet, has it?' Dania replied. 'We are not enemies, nor would I say or do anything to put our tribe in danger. I would not expect you to revenge yourself on me simply because we've decided to go our own ways, though your appearance *here* dressed like *that* puts us all in danger even as we speak.' She saw that Brannius had the grace to look uncomfortable, and she added more kindly, 'I wish you no harm, Bran. We're kin, remember? You have served the House of Women well and I have given you my protection. There is no need for this terrible bitterness.' She rose, and went to speak to him more intimately.

To her astonishment, the young man's eyes were filling with tears. 'No, lady,' he whispered. 'I know that. But things…have happened…too…'

'Too unexpected? Out of character? Yes, that's how life is.'

'And that bloody tribune, a *Roman*, in your bed. How *could* you?'

She would like to have said *ask Somer*, but she knew he would deny it. 'One day I shall be able to tell you how, Bran, but this is not the best time. Give me your trust, that's all I ask, as you've always done in the past. We've been close, you and I, have we not? Pray for peace.' Gently, she touched his arm.

'Yes, lady,' he said, 'we have. But it's not peace I'm after, it's war.'

She sighed. 'Yes, I was afraid of that. It's the root of our differences, isn't it? Go to Somer and fight with him, then, and tell him we're still faithful here. You're a brave warrior, Bran, but leave the tribune's head to me.'

He nodded. 'You'll not let me stay another day?'

'No, not another hour.'

'Then I have no choice. I may take my pony?'

'Of course. It's yours. I shall have food packed for you, and gifts.'

The enticing aroma of frying bacon and new-baked bread caught in Dania's nostrils as she returned from the stables through the garden at the back of the house. Lit by the early sun, the opening flower heads made a brilliant splash of colour against the darker greens, reminding her that she could easily have made such things alone an excuse to stay here where she could keep some control of her life, though that luxury seemed to be dwindling by the day. The sharper truth, however, was nearer to Bran's suspicions, and the deceit she was being obliged to practise was contrary to everything she wanted from life. Out of character, she had told Bran, as if that explained everything, and while she saw herself being edged unwillingly into a role she had no wish to play, Bran was being set free to follow his conscience, sure that he was the injured party.

Delving a hand into her pouch, her fingertips touched the seeds left there since yesterday and, gathering them up into her palm, she threw them across to a blackbird and a hen-sparrow. 'There, feed your little ones,' she said.

Taking advantage of their self-imposed captivity behind locked gates and the absence of guests, even daytime visitors, Albiso set the household to spring-cleaning and soon had the garden flapping with white sheets, pillow and bedcovers, towels and furs. From over the rooftops came the sounds of yelling and crashing, and plumes of black smoke rose into the sky as someone's house was torched. The ensuing pandemonium brought the cleaners to a horrified standstill as they tried to gauge how near danger was creeping. Three of Dania's women had gone to stay with relatives after Ram's funeral, leaving the remaining four to wonder how soon it would be before the place was overrun by uncouth soldiers hoping to gain entry to the place that had always been beyond their reach.

The cleaning kept the household well occupied that day, and it was late afternoon before they discovered that Dania's stables had been searched and that, apart from a frightened young stable-lad, a few spilled sacks of oats and a door torn off its hinges, nothing else had been damaged. A few hours earlier, and they would have found the clothing and weapons that Brannius kept there.

Troops passed, people hid, and abandoned waggons cluttered the streets, but no one attempted to break through the wrought-iron gate that led to the House of Women's courtyard where Dania and Etaine, with turbans swathed round their heads, were stuffing pillows with goose-down. Sitting on the verandah steps beside them, Astinax watched and listened. Each of them felt Ram's absence keenly for, though he had been a quiet man, his immense form had always been linked to his friend like a pair of guardian twins. Now they had lost both Ram and Brannius within twenty-four hours, and the feeling of vulnerability was very real.

'Do you think Bran will have reached Boar Hill safely?' said Dania. 'Should I have waited before sending him off? Was I too hasty?'

'He'll be all right,' said Astinax, watching a tiny white

feather float on an updraught. 'He'll know a dozen different ways of getting there without being seen. It's Con who'll have problems getting away. He's harder to disguise, and he was injured, too.'

'Where would he go?' said Etaine, blowing a feather off her nose.

'I think,' said Dania, 'he'll make his way north through the Wall to reach my sister Mona. She's the fosterling's mother, you know.'

'You think he'll take young Dias back to his parents, then?' said Astinax.

'Well, I do,' Dania replied. 'Mona's husband and Somer's wife Morning Star are brother and sister, remember.'

'And she's just had a wee lad too,' said Etaine.

'Yes, and I believe Morning Star may have helped Con's wife to flee while Somer was away fighting. Con's wife told me she was sympathetic.'

Astinax was sceptical. 'And how could Con the Silvertongue know where his wife's gone when he was in Roman custody?'

Etaine spoke quietly as if to a child. 'He tore his house apart, Astinax,' she said. 'He'd be desperate, and there'd be somebody there who'd want him to know where they'd gone, believe me.'

'Would there?' he said.

'Yes, it's called woman-sense. Some of us are blessed with it.'

The bluff giant found no reply to that except to watch the graceful arch of Etaine's neck as she bent over her task.

Dania broke the silence. 'Astinax, do you think you could get a message to Metto Lentus for me? Tonight, after dark?'

'Is he still in Coria?'

'Yes, he's staying at the inn down near the bridge.'

'Sure, I can get a message to him. You want Eneas to write it?'

'No, word of mouth. It's quite simple. I want to know if anyone has arrived at Flynn the Redhair's settlement seeking hospitality. That's Mona's husband. Metto will be on his way north in a day or so. He knows where to find them. Flynn sells beaver pelts to him.'

'And Metto Lentus the leather merchant knows that this Flynn is married to your sister?'

Dania tightened her lips and sent him a scolding glance. 'Tch! What do *you* think, you great lummock? Course he doesn't.'

Astinax thought that these two were quite a pair.

Having exclusive use of the bath-house so late at night was a luxury for Dania, for at that hour the vaulted roof would be ringing with men's laughter and the sound of music, and the water would be clouded and tepid with their sweat. Now, it was clear and cool as Dania and Etaine rippled the lamplit surface, their eyes half-closed in delight as they listened to the distant chords of a harp and let the water caress their arms.

The house was sparkling at last with refreshed colours, the two days and nights without men had been very bearable and, sensing that this peace could not last much longer, both women kept any predictions to themselves for fear of breaking the spell. For Dania, thoughts of Tribune Fabian Cornelius Peregrinus continually invaded her mind, however much she fought them. Berating herself for a fool all the while, she re-lived that brief blissful night in his arms and blamed herself for so easily giving in to his skilled lovemaking after years of dogged resistance. Astinax and Ram had warned her that he was unlikely to be infatuated, that he was ruthless and clever, that she should beware his methods and, on looking back over their meetings, she was bound to admit that, so far, she had gained nothing of any real value to Somer. If anything, the situation had deteriorated. Because of the tribune, she had lost Bran and her brother's support. Con and his family were in exile, and the whole of Coria was in turmoil as a result. It would be better for them all if her association with the tribune was discontinued and her energies channelled into giving aid to those whose lives she had disrupted.

Yet there were still questions that must be answered, like why the House of Women and the two shops had been untouched by searchers that day. Would Fabian Peregrinus return at night, long after dark? Was it her he wanted to see or was he, as she was beginning to fear, following a totally different line of enquiry? In trying to please her brother, had she thrust her hand into a hornet's nest and, if so, would she be able to retreat without injury?

No, I have gone too far. I am already injured.

Attendants brought them warm towels and, through the deserted corridors and ante-rooms of the bath-house, the two half-wrapped women wandered, rubbing their hair and hardly daring to tempt fate by making plans for the next day.

Albiso appeared, coughing discreetly. 'My lady, I'm afraid you have a visitor.' He wore a sorry expression as if he were personally responsible for the intrusion.

Dania threw back her mop of damp hair and stared in surprise. 'Did Astinax forget to lock the gate behind him?' she said.

'No, my lady. The guest came round the back, from the stables.'

'Bran? Already? Is it bad news?'

'Not Brannius, my lady, but Tribune Peregrinus. He awaits you in the entrance hall.'

Joy and fear raced each other to her heart.

Etaine's eyes widened. 'I'll go and get you something,' she whispered.

Dania knew what she meant. 'No, I won't need anything,' she said in a voice too low for the steward to hear. 'There'll be no more of that, Ettie. I'll be there directly,' she told Albiso. 'Give the tribune some wine, and tend the lamps.'

But she was not allowed to keep the tribune waiting as long as she had intended, and she was still half-wrapped in her linen towel when, as if he had anticipated the delaying tactics, he entered the changing room without knocking, caught her under the knees and tossed her up into his arms before her protest was more than a yelp. Witnessing nothing she hadn't seen before, though not to her mistress, it had to be said, Etaine obligingly held the door open and closed it after them, thinking that her mistress was more than capable of making her objections known, if there were to be any.

There were. The brand on Dania's naked back was easily forgotten by Etaine but not by Dania herself, who hissed and struggled frantically all the deserted way to her room, saving her loudest protests until the door was shut. This was a matter in which she dare not summon interference.

'Put me down!' she yelled. 'Damn you…put me *down*!' With one incredibly agile twist against him, she freed herself and, clutching tightly at the loose towel, backed away in the direction of the tall basket chair where she sat fuming, quickly losing her fragile hold on her temper. 'How *dare* you do that?' she went on, pulling the towel up as far as it would go.

Two green eyes blazed angrily, and the tribune's initial doubts about the genuineness of her fury faded before their fire. Once again, she was the wild native woman fighting for her honour, cornered, spitting with rage. And he had misjudged her reactions yet again.

Having come straight from the emperor's house, he was formally attired in military-style white belted tunic that came some way short of the floor, a white woollen cloak thrown over both shoulders and the wink of gold on both arms. The stable had been his first call and, from there, one of his slaves had discovered the path into Dania's garden. Privatus and Ajax were still out there on the verandah, their hopes of pillows and warm drinks fading with each passing moment.

Fabian was not, however, completely at a loss, though he pretended to be. 'What is it?' he said, shedding his cloak and taking a step towards her, well aware of how she would find that provocative.

'Stay away from me!' she snarled. 'You have no business here, Tribune. You've done enough damage already, and my life will be in some danger if it's known that my name is linked with yours. I am well known here in Coria and I have friends out there who are being made to suffer because of what happened to my servant.' She pointed with one hand, using the other to hold the towel up.

'Ah, yes, it's not been a good day for Coria, has it? Until we find that Boar Hill barbarian it's going to be difficult for us all, one way or another. And I regret the death of Ram. It was an unfortunate business.'

'Unfortunate?' she replied, savagely. 'You knew when you were here last exactly what was to happen, yet you said nothing of it, did you?'

'Well, no, lady. If you recall, it was hardly the time or the place to be discussing the finer details of who would fight whom. As it was, I seem to remember you being deeply affected by knowing that this particular captive was expected to put up a good show. I wonder why that was.'

'I was anxious for them *all*,' she said, throwing a heavy mane of hair away over her head to fall down her back. 'They're my countrymen.'

'And this red-haired countryman we speak of, the one the crowd helped to escape after he killed your guard. I don't suppose you know where he might have gone?'

'Correct, Tribune. I don't know where he's gone. How could I? Surely he'll have returned to his home, wherever that is?'

'No, we've been to Boar Hill. He's not there.'

Dania's throat dried, and instinctively a hand went to comfort the burning fear that stopped her breath in her lungs. 'You…you *looked*. You went to…to Boar…?' The last word failed to emerge.

'Boar Hill. Yes, my lady. Quite a sizeable place, isn't it? Well hidden, too. Are they all your kin, or is it only the black-haired ones?'

Beside her chair lay a long basket-work box in which she

kept her spinning equipment where also her dagger lay hidden amongst the spindles in case of danger. One hand over the side of her chair sought the boar-tusk handle while her body tensed, ready to spring like a wildcat upon a marauding stoat.

But the dagger, unused for so long, had become tangled in the strands of unravelled wool and, as she jerked it upwards, the contents of the box came with it, spilling with a clatter around her feet as she leapt towards Fabian, delaying the hand that stabbed just short of its target. Then it was too late for another try for, although she reached him in one bound, she was already off balance and tripping over wooden spindles, her hair blinding her, the towel giving way to gravity at last. At his brutal grasp on her wrist, the dagger flew from her hand as she gave a yelp of pain, and once more she was caught up in his arms, this time to be hurled bodily on to the furs that covered her bed.

Before she could bounce and right herself, Fabian was above her, throwing her roughly on to her face like a puppet and holding her there while he knelt astride her thighs, taking a fistful of hair aside to reveal the terrible scar that she had tried so hard to keep hidden. There was no more she could do to stop him, and she would not plead. Not to any man.

She felt him reach over to the small oil-lamp on the side-table, holding it aloft to illuminate her skin. 'There, that's it,' he said. 'It was too dark to see clearly at our last intimate meeting, but that's what I thought it was. The Boar Hill tusks, just like the tattoos on the chest of that strapping captive you know nothing about. Who put this mark on you, lady? Was it a punishment, or a reward? What odd things you barbarians do to each other.' His fingers traced the tusk motif as no one had ever done before. 'Tell me about it,' he said.

'I shall tell you nothing,' she growled into the fur. '*Nothing*. Do what you have to. Kill me. I shall not tell you.'

Fabian leaned over her until his mouth was upon her neck, close to her ear. 'Ah, no, my beauty. Let me explain,' he whispered, tasting her skin. 'It is not *you* who will suffer but your household, you see. Your co-operation ensures their safety but, if you refuse it, they will all be taken captive. Every one of them. And who knows what the emperor and his son will devise for their entertainment? They're quite an inventive family, though I don't approve of it, myself. Do you doubt me, Dania of Boar Hill? Shall I have to take you to him and show him my proof? Or are you going to work *with* me in this? The choice is yours.'

'No!' she shouted. 'You cannot do that. My household have nothing to do with Boar Hill. Only me. They know nothing of what I was, only—'

Without warning, Fabian sat up and pulled her round to face him, intercepting the claws that immediately began an attack upon his arms and chest. Savagely, he held her down without a hint of the tenderness she had once received from those same hands, without a trace of softness from his eyes or gentleness in his mouth. Now she saw fierce anger in the grim set of his lips, in the flint hardness of his dark commanding eyes, and if she had hoped for a shred of that earlier relationship, she now saw that he was every inch the experienced soldier they had warned her about. Her protestations meant less than nothing to him, as she did also.

'Liar!' he barked. 'Don't lie to me, woman. They are *all* of them hand-picked for their loyalty to you. They may not know your background, but every one of them is as much an enemy of Rome as you are, passing on what they can pick up every night and day. You think I don't know what kind of a place you run here in the guise of high-class brothel? I've known from the start. And you thought to draw me into your clever scheme, didn't you? Eh? Well, I'm ahead of you there, my beauty. You didn't learn as much from me as you'd hoped, did you?'

'Viper! Toad!' she whispered through the hair that covered her face. 'They do it out of loyalty and love. They care for me, and I shelter them in return. And I respect them. That's all.'

'That's all, is it? So what of your innocent Greek lad? The one who was busy writing it all down when I brought you in here a few days ago? Yes, you may well blink, lass. I took the writing-tablets he left behind in his hurry and I read his list of notes. What was it, now… thirty-one infantry off sick at Vindolanda; seven officers wounded here at Coria and twelve more with chest infections? Details of drunkenness and mutiny in the ranks? Eh? You think that kind of information will turn the tide of events in your favour, do you?'

Dania gritted her teeth to avoid crying out at the pain of his grip.

'Well?' he said. 'Who exactly uses this stuff? Who's the chieftain? Who is that half-brother of yours who looks at me with enough hate to kill me? Where is he now?'

'Gone,' she whispered.

'Where?'

'Back to Boar Hill.'

'When?'

'This morning. You say you were there. Did you not see him?'

His laugh was harsh and unkind. 'I know how to get you to respond, don't I? Just threaten your kin and you're like a wildcat guarding her kittens. Fierce, wild woman.'

'You're saying you…you didn't…get to…?'

'No, we didn't get up to Boar Hill. I lied. Worked well, didn't it?'

Rage surged through her like a roaring tide of molten lead in a white-hot crucible that spattered and overflowed in a shower of sparks, and suddenly Fabian was having to fight her again, a twisting, screaming, demented creature who bucked under him and threw him aside, rolling away with legs flying and teeth bared, ripping at his tunic and kicking madly at every part of him within reach. She was smooth and slippery after her massage under Etaine's hands: under this man's hands she was an eel, and as quick, and it took him some time and force to master her at last, though he suffered some stripes for it.

Her eyes were awash with tears of raw anger, for she knew how unskilled she was in the games of war, a bungler in the art of deceit, a mere child when it came to hiding her emotions. These were, and always had been, too close to the surface for her own good, and this clever warrior knew well how to draw them out on every level, and how to turn them against her.

'Enough!' he bawled at her. 'Enough, woman! Hold it! By the gods, you people have a discipline problem second to none, and I can see where it comes from if all the females are as untamed as you. Did no man ever take you in hand, woman? Is that why they let you go?'

She lay sprawled and half-hidden under a blanket of hair through which Fabian could see the full curve of her beautiful breasts like the peaks of pale mountains through dark cloud. She was panting with the effort, an irregular sob that showed him she was still wild with fury and by no means spent, though he felt her energy could be better directed than this. 'I shall tell you nothing,' she gasped.

'We have all night, lady.' Slipping a hand beneath his tunic, he pulled at the drawstring that tied his pants, pushing them away just in time for the next whirlwind burst of action which, while it simulated protest, did almost nothing to make it impossible or even difficult for him to catch and hold her. 'Easy,' he whispered. 'I can find a way to persuade you.'

'I will not bargain with you. I will not!'

'You've got it wrong, my beauty. There'll be no bargaining. Let's call it giving and taking, shall we?'

But if his uncompromising words sent a chill into her heart, her body could not pretend uninterest in the exciting trespass that took her breath away at each powerful thrust, and though she could have fought tooth and nail to reinforce her anger, the ecstasy that swept through her body swept her mind with it. This was what she had wanted since that last encounter, and now her greatest deceit was gone. She was once again Dania Rhiannon of Boar Hill.

'Let go of my hands,' she said through her hair.

Without question, he released her wrists and knelt back upon his haunches, watching her from a distance as she softened and moaned, throwing her hair off her face with a sweep of her arm to expose the whole length of her glistening voluptuous body.

Their eyes met through weighted eyelids sending messages that softened to desire, though Dania's pride would not shift to anything like humility. She placed a hand upon one bronzed thigh and raked her nails sleepily down the skin. 'You'll regret this,' she whispered. But her precise meaning was lost upon him, a man whose thoughts were only of the woman's beauty and the act itself, not of the new life it might generate, and his reply was as inadequate as she knew it would be.

'We all take risks,' he said, grimly.

Her mewing grew into a soft continuous wail as her body responded to his rhythm, and when she held out her arms to him, he dropped into them as a lover would, covering her face with kisses, catching her cries with his lips.

'Soft…soft, my lovely goddess,' he murmured. 'This is a part of you I have no quarrel with, as yet. Shh…lie still now. We'll talk again in a while.'

'I need to sleep,' she said.

'No, we talk first.'

'I hate you,' she said without conviction.

'So you said.'

She felt him smile against her cheek, and the ache in her heart warned her of the pain that was yet to come and of the love that was beginning to creep like a slow fire into the corners of her heart.

Chapter Seven

Captured within the rock-hardness of the tribune's arms, Dania leaned back upon his bare chest as he sat propped against the pillowed end of the bed, preparing herself for the inevitable spate of questions she had once fobbed off as irrelevant. Now, she knew they would have to be answered. Her blanket of hair lay swathed around her shoulders, and beneath its secrecy there were hands that smoothed and fondled, even while they restrained. Furs covered them in a mountain-range of peaks and troughs beneath which her fingers worked peevishly upon his warm thigh.

'Cease pulling at my hairs, woman, and answer my question,' he said, 'or I shall have a bald patch where you've been.'

'I think you've broken my arm,' she said, sullenly.

'Answer me. How did you come by this brand on your back? Your tribe don't usually do this to their women, do they?'

'If you really *must* know,' she replied, as if she had a

choice, 'it was the work of the chief Druid to prevent me from consorting with the likes of you. And so far it's been effective, but quite unnecessary.' Unaware of the contradiction, she explained, 'I didn't come here to Coria on purpose to take up with the enemy, but to help my kin. And to gain my freedom,' she added as her conscience prodded her.

'How long ago was that?'

'I've been here since I was sixteen.'

'I asked you how long.'

'Six summers, or thereabouts.'

'So you have twenty-two years. But you must have had lovers.'

'No, I have not,' she snapped, bristling.

'Then how did you lose your virginity, may I ask?'

'No, you may *not* ask. That has nothing to do with you or anyone else. I begged to be allowed to leave Boar Hill for personal reasons in exchange for sending information back regularly.'

'Spying, you mean.'

'No, not spying. All I had to do was listen.'

'You came here with your half-brother?'

'Brannius came with me as my cup-bearer. It was his task to take messages to my—' Biting the words back, she cursed herself. But it was too late.

'To your what? To the chieftain? Your family? *Who?*'

'My father, in the first place. He was the chieftain.'

'Was? And now?'

'My brother.' She felt the jolt of surprise in his arms.

'Your *brother*? He's the chieftain? Is he the big red-head who killed Ram the Gladiator? No, surely not.'

'No, that was the Druid's son.'

'Ah, so you *do* know him.' He took hold of her chin in his big hand and turned her to face him. 'You do, don't you? What is he to you, this man?'

She tried to wrench her head away, but he held her fast, swinging her sideways to lie across his thigh. 'Dania,' he said, severely, ' I intend to get answers. If you refuse to talk, I shall interrogate your household.'

'No…no! Not them.'

'Then tell me, who is the captive we're seeking, the one a cell full of Coria men are having to go hungry for?'

'Con. His name is Con the Silvertongue. He was my husband-of-one-year when I was fifteen. Our fathers wanted it. Now let me go.' Snapping like a polecat, she bit his hand and pulled it away as he flinched.

'By the gods, woman, I should beat you,' he growled. 'Did this husband of yours beat you? Is that why…?'

'I divorced him,' she said, struggling away at last. 'Do you have to know *everything*? The Druid blamed me for all the disasters of that year because he could see I was not going to stay as his son's wife and produce an heir. He wanted to offer me to the gods to restore the flooded fields and to stop the murrain killing the cattle. My father and brother dared to disagree with him.'

'So they branded you, instead of sacrificing you. A fair alternative.'

'It's the only way they'd allow me to leave,' she whispered. 'My father had lost his sight along with his power, and it's dangerous to get too far on the wrong side of a man like Mog. What he did was against all our laws.' Her anger soared, and she leapt away from him, dragging the fur behind her, too fast and too fraught with emotion for Fabian to prevent it.

Wrapping the fur around her, she went to the silver flagon that stood with a nest of horn beakers on the small carved table, pouring from it with a hand that shook, spilling the wine. Suddenly, he was taking it from her. 'Go and sit in your chair,' he said, sternly. 'This looks like being a long night.'

She took the refilled beaker and drank as he pulled the fur over her knees. 'Now,' he said, 'if my plans for your future are to succeed, Dania Rhiannon of Boar Hill, I have to know more about you. In this, you will have to trust me.' He pulled up a stool, placing it before her and taking the beaker from her fingers. 'I find it difficult to believe that you were released from Boar Hill to set up a place like this. Tell me about it.'

Seeing no reason not to, now that he knew the rest, she gave him the facts in a way that put the previous disjointed events in context. At last he sat back, downing the contents of the beaker and studying her face in silence.

'So now, Tribune, you are duty bound to take me and my story before the tribunal, and that will earn you more rewards and an extra three thousand *denarii* a year. Who knows, they may make you a governor of some other far-flung province of the Roman Empire. Shall we go?' Her sarcasm was meant to hide her fear, for now she was reminded that, even during their moments of superficial intimacy, he was as dangerously ambitious and as hard as the best of them. She could not claim to know him yet, but already she had seen that there was more to him than had appeared at their first rough meeting. Most certainly she had underestimated his keen intelligence, and now it was a crude remark made by Astinax that morning which rang truer than anything she had said.

Fabian ignored the sarcasm. 'And your woman Etaine and your departed half-brother are the only ones in Coria who know your true origins?'

'Astinax knows. He went with me on our last visit.' She thought about the recent appearance of Bran in the entrance hall dressed in the clothes he should have left in the stables, and his noisy description of the Boar Hill victory that night. If the women suspected her personal connections, nothing was ever said.

'And the weavers and tailor?'

'All hired here in Coria.' Again, they might have had some idea.

'Does the business make a profit?'

'Certainly it does,' the businesswoman replied, sharply, 'otherwise I'd not keep them on. Our cloaks and breeches are the best. Why do you ask?'

He folded his arms across his great chest. 'Because, my lady, from now on you'll simply be the owner of a prosperous cloak-making business. You're going to lose the brothel. You can call the House of Women by some other name.'

A frown drew her brows together like tracks in the snow while she tried, and failed, to find his precise meaning. 'Lose the most lucrative business and keep the other? What about me? Don't I get arrested?'

'Not yet. Perhaps not at all. It depends on whether you prefer to accept my plan or to keep to your original one. With mine, you get to keep your house and servants and your shops, your complete safety, and theirs. If your pride will not allow you to co-operate, you'll lose everything. Your choice.'

'By the gods, Roman,' she hissed, 'you mean it, don't you? Do you think it's been easy for me to establish such a successful business with nothing but the best on offer? You've seen my standards. It did not come naturally to me, you know. My revered father would not have approved and my mother lives in ignorance, but I am not ashamed of my achievements and I've saved many a life over the years. If the image of brothel-keeper and healer of women is good enough for me, why should it concern you, Tribune Peregrinus?'

He chose not to retaliate, but sat regarding her through half-closed eyes and, although he was completely naked, she glimpsed again the stony-faced hard-bitten officer in the plumed helmet, the cavalry leader mounted on the plunging grey steed, the elegant guest at her dinner party and the would-be lover telling her she should be in a better place than this. By his side, for preference.

'Shall we stick to the point?' he said, softly. 'Either I turn you and your accomplices over to the emperor to do with as he wishes, cutting off all connections with your tribe in one stroke, or you see to it that all the information you send to your brother the chieftain is reconstructed by me and that I receive word of what he is planning against the Roman army.'

The lop-sided deal came as no real surprise, but why this man should need her help was not so easy to understand when the army's numbers had increased dramatically in recent weeks. She pulled herself upright in her chair, determined not to capitulate without some argument, at least. 'Well, I never heard such nonsense,' she said. 'You know where Boar Hill is, surely? You can hardly need me to feed you with information when you have scouts all around. You could go there any time you choose and fire the whole settlement. They've been expecting you for weeks. Well, a week, anyway.'

'Wrong, lady. You're no tactician, are you? Your tribe gallop up and down those rocky outcrops like mountain goats, even in the dark. They don't fight as we do, you know that. We fight with tight discipline out in the open and, yes, we could get up there and set them ablaze with a small troop of men, but they'd know we were coming long before we could cross the first ditch, and I'm not prepared to lose men and horses without a greater reward. You see, I don't want your brother's immediate death. That's not my objective.'

'Then what is?'

'His contacts on the other side of the Wall. That is where my lord Severus is concentrating his efforts. Your brother keeps them informed, I take it?'

Dania's stubborn silence confirmed his guess.

'So, as long as he continues to communicate with you in the usual manner, you will be able to tell us who else he's in touch with. Names. Places. Numbers.'

'I see. You expect me to betray my tribe. My own brother. Is that it?' Even as she protested, another voice hardened her heart. *He betrayed you. He withdrew his support when he saw Bran's disgust. What is there to lose now?*

'His relationship to you is not important to me except in your role as informer. I want you to become a double-agent, apparently doing what you were doing before, while actually helping those who can guarantee your safety. Us. Me. I want you to keep up your pretence of being a Roman citizen, but the intimate links of your women with Roman officers must be broken. That's too dangerous for both you and them, and I don't want my fellow officers to be punished for being loose-tongued in bed. I don't want you to be exposed to anything they might say in confidence. Nor can I have a mistress who runs a brothel, however high class it might be. That won't get me very far, I'm afraid.'

The frown reappeared with a look of incredulity. 'A *what*? Who said anything about mistresses?' she whispered.

He admired her control, knowing how she longed to leap at him and place her hands around his throat. He could see the fury in her green glare. 'Did I not say? Yes, it will be best for both of us if you become my mistress. You need a patron of some standing while you're working for us.' His eyebrows moved slightly, amused or surprised, she could not tell which. 'Did you not wonder why the shops and the House of Women had not been searched today?'

'Yes,' she said, thinking fast. It was the kind of offer she had been refusing for years from officers. But this man was a tribune with the powers of a magistrate, and how would he know whether her information was correct or not? He was offering her and her household a life, and she had a responsibility to them all, especially after the catastrophe of Ram's death. But would they accept it, or would they choose death rather than dishonour? Astinax had already adapted to both worlds in order to save himself, and would it be so great a sacrifice for her to do the same? She was already halfway there, as it was. There was, of course, another element of a more tender nature that she pushed away, locking it into the deepest darkest chambers of her heart. 'Yes,' she said. 'I did wonder why. Was it you?'

He nodded. 'My orders.'

'But my stable was broken into.'

'Yes. Unfortunate. I've seen the damage. Only slight. Done before those responsible knew it was yours. They'll put it right tomorrow.'

Already she had felt the benefits.

The primitive side of the Boar Hill woman seethed under a mantle of apparent calmness while it would have been both natural and easy to scream and hurl abuse, to make herself terrifying, to fight rather than offer well-mannered protests. But her six years of acting like a Roman had taught her another useful dimension, which the tribune apparently admired, and her common sense warned her that this was the one to display. Histrionics had its place, but this was a time for discussion.

To do him justice, he could have had the place torn apart and all of them killed for being enemies of Rome, and he was taking quite a serious risk in not immediately denouncing them to his superiors. Doubtless his motives were self-seeking as well as political, but who was she to carp about that when she too had those same opposing incentives at heart? She must remain dignified. He would be expecting an explosion. *Keep him guessing.*

'You appear to be offering me something of a…a personal nature…in return for my connections,' she said. 'I would be obliged if you would tell me exactly what I'd be letting myself in for. I might, after all, find it more comfortable to throw myself on the emperor's mercy.'

Unfolding his arms, he levered himself gracefully off the stool and stood before her in magnificent nakedness that could only have been, she thought, to remind her of his considerably potent equipment. He stooped to take her arms and to pull her upright so close to him that she could feel his warmth upon her throat and, holding her semi-captive, he slid his warm hands into her hair and gathered it to the back of her head, resting his arms upon her shoulders. Unsmiling, almost grim, he laid out his plans before her in greater detail, revealing even more of himself with every word.

'Make no mistake, my lady,' he said, 'the emperor *has* no mercy. I shall not try to persuade you with talk of pity, or admiration for your courage, or wanting to save everything you've worked for. You'd not believe that, would you?'

'No, Tribune. Not from a Roman.'

'I thought not. So perhaps the stark truth is best, now we've begun to shed a few misconceptions about exactly who we are. I am the senior tribune amongst the five who came over here with my lord Severus, and I intend to become a senator like my father. As Gauls, he and I believe that a few more of us in the senate would not come amiss. But to achieve that, I need to take home as many laurels as I can carry and I can win more by breaking the back of these troubles up here on the edge of our empire. However, my lady…' he almost smiled as he gave the bundle of hair a twist '…I don't have much time left to do it. I'm due to be moved on soon, either to one last posting or to be sent home, my military service done. I've already served more than my time in the army because I enjoy it, but now I have to move forward, and, to do it, I could use your help.'

'To win all those laurels.'

'In return for your safety and that of your household. I don't suppose that would inconvenience you too much, would it?'

'And how safe do you think we'll be when your ambition is achieved, Tribune? When everyone here in Coria discovers exactly what we've been up to?'

His eyes hardened, and Dania stifled a grimace of pain as the rope of hair tightened in his hand. 'The people of Coria, my lady, don't care a damn about what you do, or about what *we* do, for that matter, as long as they can earn a living and be left in peace to enjoy it. There is unrest at this moment because of the gladiator's death and the sympathies with both British contestants, and I have to admit that I can understand that. I never thought it was a good idea, but the Roman way is for maximum carnage regardless of who's involved. The people of Coria are a mixed bunch, like you and your employees, but they'll soon forget who or what you once were. It's your kin on Boar Hill who'll hold it against you, and by the time it matters, they'll have been eliminated or fled to other parts.' He released her hair at last, but still there was little warmth in the set of his mouth, only a grim determination to put his plans in motion. If there was another kind of desire in his eyes, Dania could not see it in the lamplit room.

Chilled to the bone, she could not help but compare the callousness of his words with the soft persuasiveness he had employed only a few days ago, and she looked beyond him rather than into his eyes, trying to halt the self-pity that threatened to cloud her vision of the immediate future. 'Then this would not be for long?' she said, half-hoping to hear a denial.

'Probably no more than a few months, at most.'

She sighed, putting forward a more understandable argument than the fragile one she had just dismissed. 'I have grown so weary of deceit, Tribune. It was only to be expected that I would have to work hard for my freedom from my brother's tribe, and I had looked forward to the time when I could leave the pretence to others and lead an honest kind of life. Healing, perhaps. Now I seem to be deeper in debt than I was before.'

His hands softened upon her shoulders as if realising their former harshness. Placing a knuckle under her chin, he brought her round to face him again. 'What pretence is this that we're talking about, Dania Rhiannon? Are you trying to convince me that you've only been pretending to be a Romanised Briton? If so, you must be the best actress this side of Rome itself.'

'Thank you, my lord. I'm flattered.'

He actually smiled at that. The terms actress and prostitute were synonymous in Roman society, and she had not needed to ask why the House of Women must be styled the House of Something-else if she were to become his mistress. It was for that reason also that he came there so late at night. 'You understand my meaning,' he said, touching her cheek with one finger. 'I meant no insult.'

'I understand,' she said. 'Perhaps it's not so much of an act these days as it once was.'

He waited, thinking that she might have more to add, then he took her arm and turned her towards the low bed. 'Come, lady. Your feet must be getting cold here. Mine are. And I have more to say to you before you decide. Am I to understand that you find it hard?'

In the shadow, he would not see her smile. 'Yes,' she said. 'Incredibly.'

He swung her legs up and covered them with furs. 'As for this act you speak of, I believe you may be having more of a problem acting the part of the Boar Hill woman than Coria citizen, hostess, manager, businesswoman. Am I correct, that it's the deceit that bothers you more than the double identity?'

Do not see so close into my heart, Tribune.

'Are they not the same thing?'

'Not when one becomes more natural than the other. I've seen both of them, remember, and I can manage the Boar Hill woman well enough. But what I need most is an intelligent and cultured woman to manage my household with the same skills as she manages this one, to be my hostess at my house and to be at my side for functions, to be a source of admiration and…well…yes, of envy, too. My woman.' He braced his arms on each side of her as he presented an attractive picture of Roman high society that would have been the goal of most women she knew here in Coria.

The doubts must have shown in her eyes for, instead of bombarding her with the benefits to herself, he waited. 'What, then?' he said, ducking his head to see deeper into her face.

'Tribune,' she faltered, 'a Roman…er…woman would have little problem with…' she sighed '…with what you propose. And I'm not rejecting it, I'm trying to…well…to make you see the difficulty.'

'Go on.'

'Well, just as your army behaves differently from ours, so your women behave differently too. I know. I'm friends with quite a number of army wives. We have rights, you see. Our women are allowed to speak to men who are not their husbands, we have some say in the laws that govern our tribes, and we come and go without being followed or forbidden access. I think you would not find me as meek and obedient as one of your own kind, my lord. I have never taken kindly to a man's rule, you see.'

Lowering his forehead on to one of his braced arms, he rumbled with laughter before taking her hands in both his own. 'From what you've told me of your background, lass,' he said, struggling to hold his words on course, 'you've never taken kindly to *any* man's rule, have you? That seems to be the cause of your present dilemma. But, yes, I'm aware of these differences. Britons allow their women more equality than is usual amongst others, I know, but I am of Gaulish, not of Roman, birth and I can deal with that side of things. Though the equality may be a little less than you're used to, under these rather special circumstances, I would not want you to change in any significant way once you became my mistress. It's a partner I need, Dania. A partner like you, not a slave.'

'Would you not take your slaves to bed, then? Some Romans do.'

He stood up and in one long stride stepped over her, buckling his legs under him as he snuggled to her side and drew a fur up. Pulling her against him and settling in, his delaying tactics ruined the immediate denial she had expected, and she had almost answered the question by the time he said, 'Would that worry you?'

'Not in the least,' she snapped. 'I would not wish to interfere in your private life as long as you don't interfere in mine.'

'Ah,' he said, grinning and sliding a warm hand between her thighs, 'but that's just what I *do* wish. You see, Privatus and Ajax are my only slaves and their pleasure is to tend to my domestic needs, not my sexual ones. They've certainly never massaged me the way you did last week, my lady. Now *that* was quite extraordinary. You'd best not offer that to anyone but me.'

Impulsively, foolishly, she flared up at the first sign of a restriction. 'I dance to my own tune,' she said. 'You had better know it, Tribune.' She caught at the hand moving slowly along the inside of her leg, trying to hold it off.

But the hand turned on her like a snapping dragon, and in one quick flip she was held, spread-eagled and helpless, with her captor disallowing her last attempt at womanly independence. 'Let us be quite clear about this, shall we?' he said, once more the conqueror and she the victim. 'The only one whose tune you'll dance to is *mine*. If you decide to refuse my offer, you are free to forfeit the lives of your household as you please, but if you accept it you'll be *my* woman in every respect, responsible only to me, faithful and loyal. And no matter how Britons are allowed to behave, that's what *I* shall demand. Freedom is one thing, lady; the kind of self-suffi-ciency you've been practising is quite another. If I save you from death, I expect all the appropriate rewards. *You* had better know *that*.'

She did not recognise the first faint tones of jealousy. 'So much for not wanting me to change. I may as well be your slave, then.'

'Call it by whatever name you choose. I need to be sure of you.'

'And afterwards, when you've moved on? What will I be called then, Tribune? A Roman officer's leftover whore?'

'You'll have a business still, and a fine house to live in.'

'Yes, and women who will look at me and blame me for it. How many of my friends have had their houses wrecked today, their men taken, and all because I'm obliged to play one side off against the other? How will I know which side I belong to when it's all over? I've told you, I'm *sick* of this deceit. Let me go, damn you. It's easier to be honest and suffer the consequences.'

Fabian had seen it coming, but already he was beginning to tire of the inevitable wavering. It was time to help her out. 'I shall not let you go,' he said with none of the sympathy Dania would have preferred. 'We've done enough of this soul-searching, my lady, and I told you not to expect my pity. Yes, you'll have your house and business intact while others will not. Well, they didn't risk everything to help their kin as you did, so perhaps you deserve a greater reward. Look at it that way and stop berating yourself. This is a military zone, remember, and you're in the thick of it. And for another thing, your time is now up. I've decided for you.'

She squirmed against his grip. 'There *was* no time limit.'

'Yes, there was. We could go backwards and forwards on this issue for ever, and I don't have that kind of time. You'll do as I say, on *my* terms, like it or not. It's much the best thing for you.'

'I cannot. I have a conscience, Tribune, even if you do not.'

'Forget the conscience. It's too late for that. You're already up to your lovely neck, Dania, and anyway, I need you.'

He could have said those three words in a hundred different ways, but the way he chose at that moment, in the midst of all the demands and orders, came to enclose her heart in soft hands and to comfort it like goose-down in a blizzard, lifting it tenderly out of harm's way above the complex web of intrigue.

'What?' she whispered, blinking back a tear.

'I *need* you, Dania Rhiannon.' His hands softened and slid along her arms from wrist to shoulder, to throat, to face, to brush away the one damp sign of heartache. 'I need you. I want you. And I shall protect you and those who work for you. You can stay here in this house, if you wish, and we'll have joint households so you can be mistress of them both. Yes?'

'What of the women? This is their home too.'

'Then they must stay. You can find some employment for all your staff, surely?' His fingers stroked her cheek and traced her eyebrows.

'Yes, plenty. I need more embroiderers and seamstresses.'

'You'll have no money problems, Dania. Yes…' he caught the frown that threatened '…I know you don't like the idea of rewards, but this is not the same. Mistresses have expenses. Everybody knows that.'

'We'll see.'

Catching the sad resignation in her voice along with the faintest promise of a future defiance, he rolled aside and eased her into his arms where her hair scattered his chest and the scent of it caught in his nostrils, reminding him most unusually of meadows in summer, vineyards and harvest time.

'Listen,' he said, even more gently, 'let's not try to fool ourselves or each other. I realise you broke your own rules to find out from me about our plans. It was a great risk for you, but you took it and lost. There's no need to feel badly about it, my lady. I told you, it came as no great surprise to me, but now we have no more secrets, and that means we can be honest with each other. You understand what we've agreed, don't you?'

'Mmm…mmm,' she murmured.

'Good. So you won't get any nasty shocks either. You're using me for protection and I'm using you for information, and no one else need be involved. To all eyes on your side and mine, we're lovers by mutual agreement, and you've decided to close the House of Women because…well, you can say that the emperor himself has decided to close it down for his own good reasons, if you wish. That would let you out of having to find an excuse. Yes?'

He watched the regular rise and fall of her breast against his skin, the chiselled undulations of her beautiful lips and the thick sweep of lashes upon her cheeks, and the smile that stole slowly across his face became almost a laugh, but not quite. His arms tightened around his prize and then, setting his internal alarm-call for dawn, he closed his eyes and slept.

By dawn, Dania's household had been gathered into the large rosy entrance hall, first to offer thanks to the gods for their safety and then to be told of the wishes of the mortal who had also had a hand in it. Tribune Peregrinus. The mistress's lover. Taken, she said, for reasons more to do with policy than anything else. If they were shocked, sceptical, envious, they were careful not to show it. In the future, she told them, the House of Women would be known as the

House of Weavers and, for their own continuing safety, there would be no more visits from officers of the garrison, no more trade in gossip with them, no more earnings from that quarter.

'What are we going to live on, my lady?' said Jovina, more out of concern for their high standard of living than any attachment to the profession.

'I intend to expand the weaving and cloak-making,' said Dania. 'We're falling behind with orders. And I need more help with the women at my morning surgery; the queue is growing longer every day. Don't worry, we shall make enough to live off, and anyone who prefers not to stay is free to leave.'

But when they were dispersed, she sent messages to the three women who were visiting relatives that, for the time being, they should not return, and her immediate plans to relocate the surgery were delayed by the overnight appearance of Roman soldiers posted outside the gates. She could not quarrel with that, for the unrest in the streets was still a threat. Innocent men were being starved while Con was on the loose, and Dania's conscience laboured to find a way out of that particular predicament without putting her kin in greater danger.

In her room, the spindles had been gathered back into their box by her room-maid, but the tusk-handled dagger was missing, causing Dania to wonder about the explanation Fabian would devise for the rips to his tunic. She had presented a blithe face to her household, but to Etaine, Astinax and Albiso she had been unable to hide the ravaging effects of her fierce confrontation with the tribune, her inevitable mortification at their enforced collaboration with the enemy, after all. Though she had been half-asleep when the tribune had stipulated that it must be a private arrangement, none of the three closest to her would believe the story about her supposed amazing change of heart concerning the future of the business. It was hard to know, she told them, whether to be relieved or rebellious, but she would need all their help in the months to come.

They were, however, less mortified than she, and far more positive about the change to their lives. It would be like exchanging one kind of freedom for another, they said, using the word in its widest sense. And nobody left.

The best antidote to the negative effects of failure, according to Dania, was work. Wasting no more time in further self-recrimination, she set herself the task of reorganising the two shops, which needed extra help to take stock, to redecorate, to repair looms and benches and to clean out the upper rooms where the workers lived.

Bringing all the wares out into the sunny courtyard, she personally selected three of the handsomest hooded cloaks for the emperor's son, Caracalla: full-length, waterproof wool bound with leather and fur, one of them fur-lined, one trimmed with tablet-woven braids, one fringed and chequered in the British style he was known to favour.

The tailor, who had done his fair share of gathering officers' idle gossip and passing it on, was too old and wise to be fooled by Dania's sudden craving for royal patronage. 'What's all this, then?' he said to her, carefully folding the last cloak. 'Taken a fancy to the old man's son, have you? Or is it favours you're after?'

Dania watched how his gnarled hands lovingly smoothed the beautiful garments and pressed the fur in the right direction. 'You don't miss much do you, Ganda? Yes, of course it's for favours. I'd not be giving your best pieces away unless I wanted something in return. Trust me.'

'Oh, I do, my lady.' His knowing beam lined the screwed-up parchment of his face. 'If this lot doesn't do the trick, I don't know what will. Let me know if it works.'

'You'll hear,' she said, receiving the cloaks. 'So much for my lord Caracalla. Now for the man himself.'

'Who, old Severus?'

'The Emperor Septimus Severus,' said Dania, smiling at his disrespect, 'who has an exceedingly painful chesty cough, according to my contacts.'

'Oh dear,' said Ganda smoothly, in mock sympathy. 'How sad. Do you have a suitable pois…er…linctus he can take? Something permanent?'

Dania leaned across the cloaks. 'It's *favours* I'm after, not an early death. Yes, I have a cure, if his taster doesn't drink half of it first.'

'May the gods aid you, my lady.' He smiled, knowingly.

'Thank you, Ganda. We shall be having our mid-day meal out here in the courtyard today. Will you and your family join us?'

The tailor's eyes softened as he watched his employer carry away his best work. 'That we will,' he said.

The prettily wrapped bottle of linctus for the emperor and the parcel of cloaks for his son were taken that same morning to the commandant's house by two of Dania's slaves with a message to Tribune Fabian Peregrinus, who would be able to vouch for the donor. As the tailor had prophesied, if that didn't work, then nothing else would.

Dania then paid a visit to the stonemason's yard to order a headstone for Ram, returning an hour later with a rather red nose.

Towards the end of the al fresco meal for her employees, she received an impromptu visit from the tribune himself with the centurion Claudius Karus and the pharmacist-doctor Vitalis. As two of them were in armour, there was no question of the usual greeting when there were no cheeks to be seen. They had not come to search, they said, only to look.

The reason behind their 'looking' was still undisclosed by the time they were ready to leave an hour later. Though she had shown them over the entire house, upstairs and downstairs including the garden and outer stores, no amount of prompting could extract an answer concerning their purpose. Dania was by then quite sure that they had something specific in mind.

Her hair was bound up in a loose turban, her faded linen tunica cross-wrapped with a blue apron that left her arms bare except for gold bracelets, and she had no notion of the appealing sight she presented to men who often longed for the domesticity of a busy wife and home. Preferably a beautiful one. To forestall the plans she suspected them of hatching, she made sure they knew of her own before they left. A larger surgery for the women, she showed them, taking them into one of the courtyard rooms, with an adjoining room for preparation and the examination of patients. There was no such thing as a hospital for women as there was for the garrisons, she reminded them, though the need was just as great. She and Etaine were the most reliable midwives in the area, with the fewest fatalities.

Still they would not tell her why they had come, even when the kindly Vitalis, impressed by Dania's array of medical equipment, recipes and herb collection, jars of potions and salves, tools and neat shelves of towels and bandages, murmured, 'Excellent. Simply excellent, my lady. Just as I expected.'

The three visitors left as mysteriously as they had come, threading their way across the busy courtyard cluttered with the produce of two shops, looms and bales of cloth, stacks of fleece, piles of garments with labels fluttering, buckets, mops and brooms, tubs of whitewash and lime-spattered workers, and Eneas at his trestle-table making lists.

Only Karus's stricken face lingered in Dania's mind for the rest of the day. Perhaps, she thought, the closing of the House of Women would hit the centurion harder than most, for now he had lost what small part of her she had allowed, and Etaine too, whose attentions to Astinax were there for all to see.

Had the tribune passed on her gifts? she managed to ask.

Certainly he had. He was sure she would soon receive their thanks.

She did, that very same evening, when she and the other women were sitting together on the verandah overlooking the garden, ankle-deep in the mess of spinning, which was intended to help the spinners who had fallen behind in their work. The dyers and weavers used up woollen thread faster than it could be spun.

'The Tribune Peregrinus, my lady,' said Albiso. 'Will you see him out here?' He looked pointedly at the decidedly un-glamorous change of occupation, then at the women's smiles, wondering if things would ever be the same again.

'No, I'm coming,' said Dania, quickly winding her thread on to the whorl. She didn't want a repeat of the tribune's impatience out here. 'My lord,' she called, walking towards the entrance hall.

He stood before the statue of Venus, regarding her, his casual half-length white tunic and gold-linked belt in sharp contrast to his earlier war-gear, his short-clipped dark hair still damp from a recent bath. As always, Dania was struck by his devastating good looks and, this time, by her own changing relationship to him that terrified her by its transient nature.

She wiped her greasy fingers down her apron. 'Forgive me. I did not expect you after…'

Turning with the smile already in his eyes, he waited for her to reach him, then put up a hand to pull her turban away, releasing a cascade of black ringlets over her shoulders. 'That was business,' he whispered. 'This time I come as special envoy from my lord Severus and his son. Time to stop work, I think. Eh?' He used the turban to gather her and to hold her head, cutting off her protest with a kiss that, for sheer intensity, left her in no doubt of his hunger. 'That's what I wanted to do earlier,' he said, 'but you'd not have enjoyed it, would you?' His voice had grown husky, his eyes darkening with desire.

'In all that metal?' she said, breathlessly. 'No, my lord. I would not.'

'And now?'

'Mmm. Now perhaps you'll tell me what this is all about?

If it was not a search, it was a very good imitation of one. What were you looking for?'

'I'll tell you in the bath-house.'

'But…you've obviously just had one.'

'You, my lady. You haven't. I can tend you, if you'll allow it. You've had a busy day. Come.' He took her greasy hand in his. 'I know how it's done. You're not going to fight me again, are you?'

'No.'

'Good. So send for some wine. I have a lot to tell you.'

Barefoot as usual, she was led back along the verandah to where the suite of bathing-rooms was situated at one side of the garden, passing the laughing eyes of the competent women, now redundant, who would have given much to be led to the baths by the tall broad-shouldered tribune whose mouth was grim with intent.

He had said he knew how it was done and Dania had no reason to doubt him even while she found it difficult to dismiss foolish images of the countless and nameless women who had willingly been undressed by him in warm changing rooms, each slow erotic unwrapping rewarded with kisses to the exposed skin. This was still a game to him, she thought, bitterly. To her, it was a serious and deadly procedure that she was unable to perform with the required lightness of heart while her mind dwelt on the men suffering from starvation.

In the hot-room, they sat naked on the marble bench with sweat running off them in rivulets while Fabian tied Dania's hair up in a bunch on top of her head. Then, taking up the small bottle of oil, he sat behind her and began to anoint her back, laughing as she twitched under his fingers.

'Keep still,' he said. 'Do you always jump like that?'

'No.'

'Oh, I see.'

She heard a low gasp of laughter and knew what he was thinking. 'Tell me about the visit,' she said, changing the subject quickly. 'Why did you bring Vitalis with you? So he could see Jovina?'

'First, I have messages from the emperor and his son. My lord Caracalla sends his compliments to you and the tailor. He believes the cloaks are the most magnificent he's ever seen and he intends to order several dozen to give as gifts to visiting dignitaries at the royal court. So you see, your name will be spread far and wide, my lady. The emperor is equally touched by the linctus for his chest. He says to tell you that, after the first spoonful, it soothed him. I'm afraid you're going to have to produce a lot more of it. They both expect to thank you personally soon.'

It was exactly what she had intended.

'Lift your arm up,' he said.

'No, I can't.'

He paused. 'Look, sweetheart,' he said, gently, 'do you want to be oiled before I scrape you down, or do you prefer to be red-raw?'

'Yes…no.'

'Well, I can't get at you unless…' He stood up with a sigh and came round to face her, sitting astride the bench. 'Unless I can…oh, by Jupiter, woman, you are so…*so* beautiful!' He put the bottle down on the floor and, with the tenderest hands, cupped her breasts and lifted them towards his bent head, lapping with his tongue at the perspiration, examining the exotic shape of the brown erect nipples and brushing across them with his thumb, gently squeezing.

A low moan made him look up at last to see Dania's head thrown back, her eyes half-closed in ecstasy, her glistening skin and squirming hips inviting him to take her without the conflict of previous times.

Needing no other invitation, he eased her back on to the bench and lifted her thighs, sliding himself inside her, standing and bending over to continue the caresses that had so quickly excited her, watching the immediate climax build and rush upon her before she was prepared for it, faster and faster in time to his own, astonishing them both by its ferocious speed. Within the first few dynamic moments, their cries were echoing round the barrel-vaulted ceiling of the small room, their sensations held somewhere in space, whirling like distant stars.

Fabian sank slowly upon her to lay his cheek against the heaving softness of her breast while she held his hair, both of them stunned by the ungovernable force that had gripped them and released them again.

Perhaps it was the amazing intensity of the experience that led Fabian to wonder, at that moment, whether this was for Dania as unique as it had been for him or whether it was merely the result of her six-year celibacy. Whatever the explanation, he needed to know. He lifted his head, hearing the uncalled-for challenge in his tone. 'So is that how it was for your divorced husband-of-one-year? Did you respond to him like that, too? Eh? Did he bring you on so fast? What's his name— Con the Silvertongue? Did he use it as well as I do, my lady?'

Floating through a sea of languor, the abrupt contact with

reality came like a sluice of cold water at the cruelty of his reminder, if she needed one, that such an experience was as new to her as minted gold, as pure as crystal, as precious as spring water. She could hardly believe what she was hearing and gasped at the wound to her heart, even while she still throbbed beneath him. 'Get off me!' she whispered. 'Get *off*!'

He heard the sob in her voice and, because he was now aware of his staggering clumsiness, and defensive, he misinterpreted the effect of his heartless enquiry, providing his own answer rather than risking hers. She had been married to this barbarian for a year. Of course there must have been times. 'Forgive me,' he said, lifting himself away. 'It's none of my business, is it? I know how you dislike answering questions.'

'You're right, Tribune. It is none of your business,' she said, swinging away out of his reach and taking a beaker of the wine. 'I did not agree to sell my past as well as my future, and you will not find me asking for details of your previous mistresses.' Even as she spoke, she heard the half-truth of her words and her imaginings about his lovers with which she had just plagued herself. Her hand shook violently, slopping the wine.

He took it from her and held it to her lips, watching in guilty silence as she drank. 'No,' he said. 'We men are such fools about our performance and size, and he's such a whacking big fellow. I've made you angry again. Forget what I said, can you?'

Had she been one of the women, experienced and aloof from all emotion, she could have laughed it off and indulged in some very crude and detailed banter about performance. But she was not one of them, nor could she be detached, and if this was the kind of pain she could expect each time her protection-payment was due, then she did not believe her heart could withstand the warlord's misplaced assaults upon it. 'You forget,' she whispered, 'that playing the whore is new to me. I have only ever been a wife before, never a mistress. Does it give you some special pleasure to possess the one-time wife of the man all Coria is seeking?'

'Hush, lass. Hush. Don't talk so.' He gathered her into his arms.

'Loose me. Loose me from this bond before it's too late.'

But if Fabian understood the exact meaning of her plea, he purposely ignored it. His fingers caressed her face as he kissed her with the softness of a butterfly until she reeled and clung to him, made dizzy with the sweetness. 'Put your arms around my neck,' he said.

Cradling her against him, he carried her into the next warm room where the deep pool held steaming water with shallow steps leading down into it. Rose-petals floating on the shining surface swirled away as he carried her down into the white mist, letting the soft silkiness creep up their bodies until it reached the valley between her breasts. And there, by rocking her gently to and fro in the sensuous cloudy warmth, he washed her hurts away with his kisses and made dripping black spirals at the ends of her hair.

Chapter Eight

The next phase to affect the House of Weavers came as less of a surprise to the household than the previous one, most of them having already drawn the conclusion that the new name was meant to mask the building's true purpose in view of the visit of Vitalis, the garrison doctor. Why else would he have been there if not to assess its suitability as a workplace?

'Yes, as hospital,' Dania told them. 'They want to take it over.'

She had gathered them together straight after their devotions to Coventina and her associates while the sun rose over the rooftops and the aroma of newly baked bread drifted across from the kitchen. On the colourful mosaic of the entrance hall they lounged and listened, trusting Dania to see them safely through this latest development.

'Do we have any choice?' said Eneas, soulfully, thinking of all the suffering. Of them all, he was the least enthusiastic.

'No, not really. I'm not in a position to refuse, Eneas. I'm afraid we have to co-operate. It could be much worse. I have to go and meet the emperor later on, so I shall know more details after that but, as I see it, they need somewhere close at hand and as big as this to take the overflow of patients. There are so many more soldiers now, you see, and not enough beds in the local fort hospital to treat all those off sick. Not enough medics, either. Don't worry, you won't have to stitch up wounds or chop limbs off. Vitalis will be doing all that.'

'They call it requisitioning,' said the cynical Astinax, leaning his massive frame against the alcove dedicated to Brighid, 'but at least we'll be dealing with fewer randy officers for a change. Isn't that so, my lady?'

Dania's cheeks bunched. 'Probably, though I don't know whether we shall get officers or ranks. Meanwhile, we shall need all the downstairs rooms for accommodation. You will all be housed upstairs. Perhaps we can make a start on that straight away.'

'Not your room too?' said Etaine.

Wearily, Dania smiled and lifted an eyebrow, remembering. It had been for her an energetic night in which she had sampled the tribune's amazing stamina and the extent of his need for her. Now she knew exactly where his longings were stored and how he craved relief, after which she could harbour no more delusions about the nature of her use to him, or to Rome in general. 'No, not my room,' she said. 'Go and open the gate, Astinax. There'll be a queue of women out there already. I hope I won't have to plead to keep my surgery going.'

Her fears were not borne out, for the Emperor Septimus

Severus was some way from the disobliging, tyrannical and vicious brute she had been led to expect. Instead, he was a tall, elegant and comely man, dark-skinned with tightly curled greying hair and a trim beard to match. She heard his racking cough even before they met, and knew at once how it must have hurt him.

Life had moved on apace since Dania's last visit to the garrison headquarters deep in the heart of the military buildings, where it appeared that several of the staff on duty remembered her enough to bow respectfully as she passed. At the side of Fabian she walked along the echoing hall where monstrous statues of Mars and Jupiter faced each other, their feet as large as stool-tops, their naked private parts fortunately too far above her head to impress. Surrounded by the Praetorian Guard, a group of men stood by a raised dais at the far end; one of them she recognised as Vitalis, one padded out with more tunics than usual under a robe and an extra scarf, the others in short military tunics, breeches and cloaks. Centurions, Dania thought, though it was getting harder to tell these days with so many versions of the standard uniform, depending on the country of origin.

Their conversation stopped as heads turned to watch her approach with the tribune, with Etaine, Astinax, Ajax and Privatus following. She was thankful then that Etaine had swathed her in an extra length of brown gold-bordered linen the end of which floated behind her like a banner. It was a sober and healing colour, fixed over her head by a jewelled pin large enough to buy a new horse. More gold peeped out from ears and wrists.

One of the men cleared his throat.

A scruffy unkempt man with a dark curly beard moved forward into a beam of light, and it was with some annoyance that Dania saw he was wearing one of the cloaks she had sent to the emperor's son.

Already he's given one away to a man such as that. What a waste.

The well-padded one, the emperor, acknowledged Fabian's salute and Dania's bowed head. He was a practical man, a soldier first and foremost with no pretensions to the god-like status so many of his forebears claimed. 'Dania Rhiannon,' he said with a wheeze. Even so short a greeting, however, sent him into a spasm of coughing that rendered him speechless and labouring for breath.

'My lord,' said Fabian, addressing the scruffy individual, 'may I present the lady Dania Rhiannon, owner of the House of Weavers?' To Dania, he said, 'His Excellency Marcus Aurelius Antoninus Bassianus, son of the Most Noble Emperor Septimus Severus.'

Caracalla! Gods preserve us. This scruffy tow-rag?

'Your Excellency,' she said, returning his scowl with a bewitching smile.

The emperor's son appeared to soften a little at that. 'My lady,' he said gruffly, 'you don't wear your own cloaks?' He would have been handsome if he had bathed and shaved and trimmed his hair.

'Not on such a day, my lord. I am a northerner, you see, and this is almost our summer. But I am honoured that you wear the cloak.'

'Hmm. Best I've ever seen. I wear whatever is best for the purpose, no matter what the fashion. No time for dressing up, but I know a good thing when I see one. Tribune Peregrinus appears to agree with me.' The smile that passed between them seemed to suggest that he meant something other than dress.

During the courtesies that followed, Dania was able to observe the father and son together. Judging by the number of times the emperor referred to his wife, who was still in Eboracum, it became clear to Dania that he was missing the comfort she would have provided.

'Oh, no…no,' he replied to Dania's enquiry about his painful chest. 'It's nothing, my lady. Your linctus is doing some good. Ah, you've brought some more. Excellent. I thank you.' Before the words were out, the spasm of coughing attacked him again, bending him almost double.

Taking that as an excuse to cut across the usual royal etiquette, Dania took a risk that only a few days ago would have been almost suicidal. One did not touch an emperor without his invitation. Supporting his elbow, she led him to a nearby stone bench and sat him down, still coughing.

She showed him her empty hands. 'Will you allow me to help, my lord?' she said. 'I believe I can.'

Red-faced and gasping, the emperor nodded, wiping away beads of sweat from his brow with the back of his hand. 'My own doctor—' he said.

'Is obviously useless or he'd have sorted this out before now,' said Dania, briskly. 'Just sit quietly, my lord. You may feel some heat, or you may not. Don't speak, if you please. I need to concentrate.' She went round to his back and laid her hands gently upon his waist and began to move them slowly upwards, over his many layers. 'May I remove your robe, sir?'

she said, sensing that her every move was being watched, that every right hand was on the hilt of a dagger, including Fabian's.

He nodded, past caring, shrugging off the outer robe and scarf, almost exhausted by the effort of breathing.

Once more her hands rested lightly upon him, moving up to his hunched shoulders and down again as if sending messages to his lungs. Then she went to stand before him, starting at the top beneath his collar-bone, moving her hands from side to side across his chest, lower and lower by a finger's breadth with each sweep, holding them where she knew the pain was at its most intense, in the centre. She kept her hands there, one above the other, drawing the pain away with her mind, enticing it, gathering it up.

His eyes were closed; the rattle in his lungs faded; his breathing eased and the mottled patches on his swarthy skin smoothed into a normal tan. He opened his eyes and looked at her, blearily, as if he had just woken from sleep.

'May I sit, my lord?' she whispered, feeling suddenly light-headed.

'Please, do.'

'May I examine your eyes?'

'Of course.' He turned to her like a child and allowed her to lift one eyelid after the other to see the whites, which were not.

'Your tongue, my lord?'

Obediently, he stuck it out, like a piece of grey fur.

'Thank you. Your diet, my lord. Will you accept some advice?'

'Most certainly.'

'Then for the time being, avoid red meat. Chicken, fish,

shellfish and eggs are good. Drink only warm goat's milk, not that of a cow. It makes less phlegm and it carries fewer diseases. Eat apples, too. One a day. To drink, take nettle-juice and barley-water mixed. Better still, my lord, I shall make it up myself and send it daily. Drink all of it to flush the system. I shall also send you a chest-rub and I shall make up a new linctus for you to take first thing in the morning and another for bedtime to help you sleep properly. Keep your body warm, and no displays of hardiness, my lord, for the moment.'

He smiled at that, and nodded. Then he took a deeply quiet breath as if to test his lungs against the amazing sensation he had just experienced and let it out slowly. Not one to display emotion too readily, his eyes were nevertheless like windows at that moment, awash with relief. 'Lady,' he said, 'I cannot describe to you what I felt…quite impossible…as the warmth came, and the pain left. I can breathe. May the gods be praised.'

'Indeed, my lord. And now,' she said, looking at his heavy bare arms, 'perhaps you should follow my lord Caracalla's example and wear long sleeves and a warm cloak until you become used to our climate. Would you allow me to send you a fur-lined one? Beaver? Winter stoat?'

'I would be honoured to wear one of your cloaks, my lady, as my son does. Gentlemen,' he said, getting carefully to his feet, 'the lady Dania Rhiannon is to be granted whatever she wishes. She is a true healer, not one of your sour-faced bleeders who can only talk about urine.' He carefully avoided looking at Vitalis. 'Do you bother with it, my lady?'

'With urine? Well, yes, my lord, I do. It's a good indication.'

'Of what?'

'Of problems within the body. There are signs to be read.'

He stared at her in silence for some moments as the growing crowd around them waited to see whether this was the beginning of an argument. But the emperor's voice was even, his head tilted as if listening for something. 'I haven't coughed,' he said. 'I haven't bloody *coughed*!'

'No, my lord. You won't be doing. But I shall also send you some socks to wear. You can't go round up here with those cold feet.'

'Gods, woman!' he yelped, bursting into laughter. 'You're as bad as my wife, bless her. Watch out, Peregrinus my lad. You've met your match here, have you not? Eh?' He slapped Fabian on the back, still without coughing. 'Come, we must talk about this new hospital wing at the lady's house. She's more than qualified, Tribune. You had no need to be concerned on that score.'

Dania's sudden green-furied glare at Fabian was intercepted by all of them except the man himself, whose stare was innocently directed towards the high rafters, and the unsympathetic bellows of laughter were predictable.

But when they had sat and discussed the numbers of patients, their eye infections, chest complaints, convalescents and requirements, the opportunity came at last for Dania to call in her favour.

In answer to the emperor's enquiry, she was able to say, 'Yes, my lord, there is something else I want.'

'You have only to name it, my lady,' he said, generously.

'Before I begin to nurse your men, I would like you to set free those citizens of Coria who are being held captive.'

The silence descended like a heavy blanket through which she could hear distant bird song, the echo of men's feet, a horse neighing in the nearby stables, and she felt Fabian stir uncomfortably, looking hard at her with an urgent warning.

'Ah,' said Severus. 'And what are these men to you, my lady?'

'They are my fellow citizens and countrymen, my lord. Some are personal friends, husbands of the women I treat, and some are related to those who work for me. And I do not believe that starving them is the best way to find the man you are looking for.'

From the corner of her eye she saw Fabian lift a hand as if to stop her, half-raised from his stool to escort her away. But Severus stopped him with the brief movement of one finger that allowed the dangerous exchange to play itself out to the end. 'Is that so?' he said. 'And what in your opinion would be the best way to find him?'

'If you would be willing to leave the matter in my hands, my lord Severus, I believe I can discover in time where he may have gone. I find it hard to accept that anyone actually *helped* the man who killed my personal assistant to escape. Ram was well known and popular. They wouldn't. They'd have been far too stunned by what had happened. The wanted man is, so I understand, a big man and very unstoppable, and the men of Coria would not remain silent, harbouring such a barbarian so well able to help himself, given the chance. It is not mercy I ask for, my lord, but for you to try a different method. That is, after all, exactly what I have done to your stubborn cough. Tried a different method. Sometimes that yields quicker results. It's a gamble. It requires trust.'

At last, when the ensuing silence became almost unbearable, Severus pressed his fingertips together and spoke, at first to his fingers and then to her. 'If I did not have a remarkable woman for a wife, Dania Rhiannon, I would find it hard to believe that such women exist outside our fancies. They are rare indeed. A healer. Businesswoman. Thinks like a man. What else do you do, my lady?'

Dania tried to control the loud thudding in her chest. 'What else, my lord? Oh, I can think like a woman too, when I need to. And I can find a better cure for your men's eye problems than the one they're getting at present. If I guarantee to cure them in half the usual time, would you release the captives immediately? Today?'

Again, a sound of alarm came from Fabian. No one bargained with the emperor and came away intact. 'My lord, I beg you will excuse her,' he said.

Severus barely glanced his way. 'Marcus,' he said eventually to his son, 'I told the lady Dania that she should have whatever she needs. How do you rate this request, as a need, or as a pledge to be honoured?'

'Both, my lord,' said Caracalla without hesitation. 'Anyone, man or woman, who can effect my father's cure so convincingly deserves a favour of an appropriate magnitude, especially if it's one that costs us so little. And if my men are put back on their feet in half the time, that's worth more than the miserable lives of a few captives. Free them to get on with their work, I say, and let the lady's enquiries start immediately. If she's as efficient in that as she appears to be in other respects, we should have a result in no time.'

'You think we should impose a time limit, do you?'

'No, sir. With respect, sometimes time limits can be counter-productive. The lady will not take advantage. It's not in her interests, is it?' He turned to Dania, showing her the latent cruelty in his eyes, his message warning her that the penalty for taking advantage of them would be appallingly severe.

Severus nodded. Then, with mischievously twinkling eyes, he looked at Fabian. 'You have a rare woman here, Tribune. Trust *you* to find her. Did she come easily to your hand?'

'On the contrary, my lord Severus. You can imagine.'

'I can indeed. I'm glad she's for us, not against us.' He rose to his feet, quite unaware of how his teasing words riled Dania. 'Your captives will be released, my lady, and we shall begin sending patients to you as soon as you send word that you're ready for them.' The matter of the captives was already losing interest, the fare of his own men claiming priority. He was, however, still mindful of the recent physical experience that had put his own personal power in quite a different context, transforming his attitude to Dania into that of an indulgent older husband.

He was therefore both concerned and amused to see how, in the middle distance, the tribune gripped the arm of his mistress and steered her quite forcibly to the far side of a wide stone column from where, for quite a few tense moments, their two voices were raised in heated argument. One short loud bark from the tribune ended it, and the lady was then seen to be striding stiffly by his side at a pace that could have matched a legionary's trot.

From every point of view, her meeting with the emperor and his son had been a taxing one, and to end it with a tongue-lashing from the tribune was more than enough for Dania's tightly held control. Overjoyed that she had achieved more than she set out to do, she had also managed to upset Tribune Peregrinus more than herself by refusing to acknowledge her foolhardiness. But she could have done without his unnecessary censure, just the same.

He had stomped off with a face of granite that had refused to soften even for Astinax, and when Dania emerged from her room some time later and headed across the garden with two bright spots still flushing her cheeks, Astinax braved her scolding tongue for a few quiet words in her ear.

She sat on the wall of Coventina's Well as the ex-gladiator sauntered through the dappled shadows towards her. The surface of the water reflected her touching fingertips and, resting on the pebbles immediately below, the noses of inquisitive sticklebacks nudged at the valuable gold and jewelled pin that had graced her head only that morning.

'The men will be freed,' she said, watching the ripples, 'and nobody's going to spoil that for me. I know it was a risk, but it was worth it. If you've come to tell me otherwise, I don't want to hear.'

'Aye, lady, but the tribune appears to disagree,' said Astinax, ignoring the instruction. 'Perhaps that indicates how highly he values you. He was scared stiff. So were we all.'

'Scared?' she scoffed, turning to him at last. 'Of that ill old man?'

'That ill old man and his unstable son don't share a fine feeling between them when it comes to punishing supposed offences against protocol. The tribune knows that as well as the rest of us, and it's not so much the soldier-emperor he's scared of, but what can be done to those who try to force his hand. Which is what you did. And a woman, at that. You could have been thrown in with the captives to starve. Did you not realise?'

Dania stood up, ready to walk away. 'Then it would still have been worth the attempt. He owed me a favour, Astinax, and I called it in. He knows how much it was worth, and so did his son and what you forget is that, as a woman, I pose no threat to him. At that moment, he needed a woman, a healer, and I was there. He'd not have harmed me.'

'Did you tell the tribune that?'

'Of course not. All he could think about was that I don't understand the form, that no one bargains with the emperor. They're all scared to death of him.'

'No, lady. I told you. He was scared for *you*.'

There was more that could not be said. She had also offered to find out Con's whereabouts and to let the emperor know, and that was something for which Fabian himself had hoped to take the credit. She had gone over his head. He had not accused her, but she knew that was at the root of his anger. Astinax had got it wrong, she was sure. 'No, Astinax,' she whispered, hoarsely. 'For himself, not me.'

The big man knew better than to argue with his employer when she was on the verge of tears. 'You are the bravest woman I know,' he said. 'Commanders always yell at their men after feats of exceptional courage because of the risk. It's fright. Believe me. And I happen to know that the tribune admires you.' He gave her no chance to respond. By the time she had recovered from her surprise he was halfway across the garden, waving at the approaching Eneas to clear off.

It did not take long for the news to spread, and the particular one to whom any gossip was a chief delight was Julia

Fortunata. She knew Dania Rhiannon personally. She would be the first to pay her a visit, claiming an association that was bound to enhance her reputation as a socialite.

Dania was in the newly appointed surgery mixing duck and hen fat and fresh bone-marrow with a wooden spatula in a bowl, her image far from that of her glamorous friend. A pile of chopped and split animal bones lay to one side, and Dania's hands were smeared and sticky from handling them. She whisked off her grubby apron as Julia entered wearing a concoction of clashing pinks. 'Julia dear,' she called. 'Come in.'

'What on earth are you doing?' said Julia, wrinkling her nose.

'A chest rub. Urgent.'

Julia peered into the pinkish mess and drew back. 'I *cannot* believe it,' she said. 'Everybody's talking about you, Dania. Did you know you're the local heroine?' Leaning forward, she touched cheeks in greeting.

'How did Everybody find out?'

Julia's kohl-painted lids half-closed with pride. 'My Titus Flavius was given the job of releasing them. He was there when you demanded that the emperor let them go. Didn't you see him?'

Dania took her friend by the arms in a grip of alarm. 'Ye gods, Julia!' she hissed. 'I didn't *demand*. Is that what he's telling people? For pity's sake, love, you'll get me arrested. Tell him, Julia.'

Julia laughed, a little guiltily. 'No, dear, that's me. You know how I exaggerate. You got them freed though, didn't you?

You'll have them queueing up outside to bring you gifts any moment now.' She looked down in concern at her pink silk sleeves embellished with dark fat-stains and decided that, rather than complain, she would use it as evidence of Dania's affection.

Caught between relief and dread at Julia's appearance, Dania resolved to take advantage of her own soaring popularity, however short-lived, to tell her gossipy friend about Tribune Fabian Peregrinus and the unwanted developments since their last meeting. She wiped her hands, reached for a small wooden pot and began to fill it with the emperor's anointment. 'Julia dear,' she said, 'don't talk nonsense. Of course they won't. Listen, I've been wanting to tell you something…something that concerns you…and me.' It was not going to be easy. She might have to offer Julia something to alleviate the disappointment.

'If it's about that Tribune Fabian What's-his-name, you can spare yourself the trouble,' said Julia, lightly. 'I went off him quite quickly. He shouted at my Titus and I don't like people who shout. You're welcome to him, Dania dear.'

'You know, then? How?' Holding a spatula full of pink ointment, Dania stared in astonishment. Julia must have ears like a bat.

But Julia didn't understand the question. 'How?' she frowned, sweeping the tidy shelves with her eyes, searching for an answer. 'How what? I keep my ears and eyes open, that's all. And my Titus tells me what's going on, and anyway everyone knows the tribune's mad about you and that he couldn't keep on coming here to a house of women so he had them change it to—'

'Julia…stop!'

Julia stopped. 'What?' she said, blinking prettily.

No, let her go on. There may not be the officers' gossip to pass on to Somer, but there is still the women's. And Julia's. Let her chatter.

'Don't repeat that nonsense, please, there's a dear,' she said, laying down her tools and going to sit by Julia's side. 'It's not like that at all.'

'What's it like, then?'

'It's a business arrangement, more like. The garrison needs my house for a hospital and he thinks I may need his protection, just like your Titus thinks you need his. And I don't want to refuse it because it's useful to me, like being able to help the emperor and ask him a favour. This relationship will only last until the tribune has finished up here. I shall be quite relieved when he's gone. I never wanted anything like this to happen, Julia.'

'No, you've never wanted a man, have you? Not like me.' She giggled. 'I want one all the time. It can be quite embarrassing. Poor Titus.'

'Do you want me to give you something to help?'

'Ooh, yes!' Julia laughed excitedly, setting her blonde curls dancing. 'Could you? I like Titus to do it in full armour, but it's chafed a sore. Look…here.' She pulled up a pile of pink silk to show Dania the red marks on the inside of her plump thigh. 'Do you have a salve for it?'

Dania was still chuckling an hour later at the heady mixture of Julia's sexual exploits, barrack-room tales courtesy of Titus, town gossip and some details of sufficient importance to be sent up to Boar Hill. By the time Julia had gone, gifts had started to arrive at the House of Weavers: a side of beef sent by the butcher's wife, two amphorae of Rhenish wine from the wine merchant, a box of beeswax candles from the chandler and a visit from the tearful cobbler's wife who brought her tape measure to measure Dania's foot. Others came and went with thanks, pledges and tributes while Dania sought to resolve her ever-conflicting loyalties, none of which seemed to deserve the attention she was giving them.

Somer, her chieftain brother, had proved himself to be underhand, uncaring and unreliable, and now that Bran was no longer their go-between, there seemed to be no reason not to leave them to their own devices, as they appeared to be doing to her.

Fabian was Roman and still the enemy, no matter what other feelings she had for him, using her to further his ambitions and expecting her to betray her own people. But *were* they still her own people? How much did she still care about the growing strangers on Boar Hill? Did she even care any more about what happened to Con, or was it only his wife and family who tugged at her heart-strings? Who did she care about most? And while she still had the means to send information to Somer, should she go back on her word to Fabian and do it? Would he ever know? And what of the information she had promised to find for the emperor? She recalled the hard and merciless threat in Caracalla's eyes and shivered, realising with growing dismay how at every turn her own conscience was being set aside by men and events.

She took the new batch of linctus, ointment and drinks into

the entrance hall and placed them beside the folded cloak lined with softest white fox fur that she had intended for herself that coming autumn. Two pairs of grey woollen socks lay folded on top. 'Find a basket to put these in,' she said to Etaine, 'and get Eneas to check the labels. I don't want there to be any mistakes. Then you and Astinax can take it to the emperor's house by the bridge.'

Her concerns about the promise she had made concerning Con's whereabouts were moderated just as her gifts to Septimus Severus were being carried out under Astinax's arm. Metto Lentus the leather merchant from Cateractonium nodded affably and exchanged greetings with the two messengers and carried on up the steps, two at a time, into the entrance.

He stared about him at the piles of bed linen and the bustle of servants. 'What's going on here?' he called to Dania in the dining room.

She was getting used to the question by now. 'My dear Metto Lentus,' she called. 'Welcome to the House of Weavers.'

'The House of What?' he said, waving to his slave to stay outside.

Smiling, she came forward to greet him with a kiss to both cheeks, tasting the air on his skin, fresh and cool from the moors. A panel of greying hair curled into his long ears, and his grey worldly eyes registered sadness at the obvious changes even before she had explained. Was Metto's goodwill worth making an exception for? 'I'm sorry, my good friend,' she said. 'It's taken us by surprise too. Come through here. Take some wine with me and I'll tell you about it.'

Albiso and a slave brought a tray of biscuits and beakers, a jug of wine, a pair of slippers for Metto, an extra cushion for his back, and Dania told him what had happened during his absence beyond the Wall gathering furs from his suppliers. She whispered in Albiso's ear, and soon Jovina was sitting by the merchant's side, holding his hand and his drink. It was the least they could do to thank him for the message he had brought.

'I met your friend Flynn the Redhair,' he said. 'I'm surprised you have friends like him. He's quite an ill-mannered sort, isn't he? I wouldn't wonder if he beat his wife. Wives, I should say. He has several, I believe.'

Dania felt the twinge of pain in her breast. Her sister Mona had grumbled in the past about her husband and his growing family of concubines, but she had never spoken of beatings. 'He's only a contact,' she lied, 'not a friend.'

'Well, he's had a family of refugees come to him within the past week. Is that what you wanted to know, my lady?'

'Thank you, Metto. Yes, it is. Did he say more than that?'

'Only that they were from Boar Hill and they've left for good. They actually brought Flynn's own son back to him, so he can hardly turn them away, can he? Apparently the lad was foster-son to the Boar Hill chieftain. A serious matter, you know, not to protect your own fosterling better than that. Flynn is hopping mad about it. Talking about going over there with his best men to sort him out.'

'What, to Boar Hill?'

'Aye, there are ways of crossing through the Wall at night, and the distance is nothing much at this time of year. They love an excuse to go raiding, these people, to capture the youngsters and sell them for slaves. If they can't find a good excuse, they'll invent one. But I'd say that any man who lets his foster-son get kidnapped without a chase deserves all he gets.' He took his wine from Jovina and drank deeply, handing it back to her with a smile and a pat on the knee. 'But I've brought some lovely beaver pelts from him. Marten skins and squirrel, too. A whole lot of hides. Foxes, and some good calf-skins for vellum. Just wait till they've been prepared and I'll see you get some.'

'It is I who owe you, Metto,' said Dania.

He smiled sideways at Jovina and winked. 'No, you don't,' he said.

Metto stayed on to dine with them, and they were still laughing uproariously at his tales when Albiso came in to whisper a message to Dania. She excused herself and followed him to the entrance hall, purposely dismissing all signs of laughter from her face, though it could be heard easily from where the guest stood by the shrine of Brighid, his hands behind his back.

Her bare feet made no sound upon the floor, and the light from the dining room behind her made a halo that shone through the edges of her white tunica, softening the outline of her loose hair. In luxurious waves, it tumbled about her shoulders and, because there were no guests she wished to impress, she had left it unbound since her bath. Gold cords crossed her breasts and tied beneath them and, if she had intended to give an impression of wantonness, she could hardly have done better.

At their moment of meeting, Metto's loud laugh reached a crescendo, followed by Astinax, then Etaine's shriek.

'Tribune?' said Dania.

Fabian looked beyond her, his face as grim as before. 'You have guests,' he said, accusingly. 'I should not have come.'

Like a mother with a truculent child she wanted to reassure him, but she was still sore and confused by what she had heard since the morning, and her feminine streak of pride and cruelty, hearing the uncertainty in his voice, could find no good reason why she should dispel it. She felt dizzy with fear as she deliberately withheld her understanding. 'Yes,' she said.

'Dressed like that.'

'As you see.'

'I think I do see, lady.' His voice was brittle almost to the point of breaking as he turned on his heel. 'Dania Rhiannon.'

Fabian, come back. Come back.

His cloak swung behind him, and the sight of his broad back and proud head departing so abruptly was like a pain for which there is only one cure. But this time, she would not move to cure another wound of his making, not for either of their sakes. He had misunderstood. Well, that was his own fault for which he deserved to suffer.

She clung to the wall to stop herself from chasing after him and, when Albiso reappeared, apparently needing no explanation for the brief visit, she drank the glass of wine he brought her in one single draught and went to rejoin her friends and their guest, looking flushed but no worse for the incident.

That night, the ache in her breast was remorseless, filling her with dread. But she told herself that she had better get used to it, for this was how it would always be: longing for him, yearning for him, hating him, loving him.

Chapter Nine

It had rained heavily during the night and, in typically northern fashion, the squalls had grown into a fully fledged gale that lifted rooftops like cot covers, flattened fences and uprooted trees, filling the rutted tracks with rivers of thick brown water.

Two women had walked through the night, then at dawn had hitched a ride on a waggon amongst jars of olive oil and fish sauce, arriving at Coria just as the shopkeepers were wrestling with their shutters, half-drowned by the sleeting rain that was no warmer in May than it was in December. The younger of the two women had only needed to ask once where to find the house of Dania Rhiannon, but the effort of walking those last few muddy yards down Weaver Street had been too much for the elder one, and the oil merchant himself had carried her through the courtyard and deposited her on the verandah.

Astinax, having no idea of their identity, was about to direct them to the new surgery rooms at the side of the courtyard when the upright one, breathless with exhaustion, managed to raise her voice against the howling wind. 'Dania's *mother*,' she yelled at him, clutching her wet cloak across herself. 'I'm her sister. Please...let us in.'

Without further encouragement, Astinax picked up the huddled body and its meagre bundle of belongings and carried it into the safety of the house, bellowing to the astonished Albiso, whose mouth was full of oat porridge. 'Fetch the lady Dania...quick, man! Hurry! It's her mother and sister.'

There had been no time for questions then, Rhiannon being too ill and Mona too relieved to speak through chattering teeth and tears of joy. Nor did Dania show much surprise after what Metto Lentus had said, for it was obvious what had happened, and not before time.

'Hot towels,' she called to her maids, 'blankets and warm milk. Turn the beds down in the double room next to mine. Albiso, take braziers in there, and lamps too. Etaine, they need food. Something soft, if you please.'

'I'll see to it,' said Etaine. 'Astinax, carry the lady through here. Come, my lady, leave your wet shoes there. Someone will dry them.'

'A fine place you have here,' Mona whispered. 'Is it all yours, Dana?'

Dania chose not to answer that. 'Come on, love, you're safe now. You have come to the right place.'

Nevertheless, this was so unlike anything Mona was used to that she was careful not to step on the faces in the mosaic floor.

As the gale continued to batter the building, it became clear to Dania and her assistants that her sister and mother's flight from Flynn the Redhair had not come a moment too soon, for Rhiannon was very poorly and had no strength left to fight off the pain that crippled her. They put them into soft beds with furs for their feet and shawls of wool for their shoulders, they spoon-fed them with nourishing gruel and bread, and Rhiannon was given a potion made from the juice of poppies to help the pain. It put her immediately to sleep. It was only when Mona's dark head lay back against the buttress of pillows, her hair tidied, her face at peace and her green eyes moving from point to point around the beautiful room that Etaine and the others noticed how remarkably like Dania she was. Except for a more worn complexion, a few silver hairs and eyebrows that needed some attention, they might have been twins.

She was, in fact, two years older than Dania, though the rough living and emotional disputes with her husband Flynn, his three concubines and their squabbling rival families had taken their toll of her. She had once been assertive and confident; now she had grown tired and wary. Her only son Dias had been accepted by her brother Somer for fostering, as was usual, but she had had no more children and had not been allowed contact with her son. Flynn had taken other women to his bed, but rarely Mona, whose name meant moon.

When her mother Rhiannon had come to her from Boar Hill after Brigg's death, things had eased for Mona, comfort had arrived. But Rhiannon's health had worsened, and Mona had none of Dania's healing skills. There had been only one thing left to do, and Flynn's permission had not been sought. He would believe they had returned to Boar Hill, to Somer, to her young son Dias.

Dania could not bring herself to tell Mona that her son was now back with his father and that she had missed him by only a day or so, if not hours. It had taken the two women much longer to walk to Coria than either Con with his waggon or Metto Lentus with his, and the news would do nothing for Mona's recovery. It would have to wait. Still, Dania found it ironic that, although Flynn had told the leather merchant about the new arrivals, he had said not a word about the loss of his wife and mother-in-law.

With the last bandage of the morning in place, Dania set about tidying her new surgery, giving instructions for the infusion of more nettle-leaves for the emperor's daily tonic. The high winds, determined to strip the may-blossom off the courtyard tree, sent a snow storm of petals to swirl across the cobbles and beneath the bounding hooves of a large grey horse whose rider swung to the ground before the creature could come to a standstill. Passing his reins to one of his panting slaves, he leapt up the verandah steps and disappeared inside the house.

'I'd better go,' said Dania, unwrapping her apron.

Fabian turned sharply as she entered behind him, his face drenched, his hair and shoulders blackened with rain. At the first glance, it was clear to Dania that his mood had not softened, that their anger stood between them as firmly as if they had never been lovers, as if they had moved backwards to that time of dangerously attractive hostility when they had known nothing about each other. With regret, she saw that she knew as little about him now as she did then, except that he would never be hers. He would have come with some information for her to pass on, or yet more demands, and she would have to pray to the gods that she could do it without tying herself in knots over the deception.

'My lord?' she said, pushing her wet hair out of her eyes.

'Greetings, Dania Rhiannon.' He threw his wet cloak across to Albiso as he spoke with an impatience she was beginning to recognise as characteristic, as if he could not stand still long enough to grant her a courteous greeting.

Tetchily, she did the same, throwing off her cloak with an even more dramatic flourish which the astonished Albiso had to drag off his head before he could move. 'Greetings to you too, Tribune Fabian Cornelius Peregrinus,' she snapped, marching past him. Her wet sandals went flying across the floor to land under a couch. 'You are most welcome. Please *do* come in. You will have come for my news, of course. Give the tribune some wine, Albiso.'

Shaking her wet hair with one hand, she stalked off to the far end of the dining room where, through panes of greenish glass, ghostly foliage could be seen thrashing around the garden while the rain lashed the verandah with unrelenting force, feeding the disproportionate anger bottled inside her. It was not like her to hold on to a quarrel for so long, or to respond to so small a provocation, to be unduly rattled by violent weather or to feel tearful and unsettled and out of control.

Picking up a thick woollen shawl that draped the back of her basket chair, she threw it round herself, refusing to turn at the slow and quiet steps that he would think she couldn't hear. She could have heard a bat sneeze or a toad sigh; she could sense his intransigence, but she could not trust herself to speak first, she, who had always known what to say to a man.

'I came to tell you,' he said, quietly, 'that I have arranged for us to go over to Vindolanda and the garrison further along the Wall to visit the hospitals with the doctor Vitalis. It may not be convenient to you, but…'

'It *isn't* convenient,' she said, shakily. 'I have guests.' She felt the air between them crackle with frost.

'Yes,' he said. 'So I discovered. Did they stay all night, these guests?'

'That's my business,' she said. It was a mistake. She had not learnt how far to push him, nor did she know in the slightest how she had the power to fan the growing possessiveness that had smouldered inside him since their first meeting.

His hand took her shoulder in a grasp that bit through the thick wool of her shawl, swinging her round to face his blazing eyes in which, for all her sensitivity, she did not recognise the raw pain of jealousy. 'Then you will have to make it *my* business too, my lady,' he snapped, 'since you may recall an agreement you'd be unwise to ignore. Who are the men who stayed here last night?'

Furiously, she brought up her forearm and knocked his hand off her shoulder. 'Agreement? Is *that* what you call it? Well then, Tribune, you had better hear the simple truth, however you may wish for something more exciting. The two men who took their dinner here were Astinax and the leather merchant Metto Lentus who you met once. *Now* do you understand?' She saw his tight jaw relax, his eyes become more watchful. 'The two guests who arrived at dawn are my mother and sister. No threat to my virtue, you see. They came to me for shelter when the lease of their tenancy at Cateractonium ran out.' Thinking on her feet, she hoped he would not try too hard to verify her story and that her sister would agree to have come to Coria from some unknown town. 'My mother is ill and my sister is exhausted. They're in there…' she nodded towards the door '…sleeping. I cannot leave them to go looking at hospitals. Vitalis will have to tell me what I need to know.'

Expelling his breath slowly, he dropped his tense shoulders and looked away. 'I beg your pardon,' he said. 'I thought…' Facing her again, his eyes softened, travelling over the lovely features in which, since yesterday, he had seen nothing but a mask of resentment. 'I thought—'

'You astonish me, Tribune,' she said, acidly, moving away from his gaze. 'I could have sworn you did not. Perhaps you'd better leave the thinking to others if that's the best you can do.'

Rather than retaliate, which she feared he might do, he appeared to be digesting her rebuke and, when he remained staring at the turbulence outside without speaking, it was as if an obstacle had been removed at last, allowing them to move forward. Dania went to sit down and was glad when Albiso brought wine and water and poured it, giving them time to recover.

Fabian took a sip and replaced his beaker. 'You say you have news of the man we seek,' he said, carefully avoiding his name. 'Have you let the emperor know yet?'

Until then, the news had entirely slipped her mind. 'Not yet. You can tell him yourself, if you wish. It really doesn't matter.'

He came to sit opposite her on the edge of a couch, resting his arms along his thighs and exposing his muscular forearms bound with gold awards. 'I thought it did,' he said. 'It was part of your agreement with him. Your information for the release of the captives.'

'It was. But if it will make you feel any better, let it come from you. I don't think I owe him anything after what I did yesterday.'

'Tch! This is not about making me feel better, or him, come to that,' he said, looking over his shoulder to check that they were alone. 'And you still don't understand how close to the wind you sailed yesterday, do you? Well, now we've calmed down, I'll tell you, though I didn't intend you to know. After we'd gone, Caracalla had a woman flogged until she died. Shall I tell you her crime?'

Dania's eyes widened in horror. Speechless, she nodded.

'Because her small child ran out under his horse's hooves and made it rear. It gave him a bloody nose. The child was killed by one of the Praetorian Guard, and Caracalla had the mother taken and flogged. *That's* the kind of man I serve, Dania, and if my criticism is reported, I shall suffer an even worse fate. Much worse. And don't tell me he can't do that, because he *can*, and he *does*, and my lord Severus will do nothing to prevent it because he and his son share the power between them. There's a younger brother, Geta. You should see the tricks they play upon each other. You'd never believe it. That's why their parents keep them apart, but the gods only know what will happen when Severus goes. They'll probably kill each other. Neither father nor son feel any degree of compassion, lass, and if you think that being a healer, a woman, and my mistress will save you if you cross their fine line, you're wrong. It won't. You're not dealing with reasonable men here, you're dealing with emperors, and if I'd had my way I would not have let you meet either of them. It was Vitalis who told them of your skills and your big house. I had very little say in the matter.'

'Vitalis? I thought it was you who wanted it.'

'Never to meet Caracalla. I saw how he looked at you.'

So Astinax had been right. Fabian had been so afraid for her safety that relief had overwhelmed him even before they had left the building. She saw again the cruelty in Caracalla's eyes as if he only waited for her to make the smallest slip which, in fact, she had come so close to doing but for its benefit to his father. She felt the blood drain from her head, the room sway, her body shake with fright.

'Here,' he said, holding a beaker of wine to her lips. 'Take a drink.'

She obeyed, placing her hands over his and feeling her own wretchedness at the needless loss of life, the brutality, pain and anguish. She could not understand how such things could happen when she herself had spent years trying to keep women and children healthy, only to have their lives snuffed out at the whim of a maniac. The woman might even be someone she knew, one of the many who came to her door every day of the year.

And what of the message to the emperor in which she was expected to betray Con's whereabouts in exchange for healing the old man's cough? Would Ram have approved, having given his own life to save Con's?

'The message,' she said, pushing back her hair. 'Could you help me to write it, my lord? Then perhaps you could take it to my lord Severus, to show him how I've kept my word?'

'I think that would be best.'

She sent for wax tablets and a stylus and, at her dictation, Fabian wrote that news had reached her from well to the north of the Wall that the man they sought, known as Con the Silvertongue, had recently been taken captive by a remote tribe of the Caledonii. It was believed that the man's fiery red head was already decorating the chieftain's hall.

Fabian paused, tapping the wooden frame with the stylus. 'Is this true?' he said.

'Yes,' said Dania, not looking at him. 'He's well beyond anyone's reach now.' She went across to her room and came back a moment later with a large gold and enamelled armlet she had brought with her from Boar Hill when she left, the last useless gift from her father. It had the mark of the Boar Hill engraved into the swirling design. 'See,' she said, passing it to Fabian, 'that's what I've received as proof. The man wore it on his arm. Do you remember?'

Fabian looked closely. 'Yes, I remember well. At least, I shall *say* that I do.' He held her green beseeching gaze as the truth of the matter was shared between them, and then the subject was closed, the wax tablets tied together and put away with the valuable armlet, the next problem brought out ready for discussion. 'Have you seen anything of your half-brother since he left?'

'No, Brannius has not been back.'

'When he does, perhaps you can tell him that you've heard the emperor is about to take his army much further north, and that the local tribes around Coria will not be molested unless they choose to make trouble.'

It would, of course, mean quite the opposite. 'I'll tell him,' she said.

'Good. Now, can we be friends again?'

Temporary friends, beloved enemies. Yes, my lord. That's all I can expect. 'Is it true about Somer being left in peace?' she said.

'Yes. As it happens, it is.'

'And you? You'll be going with the emperor's army?' The question, apparently artless, hurt her, and his reply would be more than she could bear.

Fabian stood in a swift impatient move that swung him away to the window before Dania could see his thoughts. It was the return of the tension to his shoulders that warned her of the conflict within.

A dark menacing dread stole over her in a half-remembered nightmare, while beyond his dark silhouette the wild trees tossed like tormented spirits. Somewhere in the future, ahead of them both, was danger. He was needing her help, and she was being obliged to watch and do nothing. The premonition hung over them, then dissipated, and her skin crawled with fear as a magpie, as big as a cat, came to perch on the rail of the verandah, blown by the wind to seek shelter. It was an omen of disaster as clear as any.

'Gods have mercy,' she whispered. 'What is it?' She went to stand at his back, pressing herself against him with her hands over his chest to feel the deep hollow thud of his heart, the lift of his ribcage, the comforting warmth of him. 'Something's wrong,' she said. 'Where are you going?'

He placed his hands over hers and, because he did not instantly deny her questions or pretend ignorance, she knew that he had been as aware of the menace as she. He spoke dreamily, as if to the tempest outside. 'I don't…think…I'm going…anywhere.'

'Then you're not going north with Severus?'

'It's difficult,' he said, caressing her wrists.

She spoke into the deep valley of his spine nestling between craggy shoulder-blades under his tunic. 'Difficult? You mean… dangerous?'

His short laugh held no mirth. 'No! Not that kind of difficult, my lady. It's the choice that's difficult. To march and fight with Severus and to command part of his army is where I'll win my laurels. But for the *life* of me…' He sighed.

'What? You don't want to go? Is it Caracalla, the son?'

'Oh, this is treasonous talk. I must not even *think* it.'

She slid round to the front of him, taking his jaw into one hand to make him look at her. 'Think it,' she whispered. 'Don't speak, just think it. Let me see what this is all about.'

He could not stop his thoughts, for they had begun months ago in Gaul to slowly sour his views of glory. Here in wildest Britain, disillusionment had begun once more to eat away at his ideals since the arrival of Severus and his son, but it was mainly Caracalla's intolerable depravity and total disregard for human life that had worn through Fabian's standards of fairness until he had begun to question how much longer he could serve under such a monster. Many men did, but they were either mindless rabble or men too far gone in their quest for power to have any scruples left, and Fabian was not amongst them. Ambitious, yes, but not at any price. Not if it meant trampling over good innocent people and taking their lives for sport. Even Caracalla's own brother was not safe from him. Some of the men had started to mutter in discontent. Others had deserted, risking the punishment of an unspeakable death. Fabian himself was more fortunate.

'I'm being offered a choice,' he said. 'That's all I can tell you.'

The hand that held his chin began a caress along his cheek. 'You don't need to tell me,' she whispered. 'I can see. Do you need help?'

'To make my mind up?' His arms tightened around her. 'Ah, lass…you are a siren that lures men into deep pools with your song. I hear you. I cannot resist you.' Plunging a hand into her hair, he whispered the words upon her lips, stealing the laugh that played there, drinking in the sweetness of her mouth to remind her of what she would lose, one day soon. 'You're offering me help?'

'You were speaking of deep pools,' she whispered. 'I know of such a one. 'Twill wash away some of these doubts, perhaps?'

He lifted her and strode with her in his arms through the passageway to the tepidarium where she peeled off his already damp clothes, laughingly fending off his searching hands as she did so.

Then, protesting mildly at the lack of preparation, she was carried through to the steaming pool and set upon the water with her arms and legs wrapping him, enfolding him in a plea to be one with her, never to leave, never to part, never to sorrow her with deception as she was being forced to do with him.

Like serpents they coiled, submerging and surfacing with sleek silken skins wreathed in vapour, parting and meeting through streamers of black hair, fusing underwater at some mutual signal, panting, gasping, laughing at the slipperiness of parts. Then the surface was still except for delicate ripples as the two lovers became quiet and intent, lost in the sensuous warmth of the water and in primitive rhythms too instinctive to need any thought, making them forget, while it lasted, their earlier forebodings and the omen of the solitary magpie.

One for sorrow…two for mirth…

If Brannius had been with her still, Dania would have sent him immediately to Boar Hill with the news from Julia Fortunata, such as it was, and the good news from Fabian himself. But for reasons she could neither explain nor justify, she did not, almost changing her mind several times during the day while remembering Somer's increasing remoteness from everything she wanted. Eventually, it seemed to be less important to her than the new responsibility of her sister and mother.

That same afternoon, she and Mona tucked themselves away from the howling gales and the chattering spinners to talk as they had never done before. They kept a constant vigil over Rhiannon, fed and bathed her and watched her breathing ease into a more normal rhythm and saw a tired smile appear at last with the words, 'Thank you.' By bedtime, Mona had sampled Dania's heated bath, had been massaged and beautified, had tried on Dania's robes, adopted a new coiled hairstyle and become so like her younger sister that, to their amusement, Albiso himself addressed the wrong woman.

As for the new background that Mona and Rhiannon must adopt for their safety, Dania found that her sister was content to accept whatever changes had had to be made, as long as they could all stay in Coria, together. Mona was willing to help in any way she could, gladly accepting the offer of the old surgery further along Weaver Street. If Dania wanted them to say that they had come from Cateractonium that was all right, if only Dania would tell her something about the place.

That was not the only thing Dania told her sister, for now the story emerged about Con's inexplicable capture, the gladiatorial fight with Ram, Con's escape to Boar Hill, the Coria men taken as hostages, the reprisals and her own part in the men's release, Con and his family's flight across the Wall to Mona's husband, Flynn the Redhair, taking the fosterling with him.

Mona was upset and afraid, but philosophical. She told Dania, 'One thing that's sure to happen now is that Flynn will have no excuse to hold back his attack on Boar Hill. He's been wanting to rob Somer of his influence for years. Now our son is safe with him, Flynn will take his warriors over there and, after what you've told me of our brother, it will be no more than he deserves. Somer has treated you ill, sister. You did well to get away.'

'Even though that threw me into the tribune's path?'

Mona helped herself to a grape. 'That would have happened anyway.'

Albiso the silver-haired steward suspected that there might be fireworks when young Brannius turned up two mornings later at the House of Weavers and stood for a moment in the entrance hall as if he had entered the wrong house by mistake. Albiso noted that, this time, he'd had the good sense to dress like any other Coria citizen, in tunic and cloak against the fine drizzle that followed the recent storms, and instead of taking his pony round to the stable, he had ridden him into the court-yard and tied him to the tree for shelter.

'Brannius?' said Albiso. 'The lady Dania is not at home.'

Beyond them, a woman fitting Dania's description moved across the dining room to attend an elderly lady sitting on a couch with a rug over her knees, adding to Brannius's confusion. 'She's there, man!' he said, angrily. 'Is the House of Women closing down?' He noted the wicker hampers piled up along one wall and heard the chatter of women who would normally have been asleep at this time of the morning.

'The House of Weavers,' Albiso corrected him. 'And the lady you see is the mistress's sister Mona. Perhaps you will not remember her.'

'Mona? Of course I do. What's *she* doing here?'

At the sound of her name, Mona approached, giving Brannius enough time to register some of the more obvious changes since their last meeting on the day of her marriage to Flynn the Redhair. Then, she had been swathed in bright plaids and hung with gaudy beads and bracelets, and her hair had not been bound in neat shining coils as it was today. Nor had her feet tapped in brief sandals over mosaics, her body elegantly clad in folds of soft linen and wool. He stared, spellbound at the transformation, forgetting his manners.

'You've grown, young man,' said Mona, putting him in his place.

'My lady. Mona Rhiannon.' Unlike his former relationship with Dania, his feelings for the elder half-sister were less cordial, more abrasive, and often he had been on the receiving end of her sharp tongue.

She could afford to make Bran squirm in a way that Dania

would not have done. 'Don't tell me you've changed your mind *again* about who best to serve,' she said, dispassionately. She wound a long gauze scarf around her black hair, imitating Dania's nonchalance. 'You'll have us all dizzy with your to-ing and fro-ing. Did Somer send you back?'

Brannius flushed. Not only had he been taken completely unawares by her appearance, but to have the situation read so easily by his acerbic half-sister had lifted the wind quite out of his sails. 'Leave us, Albiso,' he snapped.

Albiso looked at Mona, who said, 'Stay, if you please, Albiso. No need to take orders from visitors. What's your business here, Bran? State it, and then go home.'

'I'd rather wait for Dana,' he said. 'I must speak to her.'

'You can't. She's at the barracks—'

'Hah!'

'Looking round the hospital.'

'With the tribune, I expect.'

'The tribune and the pharmacist. Is that a problem?'

Tight-lipped, Brannius looked away. 'It's a problem when she appears to have forgotten where her loyalties lie. Did you know that she and this…this Roman tribune are lovers now?'

Imperceptibly, Albiso moved backwards so as not to be noticed.

'Yes, we all know that, Bran. And if her loyalties are in conflict, as I suspect yours are too, who can blame her when both you and Somer, whom she relied on for stability, have left her to fend for herself? She's given you her protection these last six years, Bran, son of Brigg. Is it too much for her to expect your support in return?'

The rainwater ran down his face as he glared angrily at her, though his eyes also reflected a picture of disillusionment. 'Why would she need my support when she has a *Roman* to protect her? We didn't any of us believe the Druid at the time, but this is exactly what he warned us of.'

'Grow up, Bran,' Mona snapped. 'How old are you now? Twenty? And you still think the only reason one of our tribe takes the enemy to bed is for protection? Where have you been looking these past years if you can't see further than that? Has it never occurred to you that tribunes can be made to part with important information? Hasn't it entered your numb skull that that's what it's all about?' She held out a hand to Albiso as he began to sidle away and, with hardly a glance in his direction, bade him witness the heated discussion.

'That's what she'd have us believe,' said Brannius, 'but it goes against all our principles. I thought it would have gone against hers too.'

'And is this what Somer tells you, that it goes against his principles?'

'That's what he tells me. He's shamed by it, Mona.'

'Well then, young man, let *me* tell you *this*. That Somer was the one to instruct Dana to take the tribune as her lover. He needed more accurate information, he said, and when she objected, he told her to forget her conscience, that this was war and that if she didn't obey, he would change his request to an *order*. Now, does that sound like support to you, or does it sound more like big-brother arm-twisting?' She leaned towards him like a scolding parent, sure of her stand.

Too stunned to speak, Brannius met Mona's eyes as if everything he had ever believed in had been a lie. But Mona had even more to tell him before he could begin a recovery.

'Let me tell you something else, Bran, before you return to our so-badly-shamed brother. That because of Somer's insistence, the tribune has discovered Dana's identity, and the tables are now turned. Remember the brand on her back? She's now being obliged to work for the Roman military. This place is about to become a hospital for soldiers, and Dana has had to agree to supply him with any information she gets, otherwise the whole household will suffer. So perhaps it's best if you don't give her any, to spare her the burden. Out of the frying pan and into the fire, Bran. Are you proud of yourself now? Still feel wounded and betrayed? It's a tough world, lad. You'd better start thinking for yourself, hadn't you?' Disgusted, she began to turn away but threw in a last parting shot. 'Get off home, Bran. You and Somer deserve each other. Dana would not tell you any of this, but I will. She's not proud of it, you see. Not the way you thought, eh? Well, you made your bed, so now you can go and lie on it.'

Dazed, and now convinced of Somer's treachery, he had no choice but to accept what Mona said. Sickened by his own failure to trust Dania, by his misplaced loyalty to Somer, by his appalling mistakes, he could only plead, 'I'm sorry, Mona. Please…will you tell her?'

She could have diverted his pain by telling him of the feelings Dania had begun to harbour for her Roman warlord, but it was doubtful now whether Brannius could be trusted with that. Better to let it come from Dania herself, if ever the time came. 'Yes, I'll tell her of your regret, Bran. It's too late, but I'll tell her.' She watched him step into the courtyard that shone with weak sunshine through the drizzle, while memories of their innocent childhood caught softly at her heart. 'Do you have a woman, Bran?' she called, slowing him down.

Brannius looked as if he was not sure of anyone or anything, even of himself. 'Yes,' he said. Her name was Harvest because that had been the time of her birth and, by coincidence, her hair was the colour of ripened corn.

'Then see that you give her your trust. If she's worth your love, she's worth that, too.'

Sadly, he nodded. He went to untie his pony, knowing that she watched, wondering after that last exchange whether to tell her what he'd come to tell Dania. How his suspicions about Somer had been gnawing at him since the departure of Con the Silvertongue and the battle at which he himself had been present, suspicions shared by many of the men at Boar Hill who had fought alongside them when Con had been captured. They were saying that Con could have been saved, but for Somer's orders to leave him to it. Too dangerous, Somer had insisted, like a coward. It began to look, Brannius thought, as if Somer had been drinking a bitter brew for years, as far as Con the Silvertongue was concerned.

For her part, Mona could easily have warned Brannius that her husband Flynn might even at this moment be considering an attack on Boar Hill, now that Dias was no longer there. But, like Dania, something held her back. Let them sort it out between them, she thought.

Mona's adventures for that day, however, began by spiralling out of her control at an alarming speed. Before Brannius could make his exit from the courtyard, a surge of clattering horsemen flooded through the passageway, filling the sunny space with an intimidating presence. Red cloaks swished and helmets flashed as three of the six dismounted and surrounded her, their anonymous features clamped between cheek-guards, brawny arms ready for trouble.

Like her sister, Mona was not to be cowed easily and she stood her ground, unimpressed and dignified and wearing, by chance, the same loose robe that Dania had worn only a few days earlier on her visit to the emperor. Her black hair had been bound up in luxurious coils by Dania herself while they had giggled at the confusion they were causing her many acquaintances, never thinking for an instant that it could create any serious problem.

'Lady Dania Rhiannon,' barked the nearest soldier, 'you are to come with us.' It was no way to speak to a lady.

'You're mistaken,' Mona snapped back, tossing her head. 'I am not—'

Whatever it was, her denial was not listened to. Glancing behind him at one of the mounted officers, the soldier received his nod and the assurance, 'It's her. Take her.'

'No!' yelled Brannius from the sidelines. 'Leave her! She's not—'

But his protest was ignored along with Mona's fierce yells and struggles as she was caught roughly around the waist and thrown up on to a saddle where arms like house beams clamped her into an unmerciful embrace. When Brannius made an attempt to catch hold of her…the horse's bridle… anything…he was knocked brutally to the ground and trampled, his cries of fury drowned by the thud of hooves and the menacing rattle of weapons.

'Where are you taking her?' he screamed, staggering to his feet.

Albiso and the women came running. Astinax too. 'Who will not know that the Lady Dania is already there, at the barracks?' he said, glaring at the terrified steward.

Albiso paled, his eyes widening, registering the answer.

'Yes, bloody Caracalla. And it won't be for some healing he wants of her, either.' Hitching his wide studded belt a notch tighter over his tunic, he strode across the courtyard, breaking into a trot before he reached the street.

'May the gods help us,' whispered Albiso, holding an arm out to the limping Brannius. 'Come, allow me to tend you.'

'I must go too,' Brannius insisted.

'No. That's the very last thing you must do, believe me. Come.'

There was no point, Mona told herself, in trying to explain whilst being jogged uncomfortably on the pommel of a saddle with her ribs about to break under the pressure of an arm. She knew, of course, that someone was in a hurry to see Dania and that her forced march through the echoing corridors of power past guarded doors, silent slaves and shifty-eyed scribes was clandestine, for Dania had told her of the first visit here and this was nothing like that. A heavy door closed behind her and, flanked by two of her abductors, Mona stood inside a dark red and yellow-ochre painted room with windows too high to see out of and a floor littered with papers, boxes, saddlery, hobnailed boots, piles of clothing and rolls of bedding. It was not what she had expected to see, nor indeed was the half-dressed unshaven swarthy man who came through a doorway on the opposite side of the room with one arm held up in the air so that he could scratch his armpit vigorously. The sound made her wince.

Surely Dania would not know a man such as this?

Behind him through the half-open door Mona could see an untidy couch scattered with furs and a grey-white sheet that slowly slid across the floor, pulled by an unseen hand. Yawning noisily, the man lowered his arm and rasped dirty fingers around his jaws, and then Mona knew from her sister's description who he must be, and why the hurry, and what he probably wanted of her. Her skin crawled like new-formed frost.

Though she quaked inwardly, her presence of mind was remarkable and, though disgusted by the state of the room, she bowed her head while thinking furiously how to address this monster. His bare feet, she noticed, were dirty and callused.

'Come forward where I can see you,' he said, squinting at her.

'My lord,' she murmured, moving two paces nearer. His smell stopped her taking a third pace.

'Well?' said Caracalla, nastily, resting his hands over his hips. 'You had plenty to say when we last met. Silent now, are you, without your tribune for protection? So, can you perform for me as well as you do for him? I wonder if I might spoil you a little before he gets you back, eh? By all accounts you don't take on common soldiers. Well, as you see, I'm a common soldier.' He glanced around the disordered room. 'I do what I expect them to do, and they do what I do. See? Courtesans, whores, they're all the same. How does the idea appeal to you, *lady*?'

'My lord, my sister the Lady Dania Rhiannon would

answer you if she could, but at this moment she is visiting the barracks hospital with the Tribune Peregrinus, the physician Vitalis and the centurion Claudius Karus. I am her elder sister, Mona, recently come from Cateractonium to be treated for the pox.' Her heart, she thought, was beating louder than her words. He would never believe her.

She was right: he threw back his head and bellowed with laughter at what he saw as one of the world's oldest excuses. Gasping, he pointed at her. 'Her *sister*…with the pox…well, that's good. The tribune has two of you then, does he? Lucky man. So, my lady, come closer and I will show you how I reward women who presume to touch the emperor's elbow without permission. Time you learned some manners, whore. Come…?' Reaching out to her, he beckoned with scrabbling fingers while turning his head aside to call through the half-open door, 'In here!' He took Mona around the waist and pulled her cruelly hard to his reeking sweaty side, kicking the door further open.

Swathed in a grubby linen sheet that trailed behind her, a young woman appeared, walking with difficulty. Her long fair hair was matted, her face blotched and streaked with tears, her blue eyes red-rimmed and empty except for some lingering pain. Child-like hands clung to the sheet in an attempt to cover her nakedness, and Mona could see that she was barely mature, and visibly trembling.

'Turn round!' Caracalla's command cracked across the room as if he had ordered an army.

The girl jumped and turned, and with one savage snatch at the sheet Caracalla bared her back to the audience while squeezing Mona's waist in anticipation of her shock at the terrible sight. Deep cuts criss-crossed the tender skin from shoulder to knees. Blood still oozed. Matted points of hair stuck. But Mona would not gratify him with any horrified reaction nor, even by the flicker of an eyelid, would she betray her revulsion, or pity, or fear. She had seen beating a-plenty and knew of some men's pleasure in the smell of a woman's terror and, out of respect for the girl's quiet courage, she would not indulge in empty pleading with such a perverted beast as this, knowing what she did of his kind.

'Turn!' Caracalla commanded again.

Mona had had enough. Without a thought for the danger she was in, she stepped away from the man's fumbling embrace to pick up the pile of linen, covering the girl's shoulders with it before she could obey, shielding her from the lascivious stares of the three men. Briefly, their eyes met to exchange despair with compassion before the swollen eyelids drooped and the lips compressed against more pain.

Deprived of Mona's expected response to his blatant threat, Caracalla picked up a horsewhip from a nearby chest and flourished it, cracking it expertly between the two women as if they had been quarrelling hounds. Mona refused to flinch. Standing before the girl and summoning every grain of courage she possessed, she spoke calmly to the emperor's disgusting son, just as she believed Dania had spoken to his father when she healed him, hoping to tap some hidden well of reasonableness within his warped mind. It was clear Caracalla could not accept that she was Dania's sister.

'My lord,' she said with all graciousness, 'I see the maid has offended you in some way. Will you allow me to remove her from your sight? I could use her to help me prepare the emperor's next medication. He is expecting me to visit him again in a day or two to see how he progresses. Your exalted father's health is my chief concern, my lord. If you will allow me?' As she knew Dania was quite capable of doing, she fixed him with the full unremitting stare of her green eyes that, of all things, had even stopped Flynn the Redhair in his tracks. Now she poured all her will into the hypnotic gaze to burn through his malicious mask, forcing him to stay his fidgeting hand upon the whip, to throw it aside and gradually to lower his eyes against the uncomfortable green penetration.

His father would be needing her. He himself had witnessed her power over him that day. He had intended to chasten this proud enigmatic healer and had failed. He knuckled his eyes like a child. 'Take her away, then!' he snapped, stalking past them into the room beyond. 'Get them both out of here!' The door slammed, shaking the walls.

Even as he spoke, Mona made a grab at the sheet, pulling the girl towards the door where the two soldiers could scarcely open it fast enough. The corridor outside was already filled with people, and a man's heavy fist was raised, ready to knock for admittance. Behind the fist stood Tribune Peregrinus, Astinax, two other men…and Dania. The expression of utter astonishment on the faces of Mona's two abductors would have been hard to beat but for the incredulity of Claudius Karus.

Dania rushed forward with open arms. 'Mona! Thank the gods! Are you hurt? Who is this?'

'Take her, somebody,' said Mona, 'before she passes out.'

Dania looked more closely, her heart wrung with pity and anger and relief, her eyes clearing in recognition. 'Oh…no!

No…it cannot be,' she whispered. 'Is it…Lepida? Oh, my sweet child…what has he done to you? Come, Astinax.'

Lepida was caught before she hit the floor and, mercifully unconscious, was carried back to the House of Weavers, parting the angrily muttering crowds like the Red Sea. She was known to Dania as the lovely daughter of a centurion who had wanted no more than fun and fine friends, and had once approached Dania herself, in rebellion, for a taste of the high life. Sadly, she had been noticed by the emperor's son, and her father's rank had been no proof against such a demand, issued only that morning.

By the time her distraught parents arrived, Lepida had been sedated, cleansed, salved and bandaged, though not even then dared any of them breathe a critical word about the maniac who had wreaked such injuries for his own sadistic pleasure. It would take days before Lepida was able to tell them the full extent of her wounds, while Mona's reputation spread throughout Coria faster than a moorland fire.

Her introduction to Claudius Karus was even more successful than Dania had hoped: she was not only available but more than ready for friendship with good-looking well-mannered males of whatever persuasion who would offer her just a little more attention than she was used to.

Karus, especially, was willing to offer her more than that, though he could not be expected to accept the supposed connection with Cateractonium as easily as he pretended to. Right from the start of the tribune's duties in Coria, Karus had been warned of a possible connection between the young Brannius and Boar Hill, and though Dania had not directly been implicated in these misgivings, Karus had also been warned not to rule out the possibility. It had come as a shock to him, made worse by the tribune's success where he himself had failed. Mona's coming changed all that.

That same night, Etaine took Astinax by the hand and led him upstairs to her room because, she said, it would be warmer for him than sleeping on his own.

Before Metto Lentus returned to his tannery with his waggon-load of pelts, he was met, quite unofficially, by the centurion Claudius Karus who asked him about the rented properties in Cateractonium, the town where he lived. Karus discovered that Metto himself owned many of them, and the detailed information made him think, and then to smile, and then to make enquiries up at Portgate where Dere Street passed through the Wall. The sentries there were well known to him, and reliable, and they clearly recalled the oil merchant's waggon carrying two half-drowned women among the amphorae, one old and one with most unusual green eyes. At dawn, they said, on the day before yesterday.

Having gathered together enough information to make an interesting picture, Karus decided to keep it to himself, not being the kind of man to use information like that to gain a woman's favours. Nor, by the look of things, would he ever need to. It was just that he liked to know exactly where he stood, for once.

And once again, young Lepida was returned to her grateful parents.

Chapter Ten

Gifts and messages continued to pour into the House of Weavers from the liberated men, their families, relatives and admirers who understood that the change from brothel to hospital was part of the price Dania Rhiannon had had to pay. As former manageress of the House of Women, she had not realised how affectionately she was regarded; as the saviour of the town's menfolk and the healer of their women, the affection rose to adulation; as restorer of the emperor's health, the reputation of the tribune's woman became almost an embarrassment to her. In the market place, she would be greeted by smiling strangers who knew her name and business and would then launch into a full description of their complaints, expecting her immediate advice. When Mona ventured into the market place, the hero-worship became more of a problem to which the solution was obvious. She would have to take lessons in healing. She began immediately.

The first influx of patients from the local forts was soon settled in a series of small pleasant rooms on the ground floor, though some of the men were unable fully to appreciate their surroundings due to the chronic eye inflammation that Dania had promised to cure in half the usual time. Others suffered from the same chest problem as the emperor, while others needed to recuperate after surgery. None of the cases required intensive nursing, and all responded to Dania's unique and closely guarded remedies far too quickly for the patients' satisfaction. To their dismay, and to the relief of Caracalla, they were soon included on the 'patients dismissed' list.

Using every daylight hour to prepare for the forthcoming northern campaign, the army kept Fabian well occupied, his visits to the House of Weavers both infrequent and brief. Late at night, when he and Dania were too tired to talk, they would fall asleep in each other's arms, sometimes waking to make love before sleeping again. Often Dania's nights were disturbed by a feverish patient, and rarely did either of them linger in bed after the first light of dawn. Dania was convinced that Fabian would go with his men and, in the few hours they shared together, nothing was said to dispel her fears. Worse, Etaine added to them by asking, quite casually, what had happened to her courses that month.

A week or so later the routine of the busy day was disturbed, not by any announcement from Fabian or the emperor, but by the unexpected arrival of Brannius's distraught woman, Harvest. She came to the House of Weavers as the first glow of light appeared on the eastern horizon that coincided with Dania's shuffling meander across to the wash-basin. Albiso's urgent rap upon her door was answered by the naked Fabian before she could reach it.

'What is it, man? One of the patients?'

'No, sir,' said Albiso, keeping his eyes level. 'A woman for the lady Dania. From Boar Hill, sir. She's in a bit of a state.'

Hurriedly, Dania wrapped a towel around herself and tucked the end between her breasts. 'I'll come,' she said.

'If she's from Boar Hill, she'd better not be seen,' said Fabian. 'She'd better come in here, hadn't she? Show her in, Albiso.' He pulled on his calf-length leather breeches as he spoke, snatching his tunic off a stool and nosing his sandals into position with one toe.

Before the tribune's belt was buckled, the young woman was in the room and standing in the dawn light like a vision from Dania's past, clad in chequered wool of muted browns and greys, her hair pulled back into a knot of shining gold. A precious band of metalwork was set across her forehead. She was little more than sixteen summers, and very beautiful.

'From Boar Hill?' Dania said, going to her. 'Did anyone see you?'

She was, as Albiso had said, in a bit of a state. Her voice was breathless and trembling as the first words of Briganti dialect tumbled headlong into the room, almost too fast for Dania.

'No…no, it's Bran,' she sobbed. 'The Druids have taken him. They're going to—oh, my lady, you *must* help. You're the only one who can.' Her plea dried in the panic, though it remained in her wide blue eyes and in the contortions of her mouth.

Dania half-recognised her and saw how the months had rounded her features and body into maturity. 'You're Harvest?' she said. 'Bran's…?'

'Yes, I'm Bran's woman, and he's been taken. Please… help him.'

'Did my brother send you?'

'Oh, no,' she whispered. 'I went to my lord Somer to plead for Bran's release, but he says he cannot interfere. The Druids have spoken. He's being…being…*prepared*.' The last word was only a breath.

Dania felt the chill along the nape of her neck. That had almost happened to her, and now it was Bran's turn.

Standing to one side, his fingers splayed over his hips, Fabian frowned at the dialect, listening intently as he tried to understand the gist of what Harvest was saying. The ancient dialects of Gaul were not so very different, and he had developed a good ear for the languages spoken by Rome's armies. 'It's a trap,' he said, in Latin.

'Trap or not, I have to go to him,' Dania replied. The same thought had crossed her mind, but when a life was at stake there was no time for doubts. Somer was unreliable, and Bran was confused and impulsive. It was entirely believable that the Druids were insisting on a sacrifice to appease the gods, and perhaps Somer himself had nominated his half-brother as the victim. Who could say what was in Somer's mind, these days?

Fabian caught at her hand and shook it gently. 'Listen to me,' he said. 'This *is* a trap, as sure as I'm standing here. This lass will have been sent to get you back to Boar Hill and your brother knows that this is the best way to do it. You can't fall into it, Dania. They'll not harm the lad. He's kin.'

'So was I,' she retorted. 'And they will. They don't choose victims from the lower orders, Fabian, but from the nobility, or prisoners, and Somer won't stop them if he values his position. *You* don't argue with emperors; *we* don't argue with Druids.' There had been an exception once, but everyone had known of Mog's artificial reasons on that occasion.

'So what good will it do for you to go?'

'Rescue,' she said, taking her hand out of his. 'I'll take Astinax with me and get Bran away, somehow. I can't just leave him to it, and I don't believe this young woman is making it up.'

'Of course she isn't. She believes it too. But this is sheer madness.'

'It might be, but what do I have to lose by it?'

'Your freedom?'

'Oh, *that*,' she said with contempt. 'Would I notice?'

'You're quite determined?' he said, ignoring the jibe.

'Yes. Give me leave to go, Fabian.'

Instead of continuing the argument, he swept his cloak up in one fist and strode to the door, though when it did not slam, Dania assumed it was for the sake of the patients. It was a sad, abrupt and unsympathetic way to say farewell, she thought, and not what she would have expected from him, for all his natural urge to command.

With the help of Harvest, Mona and Etaine, the conversion from respectable Coria citizen to Boar Hill woman took very little time when her garments were to hand. She wore all her noblewoman's jewellery of jet, amber, glass, shell, bone and gold, her fine women's tools hanging from her girdle and her pouch of silver trading-coins for bribery. Her hair was plaited and coiled to the back of her head with her gold fillet set across her brow, her feet shod in best hide, fur-trimmed and tooled. With a brooch as big as a goose-egg, they pinned her best woollen cloak on her shoulder and held her sleeve-openings together with gold clasps at the wrists and, although this might have seemed unnecessary to some, they knew that anything less would have been unimpressive, even insulting.

As she dressed, she told Mona and Etaine what would have to be done in her absence. Mona begged to be allowed to go too, but it was better, Dania said, if her presence here provided some pretence of normality while her own absence could be explained away as a minor indisposition. As for how she would go about freeing Brannius, she had no idea but would take advice from Astinax. Where was the man when he was needed?

He was on the courtyard verandah talking earnestly and signalling with his arms as if to explain some kind of construction to a powerfully built man dressed as a local tribesman in long plaid trousers, belted woollen tunic and fringed cloak fastened on his right shoulder with a large silver and garnet pin. A long decorated scabbard was suspended from a chain on the left side of the man's belt, and in his hand was a javelin, which Dania recognised as one belonging to Astinax.

She hesitated, about to reprimand Harvest for not telling her about the man, but something about his stance and the dark head held her back. With a hand on the girl's arm, she said, 'Fabian?'

Slowly, the man turned. 'Gallia,' he said. 'Not Fabian. Gallia.'

A few moments ago she had almost wept at his departure; now she wanted to weep for joy that she was not to lose him so soon, after all. She knew from experience that there was no place in his heart for sentiment, however, so she stifled the tears beneath a veneer of practical restrictions. 'And just how do you think,' she said, 'you're going to get away with *that*? You won't understand the dialect, for one thing. And your hair, for another.'

'I am Ram's replacement,' said Fabian-Gallia. 'Astinax doesn't speak the dialect either, but he managed to get by when he went up there, as I shall with my Gaulish. It's not so very different. I could understand much of what the lass said.'

'But presumably if you believe this to be a trap, you're going to walk into it too. Somer is bound to guess who you are.'

'No, he won't. He'll never expect a Roman tribune to speak in dialect, will he? And he's not going to know mine is Gaulish, not British. You can tell him I'm from Londinium, if you like. It's worth the risk, sweetheart, and I'm not letting you go up there on your own.'

Her heart skipped and turned a somersault, and the forbidden smile escaped at last. 'You've been waiting for a chance to go up to Boar Hill, haven't you? Admit it.'

'I admit it. Now I have an excuse, but this young lady will stay here. Tell her, will you?'

'Stay behind? Whatever for?'

Astinax, sensing the beginning of another argument, took it upon himself to explain. 'It's best, my lady,' he said. 'She's seen the tribune and knows him to be a Roman. Your man. There's nothing to stop them getting that information out of her, and then this will all go for nothing.' He indicated

Fabian's disguise with a tip of his head. 'As for his hair, well, he's in your service, isn't he? Perhaps he had a slave's shaven head and he's just growing it back. That would explain it.'

She saw by their conspiratorial smile that she was outmanoeuvred. 'Then you must keep Harvest safe until we return with Bran. It may take a day or two. Take her, Mona, if you please, and explain to her. Come, are we ready to go?'

'Ready,' said Fabian. 'You know where we'll be, Astinax. If we're not back in two days, come looking for us. My men will join you.'

'Sir.'

Dania and her two closest friends exchanged glances that said far more than the cheery instruction, and only Dania herself felt the shiver of premonition as she recalled the omen of the magpie. There was only one more duty to perform before they left, and not one of the gods was left out.

Slipping quietly through the suburbs of Coria at that early hour, the well-dressed local couple met only a shepherd boy and his flock of leggy sheep on their way up to the moors. Beyond the last thatched house and its small plot lay the people's cemetery where Ram's new grave-marker caught the low sun, still surrounded by flowers and tokens, where the couple paused for a moment to tidy them before moving on. 'This should never have happened,' Dania whispered.

Fabian could not disagree, but his own thoughts were more of the dangers ahead, of the trap they were surely walking into, of how they would be received courteously and fed, even before anyone asked who he was, and of how Dania would have come by herself, even if he had forbidden it. Such was her sense of responsibility to Brannius, who could not bear to see another man where he would like to have been. It took a man, sometimes, to see what a woman would rather remain ignorant of.

That Brannius really was in some kind of danger he, Fabian, was reasonably certain, for he did not think that Harvest could have put on such a convincing show of distress, had it been otherwise. At the same time, the chieftain's attempt to remove his sister from the clutches of a Roman tribune was understandable, and Fabian was satisfied that Somer had had a hand in the lad's predicament. For Dania to manage a brothel where officers could be induced to part with information was acceptable, apparently, but to be obliged to nurse those who had no useful information to pass on was not. Fabian could quite see that it was time for Somer to get her out of there.

There was yet another line of doubt, concerning Dania herself, that niggled at Fabian as they clambered through slippery pathways and wound their way round boulders. Never in his life had he met such a complex and fascinating woman, intensely passionate about everything she did, talented, intelligent and capable yet disarmingly unaffected by the success of her business ventures. For that, she insisted on giving the credit to the goddess Coventina and the loyalty of her friends. But Fabian knew how Dania's loyalty to her own people was a real obstacle to their relationship and that, no matter how well she responded to his lovemaking, the Boar Hill woman was revealed every day by a thousand tiny resentments, her recent barbed remark about her freedom being just one, Ram's unnecessary death being another. To expect that she would not, at this very moment, be wondering how she could remain safely at Boar Hill and rid herself of him at the same time would be foolishly innocent. She would know, of course, that the reason he'd insisted on going with her was to make sure she came back again. With him.

'You are quiet, Dania of Boar Hill,' he said, hitching the pack further on to his shoulder. 'Are you having second thoughts?'

'About rescuing Bran? Of course not. About taking you to meet my brother…well…yes. You'd pass for a tribesman, at a pinch, but you know little about our ways. Why would a Roman bother to learn?'

'Because my ancestors, oh doubting one, also came from a province that Rome conquered, and the memories and ways of the tribes are still quite recent. As a child, I spoke the language of my grandfather, and the local dialect too, and when I return I shall understand the Gallic ways once again, just as you do when you visit your people. It will take another few generations before those ways fade altogether, and by then who knows what might have happened?'

'I thought Romans were sure of the future.'

'Some might be, but realists less so. Nothing is certain.'

'Not even *your* future? You said you had a choice of going north with the army or not. What's the alternative?'

'A short administrative post at Eboracum, then an honourable discharge. Home, in other words.'

'Have you decided?'

The path was getting steeper and Dania could not tell whether the reply was a laugh or a grunt of effort. 'Let's get this trip over with first, then we'll see.'

Knowing how quickly he made decisions, she could not take his dithering seriously.

'How much further?' he said, looking back over the way they had come. Coria, being on the slope of a hill, had disappeared from view, and the land rolled away like the sea into a shimmer of morning haze. Ahead of them were thickly wooded hills and miles of lonely moorland and, above them, the curlews cried a haunting song like a distant warning.

'Listen,' she said.

He had no need to ask what, and together they stood to search the sky for the lone-crying bird and its mate and to watch their low flight towards Boar Hill. 'Beware…beware!'

Fabian lowered his pack to the ground and turned to face her. 'You *are* having second thoughts, aren't you? Do you really care that I may be recognised? We shall be playing a different game up there, you know, and you're going to have to stick to your story. Can you do it?'

It was too late for such questions, for she had already agreed to put his life at risk for Bran's sake, and the enormity of it threatened to shatter her determination. How did one choose between loyalty to kin and loyalty to a lover? Yes, it was too late for denials. She loved him, and that would colour her behaviour while they were at Boar Hill. If they hurt him, she could not remain aloof.

They were close, and she dare not offer an answer.

Sensing the struggle in her mind, he pulled her into his arms, smoothing his hands over her back. 'It was my decision,' he said, 'not yours. I am not walking into this like a fool with his eyes shut. This will be a test for both of us, and what happens up there will either bring us closer together or part us for ever.' The vehemence of her reply took him by surprise.

'No...no!' she croaked into his chest. 'Not that. No, not that.'

Her fear found its way into his arms as if a floodgate had been opened, and she was lifted into them, carried to a nearby boulder and laid upon the springy turf with her head upon his cloak, her embrace wrapping his neck, her mouth upon his, hungrily. There was neither time nor need for preliminaries, nor for more words as hands searched urgently according to their needs. Within seconds they were melded in silent communion with only the haunting curlews' cry and the haze above them.

Mutual comfort and reassurance had been their intention, but they were both at the peak of fitness with limitless energy at their call, and their hunger grew as it fed upon kisses, the warm touch of skin, the sensuous rhythm of meeting and parting, at times almost violent and wild like the moorland that surrounded them. It was all Dania could do then to keep her feelings for Fabian hidden, for at such times she was not as in control as he was, and sounds were forced from her that she did not hear in the roaring furnace of her passion.

Yet when they were still at last, breathless and exhilarated, Fabian made no comment about the state of her heart, only about her body, which, he assured her teasingly, was a beautifully designed bit of equipment that he would not mind taking anywhere. It was a flippant remark intended to lighten the mood but, even so, Dania wondered whether it was for her sake or for his own, and whether that was to be their last most glorious loving. If so, it was appropriate that it should have been out here under no one's roof.

* * *

Their coming was heralded well before they saw the plume of white smoke rising above the tree-tops, the heavy gates of the wooden palisade opening as if visitors were expected. Somer strode out to greet his sister with a semblance of surprise that neither she nor Fabian could quite believe, though they had agreed to let their visit appear more social than confrontational. A challenge would get them nowhere—nowhere, that is, they wanted to be.

It was almost noon and most of the men, including Somer himself, were bare-chested except for the spiralling blue tattoos covering their entire upper halves that, if he had not already stripped down to his plaid breeches, would have made Fabian appear over-dressed by comparison.

Introductions were not strictly necessary since no tribesman would ask a stranger for either his name or his business until they had eaten together. Nevertheless, Dania wanted her brother to know from the outset that Fabian was one of them. 'Gallia,' she told Somer, linking an arm through his, 'from Londinium. He came to me as a slave to replace Ram, and I've freed him.'

Somer took a long look at the well-muscled torso. 'A slave, eh? Then he must have cost you a fair sum. Does the tribune know you're here?'

She had anticipated the question. 'Of course. It was he who sent me with some information but...' she smiled and hugged his arm '...I can tell you a different version, then you can choose which to believe.' Conspiring like children, no one would have guessed how their minds wove around the obstacles to reach the mixture of truth and lies. 'I've not seen anything of Bran lately. Is he out hunting?'

'Oh, we'll talk of Bran later. He's quite safe, but I've had to confine him. You shall see him, but first you must see Morning Star and the babes. Come, Gallia, you too. You are more than welcome.' Again, his dark eyes swept over the tribune's tall frame as if to search for a clue before he led them into the dim warmth of the chieftain's hall.

Each time she came, the picture in Dania's mind was changed by a series of small details, new pots, new carcasses hanging in the smoke, a change of weaving on the great loom, different women passing the shuttle, one of them heavily pregnant. This time, there was something more serious, for the toddler who had staggered to meet her before, now hung back, half-hidden behind his mother, and Morning Star's usual welcoming smile was not strong enough to reach her eyes.

Something is wrong here, too. Somer looks at the floor before he looks at her. He is guilty of something, and the air between them is heavy.

Fabian noticed it also, though he was careful in his manner to betray nothing beyond that of a noblewoman's bodyguard, deferential, vigilant, protective and with a grain of servility as if he had not quite managed to shake off his yoke of slavery. He took her cloak and stood behind her as she sat next to Morning Star, a position from which he was able to observe every sign that passed between the brother and sister like metaphors for plain speaking.

It was an odd role for him to play, to meet as an inferior the man his own men had fought, to equate that screaming howling demon with this calm gold-adorned chieftain whose hospitality was as formal as in any Roman villa. The language, as he'd expected, was not hard to understand, and when he was invited to share the meal of spit-roasted duck and lamb, fresh salmon served on a bed of watercress, and curd cheese with apples, he began to see that Dania's accomplishments had not all been learned in Coria. A harpist sung to them as they ate, and mead was served in polished wooden beakers bound with bronze which he suspected were not for everyday use and, as the drink gave them extra boldness, the men wanted to know whether Fabian carried his sword and javelin for show, or did he know how to use them? It was the kind of thinly veiled challenge that would have had a Boar Hill man leaping furiously to his feet but, to Dania's relief, Fabian preferred to let them think he was not so well trained as a fighter.

They laughed, complacently letting him off that particular hook only to try another. What about wrestling? they said. Surely he could wrestle?

Unwillingly, he allowed himself to be persuaded into an outdoor arena circled by men, women and children, though it was the last thing Dania wanted when there was a more pressing matter to be settled. But this was the way men's minds worked; formalities, tests, all manner of stalling devices, and business as a last resort when they'd had a chance to judge the mettle of the opposition.

Dania stood with Morning Star some way behind Somer as Fabian was pitted against a strapping young man whose challenge had been the loudest. Then, as they circled, one silent, one hurling insults, she knew that Fabian's apparent ineptness was an act. She had sampled his terrifying speed and strength, and she had examined with her hands the superb condition of his body.

The over-confident young warrior rushed in like an angry bullock and was side-stepped, then caught and thrown away like a child's toy. And no matter how many holds the man tried, Fabian broke every one of them until, red-faced and breathless, the man was thrown on to his front and held down with his face in the mud.

Applauding politely, Dania glanced towards Somer and saw something that made her look away again, quickly. She looked sideways, to see that Morning Star also had noticed how her husband's hand caressed the rounded buttocks of the pregnant woman while both of them laughed and cheered.

The pain that crossed Morning Star's lovely face was like a spasm, forcing her chin up defiantly as she caught Dania's eye. 'She's not the only one,' she muttered, angrily. 'He's had all my women, and now he's after Bran's woman, too.'

'You mean Harvest? Are you sure?' There was hardly any need for them to whisper, the din being so intense, and Dania could not hide the shock in her voice. Husband's infidelities were commonplace, but a woman's adultery was punishable by death, and Somer was taking advantage of his position by flaunting his inclinations right under his wife's nose.

'Yes, I'm sure. That's why Bran's not here. Somer wants him out of the way. You've come for him, have you?'

'Yes. Where is he?'

'The Druids have him in their hut down by the oak grove. That was Somer's doing, too. Harvest must be somewhere near him, I suppose, but I've not seen her all day. When they take Bran, Somer will take his woman. I know it.' Her mouth twisted with the agony of jealousy, and her eyes brimmed with shining beads that fell through long lashes. 'Go and find him,

Dana, *please*. Get him and Harvest away from here. Somer is your brother, I know, and I should not be speaking to you like this, but you're the only one who can help.'

'I *will* help, but, tell me quickly,' said Dania as she saw Somer turn towards them, 'do you have sleeping potions? Poppy heads. Henbane? Eringo seeds?'

'All of them. In his ale? Tonight?'

'Yes, give it to as many of the men as you can, except mine.'

There was only time for a quick squeeze of Dania's hand before Somer reached them, still laughing. 'That man of yours,' he said. 'Shall you sell him to me, sister?'

Despite the laughter, she sensed the seriousness behind the offer. 'No,' she smiled. 'I've told you, he's a freedman.'

Fabian sauntered across to them, giving off clouds of steam into the sunshine. He was smiling, brushing the mud off his arms, and Dania wanted to run to him and wash him down, to soothe the bruises and strains. She smelled the maleness of him, felt his warmth, and had to drag her eyes away before they could show what she must keep concealed. 'Well done,' she said, coolly. 'My lord Somer wants to buy you.' She held out her palm and counted invisible money into it, pointing to his chest. 'But I said no,' she mimed, shaking her head.

Somer, however, had a reserve plan for which he did not ask Dania's permission. 'I will fight you,' he said. 'If I win, you are mine. If I lose, you stay with Dana.'

On the face of it, it was no more nor less than what might have happened at any kind of bartering. Men sorted it out between themselves. But both she and Fabian knew, and probably Somer too, that this was about more than simple ownership. She shook her head, frowning. 'No, that's not acceptable.'

'But you said yourself that Gallia is free. And he doesn't object, do you, Gallia? Object? You fight me...I win you... yes?'

'Yes,' said Fabian. 'I win. I stay with the lady Dana.' He grinned, as if nothing more was at stake than a heifer or a bolt of new cloth.

Dania wanted him to reassure her, to tell her not to worry, but he studiously avoided her eyes and, although she had told him what she could about her brother on the way up to Boar Hill, she had not warned him of this kind of event. Beware, she wanted to say. I cannot lose you to him. The two men walked off, and only Morning Star shared her deepest concerns, standing close to her as a sister would, but taking no part in the encouragement.

The contest lasted far longer than the previous one, for the men were a good match in size, weight and age. But of the two, Fabian's greater experience showed, his clever methods and quick thinking had been honed by experts, and the consistently unforgiving training of his army years was, in the end, more revealing than Somer's undisciplined brute strength. For Dania, it was a nightmare that seemed to fulfil the premonitions she had felt earlier. Her heart pounded and made her feel sick as she watched Fabian struggle inside Somer's terrible grip, and break it, and wriggle free, then impose one of his own that tested Somer's fitness to its limits.

She wished they had not made love earlier, for it was well known that lovemaking sapped a man's strength, that gladiators never indulged themselves with a woman beforehand, that all warriors took their potency seriously, whichever side they were on. She wished she dared cheer and encourage, as the others were doing, to urge Fabian to break her treacherous brother's neck, to render him useless, to silence his wickedness for ever. But her lips moved, her nails cut into her palms, and her expression did not reveal any of the agonies she was suffering for the only man she had ever wanted. Telling herself that she didn't care was useless. She did care. Desperately.

The weakness of Somer's erratic training began to show, his mistakes were picked up without mercy, his slowness compared to Fabian's speed showed them all which was the better man. Fabian did not let Dania down, but nor did he see any reason to let her brother go without a heavy fine for his presumption, and the throw that ended the gruelling contest cost Somer a broken collar-bone. It was not at all what he had expected, though he bore the defeat with a good grace, shrugging off all offers of help and calling for Morning Star to tend him in the hall.

If Dania had harboured any remaining doubts about her feelings for Fabian, they had dissolved during those frightening nail-biting moments when, for what seemed like a lifetime to her, there was a chance that she might lose him. She thought of the two-hour walk that morning, their wild loving on the heath and the sweet ease of being free in his company. She thought of last night and the bliss of wrapping herself naked around his body. She thought of facing the rest of her life without him, and the anguish churned inside her and rose up into her throat, and she had to run fast to hide behind the nearest cow-byre where she retched uncontrolla-bly, clinging to a rail for support.

Putting on a pale brave face was barely enough, however, for she was given no time to recover before Somer's equa-nimity took a devious turn, demanding from her a deceitful game that was already getting out of hand.

'What news did you bring me, sister?' he said, leaning forward to allow his wife access to his shoulder. 'Has your blonde friend with the centurion lover passed on any gems lately?' He shot a quick glance at Fabian to make sure he was listening.

She knew then that the game had begun in earnest, that Fabian had been recognised. The pretence was at an end. 'Yes,' she said. 'Perhaps I should tell you in private.'

'Oh, if you wish. What about the townswomen you treat each day? Any more morsels from them?'

Dania tried not to meet the tribune's eye, though she knew he watched as Somer deliberately exposed her sources to him. 'Nothing of great importance,' she said, lightly. 'I'll tell you later.'

'Tell me now,' Somer insisted, wincing as Morning Star eased him back on to a cushion. 'And tell me what your own friendly centurion has had to say lately. What's his name…Karus…is it?'

She frowned. 'No, Karus had no information, brother.'

'I thought he did. And the leather merchant? And that pompous little adjutant who talks non-stop? And the doctor, and the—?'

'Somer,' she said, 'I think our guest should be given a drink and a wash-down, don't you? We must not neglect him.'

'Neglect a Roman tribune? Hah! Never let it be said that our Boar Hill hospitality failed a *Roman,* sister.' He caught at Morning Star's hand as he laughed loud and long at his last revelation. 'Give the tribune some spring water, woman. You did well to deliver him to us, Dana. I knew you'd not fail me.'

Along Fabian's sweating arms the hair rose and prickled as the chieftain's offhand manner barely concealed the deadly menace. Willingly, he had come here to make sure his woman returned safely, the woman he was learning to know and trust, the woman who had changed his life in so many ways. Somer had been waiting for just such a moment, Fabian was sure, for there had been a careless desperation in his fighting and not a whit of humour in his eyes, not a hand-clasp or a nod of acceptance for the outcome. It was what he should have expected; Somer had known from the beginning, and Dania had delivered him like a fish on a platter. Nothing would be gained by trying to deny it.

Dania rose, smiling at her brother with relief. 'Well,' she said, 'now *that's* out of the way. I was beginning to wonder how long you expected me to keep up the pretence. Bran and I had a wager on it, you know. It was the wrestling, I suppose. Different style, isn't it?' She went to stand beside her brother, looking across at Fabian without a trace of regret in her defiant stare.

'No,' said Somer. 'I knew long before that, sister. Bran described him to me and, for another thing, I recognise the dialect. It's certainly not from Londinium. Did you think we never hear the Gaulish tongue spoken up here, Tribune? We're quite civilised, you know.' He looked round at the smug faces of his nobles and winked at them. 'We meet merchants and traders from the northern lands, from Gaul and Hispania, Italia and Belgica. And I can tell a Roman army sword when I see one, too. Even when it's in a British scabbard.'

'So do you still wish to buy him, brother?' said Dania. 'My price has been going steadily up since he won, you know.'

Somer's smile disappeared. 'Buy him? I have a better idea than that. He can join Bran…ah…' he turned stiffly to Dania 'you didn't know, did you? The Druids have him. Yes, they insisted it was time for a sacrifice, and since he's seen fit to criticise almost everything at Boar Hill since his return here, including me, they thought a personal meeting with our god Belenos would settle his mind and propitiate the god at the same time. We cannot be doing with troublemakers.'

'Excellent,' said Dania. 'He tried to put me straight, too. But do we need to sacrifice both of them? Why do we not exchange one for the other? I'm willing to take Bran back if you find him troublesome, but I don't want his woman as well, thank you. Nor do I want the tribune. The three-fold killing is a fitting way to thank Belenos for his protection.' *A blow to the head, then strangulation followed by drowning.*

As the discussion progressed, Fabian was mentally measuring the distance to the door, to his sword, to the gateway that was bolted and guarded. None of it was possible, for a crowd of noblemen stood too close, waiting for Somer's signal to take him.

'Well, Tribune?' said Somer. 'Nothing to say for yourself?'

'No,' said Fabian.

Dania did, before they bound him. 'Can I have Bran then, brother? He was very useful to me.'

'I'll see if the Druids can be persuaded. Take him down to

the hut. And no beating. They won't accept him if he's damaged.'

'When will the sacrifice be? Tonight?' Dania said.

'Yes, at full moon. Take him. He must be prepared.'

All the time they were binding his hands, Fabian's eyes were locked with Dania's, trying to understand her obvious triumph at his downfall. She looked pale and unwell, he thought, but still as lovely as the moon in a dark sky, the last one he would ever see. There was no sign from her that she regretted what was happening, not a hint of hope, no message of remembrance. She turned away before they took him, as if her mind was already on other matters, and he went out into the bright sunlight with his mind in turmoil and close to despair. He had told Astinax to wait two days.

'Prepare some drinks for the men,' he heard her say imperiously to Morning Star, and thought how readily she exchanged her role as his woman for the chieftain's sister. Fool that he was, he had not thought that she would obtain Bran's release at his expense.

The inside of the hut was dim and the last of the sunlight filtering through the wattle walls had changed to pink, then to grey, and now it was too dark to see much except the occasional shadow passing to and fro outside. Brannius, who had occupied the hut previously, had been too stunned by his release to make any comment, and no one had been near the place since then, only to bring drinks to the guards at the door. Now, all the sounds Fabian could hear came from the distant settlement over on the other side of the great wooden palisade, the soft sighing of oak trees, and the occasional hoot of an owl.

A slight repetitive sound alerted him, drawing his brows together. With some difficulty, he rolled and bunched his body across to the doorframe where he knew the guard to have been standing on the outside and from where the soft grunt of snores now came, low down, sonorous and regular. A Roman guard, he thought, would have been flogged and demoted for sleeping on the job. If only they had not bound him so tightly, hand and foot, he might have stood a chance of escaping.

He tried to sit upright. At full moon, Somer had said. Would the moon be over the horizon yet? Would Dania come to say farewell? Did she hate him so much then, after all? When would they come for him? Was that a movement outside? Someone…something…fumbled at the rope on the door-latch. They *were* coming for him. Panic seized him before he could control it. The door moved and slowly opened just enough to allow a slender figure through the crack. Long robes were on the level of his eyes, the kind that Druids wore.

'Fabian!' the figure whispered. 'Where are you? *Fabian!*'

'Here,' he said. 'At your feet, where all men should be.' His heart pitched and tossed like a ship at sea. 'Dania?'

'Shh! For pity's sake be quiet. Keep still. I have a knife.'

Obediently, he waited, then felt the closeness of her and the frantic clumsy sawing at the ropes that bound his wrists, the sudden spring of release and the painful gush of blood into his arms and shoulders as they swung back into position. He pushed himself up as she bent over his legs and began again to saw at the ropes around his ankles. But she was tiring.

He touched her hair and felt the ache of love. 'Give it to me,' he whispered, taking the dagger from her, feeling the trembling in her fingers. Knowing which part of the knot to sever, he was soon free to stagger to his feet and to pull her upright, close to him before she could move away. 'Why?' he said. 'What is all this about? Another trick, is it?'

Snarling, she twisted out of his grasp. 'You think I'm doing this for *fun*?' she hissed, low-voiced. 'I'm doing it because you belong to *me*, not to Belenos and not to Somer. Now, are you coming with me, or shall you stand here and argue like a senator?'

'I'm coming with you, my lady,' he said, following her. To his astonishment, a tall man waited outside with his dagger drawn against the sleeping guard. Brannius, the man who, above them all, hated him enough to want him dead, handed him his sword and scabbard intact, and his javelin. It had taken this much, thought Fabian, to get us both on the same side. 'Thank you,' he whispered.

Like woodland ghosts, the three melted into the shadows, Fabian stumbling between Brannius and Dania, who knew the path that led past the Druids' oak grove through which the sacred spring water tumbled. After two days of captivity, Brannius could hardly believe in his freedom. 'I don't know how much stuff you put in their drink, Dana,' he said, 'but I would not be surprised if some of them never wake up. Even the hounds are snoring.'

'Shh…voices carry,' she warned him. 'Anyway, it was Morning Star, not me. She's not sure of the dosage and I think you could be right. She may have overdone it. Come on, down here.'

The Druids, however, preparing for the ritual of the new moon, had not received the sleeping draught, and the two novices who had been sent to escort the human sacrifice to the grove arrived only moments after the rescue. The loud blast of horns, chillingly weird, ripped through the tree-covered night into which the silver moon had already begun her slow curving sail, rising branch by branch. But this time, instead of springing into immediate action, the warriors snored on, turning over on the benches and floor, oblivious to the yelp of the hounds, to the smiles of the women and the giggles of the children.

The howls of the deprived Druids spurred the fugitives on, but the white-robed priests were dressed for ceremony, not pursuit, and when an eerie silence brought the three to a puzzled standstill, they became suddenly aware of their scratches and gashed limbs and, in Dania's case, a badly twisted ankle that compelled her to lie across a boulder, gasping with pain.

'I can't…can't go on…like this,' she whispered. 'You two go ahead. I'll do it at my own pace.' She clasped her ankle and felt the misshapen swelling throb beneath her fingers.

Predictably, the men ignored her plea, ripping long strips off the hem of her linen undergown to bandage her. Then, Fabian said, they would take it in turns to carry her the rest of the way. It was, they all knew, an impossible scheme when they could scarcely see where to put their feet as it was.

'No, Fabian,' said Brannius. 'I know the way best; I've done it countless times in the dark. I'll run on and get help while you stay here in the shelter of this overhang. Look, take my cloak. I'll be back as soon as I can.'

So they wrapped Dania snugly and carried her to the cavernous overhanging rock carpeted with garlic-smelling ramsons and badger-droppings which, they quipped, was as romantic a place as they could expect, in the circumstances. 'It might have helped,' Brannius said, philosophically, 'if you'd chosen to fall in love with a Boar Hill man instead of a Roman tribune, Dana. It makes life very complicated, you know.'

'Yes,' she said, slipping comfortably into the crook of Fabian's arm. 'I'm sorry. I did try not to, but it didn't work. You know how it is.' She felt the arm tighten about her.

'Well then, there's nothing for it, I suppose. I'll be off.'

'The gods go with you, Bran.'

'They've done very well for me so far. Won't be too long.' He was away like a hare, silently, as if it was broad daylight.

'Dania Rhiannon,' Fabian whispered. For the next few precious moments, he fussed over her like an elderly husband, tucking the cloak round her legs, placing his own cloak beneath their heads and drawing her carefully towards him so that they lay nose to nose, breathing the same night air. His arm lay across her, his hand smoothing her back as if to prepare her for his words of love, when his gentling smiles and kisses gave him the cue.

'My woman,' he said. 'My brave and wonderful woman. I've never known anyone like you, and I'm a fool to have waited till now before telling you. I should have told you well before this.'

'Told me what, my lord?'

'That I love you, Dania. From the very beginning I've loved you, and when I thought I might lose my life today, it was you I regretted losing more. The thought of you not knowing of my love was the hardest thing, sweetheart. I cannot pretend otherwise. And when you came to free me, the discovery that you cared after all was like a pain, like a salve that hurts before it soothes. You know?'

'Yes, I know.'

'And then you said I belonged to you, not to Somer, and I wanted to weep for joy. And tribunes are not supposed to weep. Then Bran said you were in love with me. Does he know something I don't, dearest love?'

She kissed the tip of his nose. 'I tried not to,' she said. 'You heard me say that, too. The gods know how I tried, but I stopped denying it weeks ago. I *do* love you, my lord. I think I always did. Perhaps I was looking for different symptoms because I didn't know how love can be so like hate and pain and yearning and sickness all at the same time. But now I want you near me, never to leave me, and I never want to leave or lose you. Boar Hill is no longer a part of my life, Fabian. I can no longer be two people.'

'After all I've put you through, is it really true that you can love me? After the threats, the fights, the way I turned your life inside out? After all *that*?'

'After all that, my lord. It was nothing to the fear of losing you to Somer and the Druids. I could not watch you go, dearest love, or he would have seen my eyes and my heart. Without his wife's help I don't know how I could have freed you and Bran. I was helpless and scared, and I never want anything like that to happen again. Ever.' She clung to him as tears streamed down her cheeks and dripped on to his neck, and the fears and exertions of the day poured out, unstoppable. 'I know you thought I was betraying you…abandoning you…and I'm sorry…so sorry… It was the only thing I could do to deceive Somer.'

'You were wonderful, my darling. You were so convincing, you fooled even me. Hush now, no more tears. It's all over and I'm so very proud to call you mine. So *very* proud, sweetheart. You've had a dreadful day.'

'But not this morning. That was wonderful. Walking together, and talking. I was in heaven then.'

'Truly?'

'Truly, my lord.'

'Then could you be in heaven as the wife of a Roman citizen, my love? It would be a different kind of heaven in faraway Gaul, not here. Equestrian officers are forbidden to marry women from the province where they're serving, but I intend to leave the army soon, and I want to take you away with me and marry you at home. Will you come with me?'

Speechless with excitement and joy, for she had never expected to hear that much from him, she washed his face with her kisses until he rolled her back on to the garlic-smelling cloak, laughing at her enthusiasm.

'I take it that's a yes?' he gasped.

'Yes…yes…oh, Fabian…yes, my lord. But what about the campaign? Will you be going on that, or staying?'

'I've been offered a short post at Eboracum for two months before I'm given my honourable discharge diploma. Assistant to the consul. And I want you to be with me, as my lady.'

'Or as your mistress?'

'As my future wife. As anything you like. Name your terms.'

'As the warlord's woman,' she whispered, drawing his head to hers, thinking that, this time, the title had no threatening sound. Tenderly she kissed him. 'Fabian, would we reach Gaul before… say…next February?'

Thoughtfully, he paused as if to calculate while smoothing her eyebrow with his thumb. 'Yes, well before February. Why, my beautiful wild woman? What do you have to tell me?'

Rather than using words, which can be unreliable at times, she took his hand and slid it down beneath the cloak until it rested over her womb, feeling his fingers caress in recognition and hearing the long slow release of his breath. His kiss was like a jewel to adorn a new life.

'Are you sure?' he said.

'It's too soon to be absolutely sure, but I think so.'

'Then, my darling woman, we're even more complete than before.'

He rocked her in his arms as the trees talked quietly above them and let through shafts of moonlight with a wakefulness of stars, while Dania mused that Coventina in her well must have been very pleased with her lovely jewelled brooch to have brought them to this miraculous conclusion.

The two sleepless lovers did not have as long to wait for help as they had expected for, as the moon rose above them, Fabian was convinced he could see pinpoints of light weaving through the distant hillside. Dania was equally sure she could hear singing and the soft thud of feet.

'It cannot be,' she whispered. 'Bran cannot have reached Coria yet, and he'll not be back here with Astinax till nearly dawn. It will take him some time to gather enough help.'

Fabian agreed. So what were the lights? 'It looks as if half of Coria is on the move,' he said, mystified.

He was not, in fact, far wrong. Brannius had met a combined army of Fabian's men and Coria men, lads, hounds, and some women too, led by Astinax, tramping the path over the moors to Boar Hill. The faithful guard had decided not to wait, and someone had had the foresight to bring a stretcher in case either Fabian or Brannius was injured in the assault.

Surging up the moonlit hillside, the great torch-lit wave came, intent on a rescue they all knew would be inevitable when the explosive Boar Hill woman who had saved their men from starvation was foolish enough to take her Roman warlord home to meet the family. In answer to a distant piercing whistle, Astinax placed two fingers inside his mouth and blew, sending grouse and partridge flapping into the darkness. The whistle returned once more. 'Aye, that's him,' he said. 'Lead on, young Bran. The other half of Coria awaits with a feast.'

It was not easy for anyone to tell which of the two, Fabian or Dania, was the most surprised by the reception when they had believed their relationship to be not only private but somewhat out of the ordinary, too. Now, it seemed that everybody knew. Could it have been Julia, Dania's chatty friend? No matter, the day had been a long one but the night was not over until the last guests staggered merrily out of the House of Weavers' courtyard at dawn, and the last few lamps were extinguished by the all-seeing steward Albiso.

All except one, that is, left burning by the side of the warm pool in the bath-house where two exhausted bathers rippled through the steaming water like entwined wraiths. Then, according to his habit, Albiso was on hand to see the tribune carry the mistress of the house to her room (because of her swollen ankle), and to kick the door closed with one heel. The sounds of laughter were very brief.

'Tch!' said Albiso, turning away to the courtyard to watch three magpies feed greedily from the scraps. 'Three for a wedding.'

Epilogue

There were other weddings that year: Brannius and Harvest; Etaine and Astinax; Jovina and Metto Lentus; Mona Rhiannon and Claudius Karus, who stopped pretending she was Dania because he preferred her as Mona. He also grew very attached to the old lady.

But the centurion's new ménage was augmented by the unexpected arrival of Mona's young son Dias, who ran away from his natural father Flynn because he hardly knew the man, so he said. What really lured him was the idea of living in Coria near his Uncle Bran and being the stepson of a real Roman centurion. So he was allowed to stay.

Somer's fate was not so happy. The god Belenos, robbed of both the offerings intended for him, decided to take matters into his own hands by not allowing the chieftain to wake from his deep and peaceful sleep on the night of the rescue. Morning Star was far from inconsolable, nor was her brother Flynn the Redhair unhappy when he heard the news. He decided not to raid Boar Hill, but sent his handsomest young noble to make himself useful instead.

Long after the departure of Dania and her tribune to Eboracum, the military hospital at the House of Weavers continued to thrive under the efficient management of Mona and her assistants, one of whom was Julia Fortunata. Her *bona fide* reason for being there, however, tended to be misconstrued by some of the more able patients, though no one ever grumbled that the recovery rate was still pleasing to the emperor's son.

In September of the year 208, Fabian and Dania, Etaine, Astinax and Albiso reached the Cornelius family home in Gaul, where grape vines hung across the loggia over the terrace, where the distant blue hills shimmered in the heat instead of the rain, and where they married. And one mild February night, Dania and Fabian became the parents of a beautiful black-haired boy. Four Gaulish magpies (*Margot picae*) had been seen together only the previous day.

> One is for sorrow
> Two is mirth
> Three a wedding
> Four a birth. (Old Northern Rhyme)

* * * * *

Place Names

The places mentioned in this story are still there in England (which was then known as Britain), though the Latin names have now become anglicised. Eboracum is now known as York, and Londinium as London. Coria is now Corbridge, Onnum is Halton Chesters (on the Wall), and Cateractonium is Catterick, which is still an army garrison. The great Wall built from coast to coast, known as Hadrian's Wall, can still be seen, although not by any means in its former glory. Many of the ruined fortresses are well preserved, however, particularly at Corbridge and Vindolanda. Town names in England ending in '-chester' are an indication that Romans lived there, for example, Colchester and Manchester, Cirencester and Tadcaster. Gaul was the Roman name for what is now France.

People

~~~~~~~~~~~~~~~~~~~~~~~~~~~~

The Emperor Septimus Severus, his wife and two sons did visit York in the year 208, Severus and Caracalla using the garrison at Coria as a base from which to oversee the campaign across the Wall to subdue the Caledonian tribes (i.e. Scotland). They were not entirely successful, but then, no one else was either. Severus died in York in 211 with his wife and sons at his side. Caracalla and Geta ruled Rome jointly for a time until Caracalla murdered his brother, then he himself was murdered by his own soldiers.

Over the following two centuries, the Romans had too many 'internal problems' to bother with this inhospitable little island and its difficult people, so they gradually withdrew all their troops, destroyed their garrisons and pulled out. By the year 400 they had gone, leaving their beautiful villas to fall into ruin. The materials from these buildings were used by the locals to rebuild in the English manner, which is how many carved Roman pieces, even some with pagan connotations, come to be found in some of our older stone churches.

The remains of Roman occupation in Britain can still be seen today in the form of excavated villas, forts, garrisons, walls, baths, statues and particularly in museums where the period has been extremely well documented. Especially exciting are the sections of mosaic pavement showing the skills of the mosaic artists and the general knowledge of Roman citizens for popular stories of the time, and the amazing heating systems under the bath-houses made use of by Dania and her guests. But for the ultimate in public baths, visit the city of Bath in Somerset to see where the natural hot spring provides healing waters as well as cleanliness.

Although the magpie has it own substantial folklore in many parts of Europe, the rhyme I have used is the one best known to northerners like myself (i.e. from the north of England), which I remember reciting as a child. Readers may be interested to know that those who lived at the time of this story (AD 208) were even more aware than we are of such old superstitions, especially the Romans, whose lives were lived according to omens, prophecies, talismans, signs and portents. Their many and various gods were asked for favours, paid in advance and thanked accordingly with coin and precious objects and, if the god didn't perform, you changed to another who did although, of course, some were better at one thing than another. Specialists, in a sense.

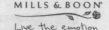

MILLS & BOON

Live the emotion

Super Historical romance

Look out for next month's Super Historical Romance

THE COLONEL'S DAUGHTER

by Merline Lovelace

She wasn't afraid to fight...
Beneath the polish of an Eastern finishing school
lies a soldier's daughter who can ride, shoot,
and deal cards with the best.

For the man...
Jack Sloan is a hard, handsome gunslinger who exudes
the kind of danger wise men avoid. And when he saves
Suzanne's life, she decides to ride with him through the
Dakota Badlands, with or without his say-so.

Or for his love
Jack wants nothing more than to put this upstart
female in her place – and in his bed. But he's riding a
tough trail, and there's no place for a woman in his life.
He's never met anyone like Suzanne, though, and
now he has to choose between avenging his past – or
finding a future in her arms!

On sale 6th October 2006

www.millsandboon.co.uk

A vivid recreation of 1850s Yorkshire, packed with romance, drama and scandalous family secrets…

Abandoned as a baby and brought up by the cruel farmer who found her, Joanna dreams of a rich family and a better life. As a potential marriage and a forbidden attraction develop, the truth about her real family lurks just around the corner —and is getting ready to reveal itself on the most important day of her life…

On sale 15th September 2006

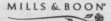

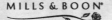

MILLS & BOON®

The *Regency*

LORDS & LADIES
COLLECTION

*Two glittering Regency
love affairs in every book*

REG/L&L/LIST

FREE!

2 Books
and a surprise gift!

We would like to take this opportunity to thank you for reading this Mills & Boon® book by offering you the chance to take TWO more specially selected titles from the Historical Romance™ series absolutely FREE! We're also making this offer to introduce you to the benefits of the Mills & Boon® Reader Service™—

- ★ **FREE home delivery**
- ★ **FREE gifts and competitions**
- ★ **FREE monthly Newsletter**
- ★ **Exclusive Reader Service offers**
- ★ **Books available before they're in the shops**

Accepting these FREE books and gift places you under no obligation to buy, you may cancel at any time, even after receiving your free shipment. Simply complete your details below and return the entire page to the address below. You don't even need a stamp!

YES! Please send me 2 free Historical Romance books and a surprise gift. I understand that unless you hear from me, I will receive 4 superb new titles every month for just £3.69 each, postage and packing free. I am under no obligation to purchase any books and may cancel my subscription at any time. The free books and gift will be mine to keep in any case.

H6ZEF

Ms/Mrs/Miss/Mr ....Initials...........................
                                                                    BLOCK CAPITALS PLEASE
Surname ....
Address ....

....

....Postcode ....

Send this whole page to:
UK: FREEPOST CN81, Croydon, CR9 3WZ